Seven Cleopatra Hill

"Holley crafts deep and meaningful relationships and then thrusts them into the depths of unmitigated madness and terror. You consistently get a double-gut-punch of romance and horror. *Seven Cleopatra Hill* does *not* disappoint."

— Brendan Deneen, bestselling author of
Morbius: Blood Ties and *The Chrysalis*

"*Seven Cleopatra Hill* is an immersive, creative tale. I had a blast with it!"

— Jonathan Janz, author of
The Siren and The Specter and *The Raven*

Seven Cleopatra Hill

by
Justin Holley

SILVER SHAMROCK

PUBLISHING

To my wonderful nieces and nephews: Zach, Shelby, Dylan, Mason, Owen, and Lux. Never grow up. Never stop believing. Never stop dreaming.

Chapter 1

Some locations felt unhospitable, even without good cause. James felt the old hotel may harbor some secrets. He didn't believe in sentience of the material, but James did cater to the idea of auras and energies and history-soaked walls. The walls before him appeared well-saturated.

The small untidy lobby smelled of old books and burnt coffee and just a hint of rose perfume as it wafted from the older woman behind the front-desk. Not entirely unpleasant. Not entirely pleasant, either.

A glance out the window showed James a slew of white flakes which floated downward like confetti. He hadn't heard any forecast of snow. Nothing to worry over, he guessed.

The white-haired clerk favored him with a smile, then returned to her tasks. She picked up a shiny metal object from a lower shelf, an item which looked suspiciously like a butcher knife. However, the item disappeared back down below so quick James couldn't tell for sure.

Why on Earth?

As if to diffuse his concerns, the clerk flashed a glance at James, and he couldn't help but notice her rather large shiny pupils. He winced. The woman's abrupt furtive movements reminded him of a ferret. Even her dark eyes were positioned closer together than one would care for. This anomaly forced her bushy white eyebrows to bunch in the middle of her face. Her long-sloped forehead allowed for this possibility.

James imagined a second set of shiny eyeballs erupting from the rather large mound of flesh, just below where it disappeared into a tangle of wiry white locks. Perhaps even a slit would form there, its edges plumped with fresh blood, a pointy second-set of white teeth inside.

Gross, James. That was his wife's voice. Even now with her sitting at a long conference table of both established and wannabe writers at

The Arizona Romance Writer's convention. This table resided right down the hall from the hotel's, and pretty much the town's, only fine dining. Sure, one may find a burger joint or an ice-cream parlor if they looked hard enough, but nothing substantial enough to call an option.

Stop sounding off like an elitist. Also, his wife's voice.

James' smartphone chirped before he could give the thought further consideration, although he would never consider himself elitist. Just practical and, he compromised, just perhaps, the slight bit discerning.

Nothing wrong with being a high-end foody.

A white triangle with an exclamation point appeared at the top of the screen, the phone now in James' right hand. Another chime erupted from the device. He clicked on the triangle to discover Jerome, Arizona beneath the blanket of a winter-storm warning which covered the entire Mogollon Ridge country. Twenty-four to thirty-six inches of snow possible, enough to make travel impossible. And this went double for Jerome, James figured. Nothing but the narrow road switchbacking to and fro, complete with thousand-foot vertical drops on the way back down. They'd close roads for sure. Even the city found itself built on a vertical cliff, each subsequent street higher than the next and looking down at the previous. The hotel sat perched like a bird-of-prey. Snow removal must comprise dumping the excess out into the abyss because no other place existed to push it. Even parking lots, out of necessity, were only small gravel alleyways.

James clicked to the radar. *Good Lord.* The band of bright blue snow appeared in the shape of a squid, reaching tentacles first, then a massive blob of blue that went on and on into California high-desert, Mojave territory. It would snow for at least forty-eight hours, so it appeared. Perhaps they should get out now.

His wife wouldn't hear of it. James knew this. Not with a room full of her peers and literary heroes. *Not a chance.* Prudence be damned.

"In for a doozy," the White Hair said. "Biggest storm in thirty years, they say." James thought she looked unduly disturbed by this news.

Not wanting for idle chitchat, James checked for the butcher knife, grunted a noncommittal response, nodded, then picked up a notebook off the coffee-table in front of him. Ghost stories written by actual guests of the Grand. Experiences of the macabre. The tablet he held felt brittle and made little noises of discontent, like old bones and vinyl-covered chairs in disrepair.

"Paranormal activity ramps up in times of weather," the lady said, as if this is what James wanted to hear.

He looked up. "What do you mean? Ghosts?"

"And then some." She looked away then to dust a curio cabinet just to her right. She added, "Seems they enjoy the extra energy the storms bring into the atmosphere. Something like that." James noticed a smirk play at her wrinkled lips. "Maybe they just like a captive audience."

And then some? He refused to ask for clarification. He thought then, perhaps, she would prove the slightest bit insane, or quirky at the very least. Then he imagined, again, that second face blossom on her large forehead, the dark shiny eyes, and this required he look away before she got the idea he may want to discuss the topic at length.

As a distraction, James paged through the handwritten installments of sightings of apparitions in the halls, ghost-cats meowing and lying on beds just like their live counterparts, the sounds of gurneys rolling by rooms at three in the morning. He wondered why the Arizona Romance Writers would choose a hotel fashioned from an old hospital, known for hauntings, in the dead of winter at that. He supposed it had all sounded romantic as hell to the planner while sitting in a coffee-shop in downtown Tucson sipping an iced mocha latte.

"We keep the worst sightings out of the book," the clerk said. "Not good for business. The name's Marion, by the way."

James' smile flashed just for a moment, then his phone dinged, again. The giant squid had developed a mouth fashioned from an even darker blue than the rest of the body. And that mouth appeared just about to swallow Jerome like a piece of meat pulled from a skewer.

Shit.

Marion reached down and rubbed her knee as if she could feel the dark-blue mouth about to descend upon them. He'd heard older folks could sometimes predict the weather by the pain in their beleaguered joints. "Gonna be a doozy," she repeated.

The elevator—one of an ancient variety that used a scissoring series of angles as a door—dinged and slid open. Nobody stepped out.

"So, it begins," Marion said. She'd dropped her duster and stared at the door like something unseen might step out.

"Somebody playing a joke," James said with confidence. "Probably kids playing upstairs and sent it down to the lobby for fun."

"Naw," she countered. "Needs a key inserted for that kind of thing."

He remembered the second key on the ring he and Victoria received upon check-in and Vic used to gain access to the elevator. Another clerk explained how they must insert the key to operate it. This ensured visitors to the hotel and restaurant couldn't access the floors which housed paying guests.

The door remained open for several moments, as if waiting for someone to enter, then closed in slow motion before clanging shut with authority. The elevator then fired up and traveled downward. Between the green and black striped carpet and the movement beyond the gate of the elevator, James felt he might get sick just from watching the flickering motion.

He closed his eyes and wondered why the thing would travel downward. No guest rooms were kept down there. Just a cement floor with a steam-boiler and several storage rooms. He knew this because he'd never found himself so bored in all his days. Exploration, such as it existed, provided his only outlet.

As if reading his thoughts, Marion said, "They claim the ghost of an old maintenance man who died down there enjoys riding the carriage. Suppose he fancies interacting with the land of the living now and then."

"Died?"

"Yep," she said. "Was working on the underside of the carriage when she broke loose and squashed his head like a rotten melon. Took 'em a while to clean him out of the gears and such. Poor man." Then as an afterthought, "Inclement weather, they say, gets him all wound up."

"And wound up entails what?"

Marion shrugged. "You know, just active. Rides the elevator. Sometimes he lets folks see his body down there. You know, how it looked...after..."

"Yes, no need to go into detail," James said with a grimace. He'd seen some kids running about. He hoped they wouldn't bear witness to any carnage.

Then he questioned the sanity of those thoughts, like any of this was real. Fairy tales from wishful guests who had nothing better to do save prowl the building's bowels looking for activity such as this. *Finding so-called evidence where none, in actuality, existed.* Things readily explained by the active steam pipes, wind in the rafters, other guests, or even strange patterns in the poured concrete basement which appeared like the outline of a body if you looked at it hard and long enough. Scientists had a word for such patterns: Pareidolia. Seeing images and patterns in random surfaces which didn't actually exist anywhere but in one's mind. Not exactly a psychosis but certainly a mania or, at the very least, wishful thinking.

The elevator dinged, again, but didn't begin an ascent, content to stay down in the dank basement which smelled like damp places usually do, with their contingent of pungent molds and moisture-laden drains. Upon his explorations below, he hadn't run into the maintenance man and hoped he never would. Very much against his will, James' mind fashioned an image of a man's melon placed strategically beneath the carriage with nowhere to go but everywhere once pressure was applied. He shook his head to dispel the grizzly imaginings.

The romance writers must have broken off because several voices cascaded down the hallway. He picked out Victoria's immediately. She then stepped out into the lobby while speaking with a robust man dressed in a suit and tie. No doubt one of the guests of honor for the conference, expected to teach the newbies something about the craft.

He said, "Your work shows much promise, Victoria."

This made her smile, perhaps bigger than James had seen in a while. A small bit of jealousy flared up but settled down just as fast. No need for that. They were all professionals. Them as writers, and him a schoolteacher. Such people always needed to keep their shit together.

"Thank you," she said in a quiet voice. The one she reserved for times she felt most humbled. Then she noticed James. "Hey, babe! Keeping busy?"

James shrugged and stood, understanding introductions were in order.

"James, please meet Jack Dowling. He's written many successful novels, the most famous of which, and my personal fav, is *When the Heart Calls Us Home*."

Home, yes, James thought. Exactly where they should head. When he glanced outside, he noticed more of the snowflakes already falling in lazy arcs. He reached out with a narrow hand with long fingers. "James Landes. A pleasure to meet you."

"Likewise," Jack said as he shook James' hand. "Your wife is quite the upcoming talent. The next generation, so to speak."

"I may be biased," James said, smile large, "but I couldn't agree more. She devotes time and effort to the craft." For a moment, he worried Jack would take that last statement the wrong way. As in, perhaps, the craft took valuable time away from him.

Thankfully, Jack missed the moment and continued, "And that's why we're here in this paradise in the heights." He spread his arms wide to encapsulate the entire Mogollon Ridge region. "We're here to stretch our wings and fly." He laughed in that social way people do when they've said something witty and want others to follow suit.

James did. And also, Victoria, he noticed. Her mouth couldn't get any wider without splitting the corners. James couldn't help but chuckle even more at her genuine enthusiasm. He wished he could fill his own students with the same. Her devotion ran deep and strong. Just as Jack looked about to heap on more praise, James said to Victoria, "A moment?"

"Of course," Victoria said. Then she turned to Jack and said, "One moment, please. My husband requires an audience." She laughed, again.

James smiled his good nature, hoping for a look of smooth contentment.

"Of course, my dear," Jack said, already turning toward the rest of the crowd which just now began to pour into the lobby to look out the rather large plate-glass windows. Snow still curled down in tight spirals.

"What is it?" Victoria asked. Concern knitted her brow, James noticed, as if he harbored bad news. News that may dampen the spirit of the convention.

"Nothing Earth-shattering," James said quietly. He attempted to sound calm and rationale. "Just that we're in for a spot of weather. Over two feet, they're saying. Came on sudden. One of their thirty-year storms if the counter-lady is correct."

"Oh," she said. "That seems like a lot of snow. Especially for—"

"Yes," James agreed before she could even finish. "Travel is not recommended in elevations above five-thousand feet. At least, not outside of the next hour." He waited for this to sink in.

"And we're at seven-thousand."

"Correct." He shrugged. He didn't want to influence her. This convention ranked high on her priorities, he knew. She deserved it.

Just then, the front door opened. An adventurous gust of wind entered ahead of the person who wore a tan uniform, a badge, and displaced several sheets of paper from the front desk. Marion dove for them like a woman half her age. James noticed with alarm that her white hair also fluttered like a graying bird and looked about to fly the coop. It stayed put with a surprising air of resiliency.

The elevator chose that moment to ding as if recognizing an audience when it saw one. Then it moved upward with flashes of reflective metal like an old movie transposing itself through the angles of the accordion-style door.

The sheriff, James presumed, closed the door the moment his narrow wiry body cleared the threshold. The ribbon of raucous wind ended as if cut. The sheriff possessed a dark and curly coif of hair and an angular stubbled jaw. Not a tough guy, per se, but carried an air of capability. His dark-blue eyes, almost violet in their way, glanced at the elevator as if he sensed a threat, but then turned their attention to Marion who still rummaged about on her hands and knees, a fist full of white and pink documents.

James walked the two steps to assist her with the papers, then to a standing position.

The Sheriff spoke to Marion, but the volume indicated a message for all to hear and heed. "I'm sure everyone's seen it on their phones and tablets, but we got a big storm on the brew," he said. "Gonna hit within the hour. Storms are a little different here than other parts of the country. Gotta make arrangements to leave now or prepare yourself to stay a spell."

James wondered how long a spell would last.

The sheriff placed a palm, out of habit James suspected, on the grip of his service pistol—a Glock by the looks. He continued, "Could be days before a plow can open her up, again. Not many places to push snow to. And the road up here, and down, is narrow as a clothesline, as you know." He shrugged. "Now or never."

Marion looked disappointed, brow furled, mouth downturned, eyes still black and shiny. James wondered if she would pull the large knife and butcher the man. "Robbie, I have a full staff on for the convention. And somewhere around forty guests."

James, after he was sure he wouldn't giggle at the use of the sheriff's first name, considered with near certainty that the Jerome Grand needed this influx of cash. Although tidy, the old place looked rough around her edges, neglected. He imagined he heard this reflected in Marion's voice.

"I'm not saying anyone needs to leave, Marion," Robbie said. "Just that they'll need to decide if they can stomach the wait. Three days on the inside. Let 'em know."

"I will," Marion said. She didn't sound excited about the prospect.

Robbie nodded at Marion, then turned to the others who hadn't returned to their rooms or went to use the bathroom. "Folks." He turned and opened the door. The ribbon of air began again until he closed the solid piece of oak behind him.

James noticed the few flakes of mere minutes ago had already turned to a light snow shower. He turned to Victoria with hope. "What do you think?"

"James, we're on vacation, anyway," Victoria said. "And even if the rest of the conference is canceled, I'd enjoy the opportunity to write in such an inspiring environment. I can feel my muse here, sweetheart."

James nodded. *Of course.* "That's just fine, Vic. Yes, we have the time to wait it out." He believed, to a strong degree, in the adage of *happy wife, happy life.* He'd abide by it, now. And he wanted her happy. They didn't have children. Vic's children were her characters and plot devices and intricate storylines. So be it.

"Thank you," she said and hugged him. Then she pressed her mouth to his ear and placed her tongue upon the cartilage within. "I shall make it worth your time. That's a promise." Then she discreetly flicked his right nipple.

James' natural systems responded with an immediacy which shocked him. He grinned with a soft smirk. He whispered, "Why, Mrs. Landes, are you making a move on me?"

"Stop with your infernal platitudes for sex," she answered. "I plan to boff you until we both cum explosively."

James hesitated. "Romance conventions suit you." Then, but only after he made sure nobody paid them any attention, he swatted her pleasant round ass. As an afterthought, he said, "On the other hand, your usage of a LY-adverb is appalling."

Her turn to smack him while maintaining eye contact and a curt smile. "Smartass."

"It's why you love me."

This is how the end began.

Chapter 2

Sheriff Robert Burk, forever known as Robbie, threw his black Jeep Wrangler into gear and considered the fact of his imminent return. A good number of the folks in this town who didn't work down below in the copper refinery, idled about or worked various jobs inside The Grand. Yeah, he'd be back and didn't think it would involve the enjoyment of a fine Cajun-rub fillet or a slab of the glazed salmon. It would involve pacifying well-meaning folk who should have gotten while the gettin' remained good. He imagined the conversations about getting back to children and jobs and whether he could have them airlifted by an inexpensive helicopter service. When would they plow the road? Why wasn't it open yet? The answer would be, of course, when pigs sprouted wings and hell froze over, because it was getting that bad fast.

Robbie rubbed a hand over his face as if washing it clean of his negative thoughts. In his five years since being elected, no storm had dumped more than a good foot on their town. This was venturing on into new territory for him. Thirty plus inches was a damn good mess of the white shit to deal with. But it wasn't the snow he minded. People often confused him. There wasn't a lick of common sense left in the world. He knew a bunch of those optimistic yet ignorant folks checked in at The Grand, at Seven Cleopatra Hill, would end up staying. An adventure, they'd think. What a fantastic vacation. We'll just stay inside and visit about cultured things like books, drink until tipsy or worse, eat until heartburn sets in, then go soil the hotel's linens with a few moments of sweaty grinding.

Robbie commanded the Jeep around the precarious city switchbacks that would soon become impassible. The sheriff's office sat on Main Street, which was five streets straight down below. He'd long ago learned to keep his eyes on the road directly in front of him. If he ventured a look out into the valley, the abyss which dropped several thousand feet in a quick hurry, he'd have to pull over and curl into a fetal position. How a man scared of heights got himself elected to a town built on a sheer vertical cliff was beyond his comprehension. He guessed he'd wanted it, and he got it. Simple as that.

He maneuvered the Jeep through a tight hairpin turn, down onto the next street. The falling snow fell so fast he couldn't see more than the next corner. For a moment, Robbie felt alone, just him, the Jeep and a lot of vertical rock and air. Then the jailhouse materialized in the snowy haze, and he wheeled into his reserved parking slot. Wouldn't be long and they'd have to move their rigs for the snowplows, but Robbie figured he had a few hours. Most likely, he'd get called back out before that.

The moment he exited the Jeep, a gust of wind sent snow down his back. Robbie hunched rather broad shoulders and stuck his pronounced chin down into the neck of the tan service jacket. Not only heights bothered him, but cold too. Summer rocked here in the heights, even spring and fall often proved pleasant, but winter could go straight to Hell. Robbie would never understand high desert. From the Midwest, he'd seen his share of snow, but this took the cake. You knew what to expect in Iowa. Here, you never knew. A dry spell could last a year and kill every crop in the valley. Range animals needed rounding up and transport to somewhere with moisture. But then, out of nowhere, the area could receive a deluge, either rain or snow, so powerful the runoff alone would flood the valley and sweep everything away with it. One insurance company even went broke because of the Mogollon Ridge area.

With a shove, he heaved the barred metal door inward and crossed the threshold. The heat from the furnace vent directly above felt like Heaven, and Robbie stood beneath it with closed eyes. He sighed.

"Ain't seen nothing yet."

Robbie, with reluctance, opened his eyes and found Harold sitting on his desk-chair, feet up on the wood slide-out. He noticed the bottoms of Harold's boots contained bits of gravel and other organic materials, some of which already had flaked down onto the wood of

Robbie's desk. "Kindly get your feet off my timber, Harold." He kept a smile on his face, although he sometimes wished Harold had retired when he lost the election to Robbie. The older man had served decades as the sheriff, but the people wanted a change. They got it.

Harold sighed and made a production of heaving booted feet to the floor with a much louder thump than necessary. Like the very act of compliance stole his dignity. "Gonna get a lot worse before it gets better. And not just the weather." He remained quiet a moment, but when Robbie didn't take the bait because he knew better, Harold added, "I've lived through a couple of these storms. You haven't." When Robbie only stared, he said, "You're a storm virgin."

"Okay, Harold," Robbie said, "okay. Impart your wisdom on me." Harold loved nothing more, Robbie knew. He always tried to balance Harold's old ways—the ways that stood the test of time—and his new ways that accounted for better metrics, accountability, and continuous improvement. All the things a modern sheriff always needed to remember or lose his job come election day.

"Better if everyone just stays put up to The Grand. That's first off."

Robbie wondered if Harold was stupid or if dementia had finally etched away at his gourd. "Are you serious? It'll take days, maybe a week, to get them out of here."

"Exactly," Harold said, a smug smile exposing his semi-white dentures which looked too big for his mouth. "Captive audience. The Grand makes more dough, then pays more taxes. Taxes pay for new uniforms and such. You get it, right?"

"My first concern is for their safety," Robbie said. "You know, the things a sheriff is supposed to be concerned with."

"They couldn't be safer than right up there at The Grand."

Robbie supposed the old guy had a point, but also found it dishonest to manipulate people to stay only to part them from their money. Although, Robbie could admit, new uniforms would be nice. After a moment of reflection, Robbie said, "I already encouraged them to take off, but I'm sure plenty will stay."

Harold donned a sour expression.

More to end the conversation than because the task needed doing, Robbie said, "Why don't you call your crony, Jeb, and see if he has that old grader greased up and ready to go. Looks like we'll need it in short order."

"Gonna need more than that," Harold said. Robbie couldn't read the guy's expression now, something between a resigned reluctance and anger. Harold stood, one hand on his sore hip, the other on his knee, then let out a pained breath while reaching for his jacket. "Want some fresh air, anyhow. I'll go visit him in person."

Robbie nodded.

The door burst open. An unhappy looking Angela ushered herself in with a hip thrust that sent the door banging against the plaster wall. Bits of said plaster sprinkled to the floor in a parody of the snow outside. She shook her mane of long black hair at the same time she slammed the door shut. Her dark brown eyes bore into Robbie's as if daring him to call her out.

"You're late," Harold said.

Angela ignored him and brushed snow off her jacket. Robbie noticed the whites of her eyes harbored a litany of broken red veins. Her cheeks looked puffy and raw. He wondered what caused this, the cold or booze. Once, he would have assumed the former.

"Back in my time, you'd be sacked by now."

"Well, it no longer is," Angela whispered, took off her coat, then treaded with noisy clomp-strides to her desk. She settled in with an immediacy that always shocked Robbie—because she was much more organized than him—and began to scribble on a report as if she'd never gone home the evening before.

"Better stop babying her, Robbie," Harold scolded and then the older man let it go before he ventured out into the winter wasteland. His last words filtered back in with a couple stray flakes, "We're gonna need all hands, on deck and sober." The flakes found their way in and floated about before succumbing to the furnace. The words lodged in Robbie's head.

Yes, he'd been allowing Angela to recover in her own time. Times change, and much had since Harold's child-raising years. Not that he ever raised any of his own. Harold didn't understand grief, plain and simple. Thought folks should just get over things right away and move on. And Angela couldn't, yet. Even after almost a year. An ongoing delicate situation in the old jailhouse.

"You drink last night?" He tried to sound casual.

"What do you think?" Angela pulled her Glock from its holster and slammed it on her desk. Robbie knew the piece, if left on her side, pushed against her ribs and made her uncomfortable.

"Easy," Robbie said. "I'm not judging."

"Sounded like it."

"Hey," Robbie said, louder than expected. "You were late, just for the record. No need to bite my head off."

She glanced up at him, eyes ablaze. "Okay," she said. Her head bobbed up and down. "I suppose you're gonna lecture me about the odds of finding a new mate at the local watering hole and how bad booze is for my liver and that I shouldn't use it as a crutch. Maybe you should tell me to find a good shrink." Her chest heaved and tears formed in her eyes.

He wanted to tell her he loved her. That's what he wanted but felt the sentiment inappropriate because she reported to him. He held the power in their relationship and that made dating off limits. That didn't mean he wouldn't, in a heartbeat, scoop her into his arms, make love to her, try to make her life better if she'd let him. Scatter all her demons to the wind. He would, too. Maybe he should quit and move away, take Angela with, if she'd go.

"What?" she asked through clenched teeth and lips pulled tight in a straight line by sheer force of will.

"Nothing."

"That's what you always say, yet I feel there's something. Fire me if you're going to."

And there was the other option, Robbie thought. God, she was beautiful, and he knew he shouldn't even let those thoughts into his mind. But here they were, all the same. He shook his head side to side knowing Angela would think he meant, "No, I would never do that fire you thing." And it happened to be true. Angela performed her job better than any cop he'd ever worked with, both before and after her unfortunate incident. Coming in late for a shift occasionally didn't negate that fact. Not even close.

"Then just let it be," she whispered. Angela started to scribble on the form in front of her as if she'd never stopped. When Robbie continued to stare at her without speaking, she looked up and sighed. "I have no idea what's going on here, but you're starting to bother me. And just for the record, I would never date my boss. Now, shoo."

Robbie understood right from wrong. And knew who stood on which side of that line at this moment. Sometimes that line could blur, and he would never find that gray-space acceptable. Neither would Angela. He respected her convictions. He nodded, because denying his feelings and thoughts, lying to her outright when she'd hit the nail on the head, would feel like a manipulation. He placed a hand, palm out, towards her in supplication. "You're one-hundred percent correct. No argument here. Back to work." *And I'm so sorry for even thinking of you that way.* He needed to consider quitting.

As if reading his mind, Angela said, "You could always quit." She stared at him for a moment—just long enough for Robbie to wonder if she meant because he sucked at being a sheriff or because he harbored feelings for a subordinate or because then they could be together. Robbie found he wanted to error on the former and allowed a small smile, then a grunt as if he found her humorous in an obscure kind of way.

Angela stared at him with no grin, then returned to scribbling on the form. Her eyes narrowed as she scrutinized her work, right index finger tapping the barrel of the Glock in concentration. Then he watched as she picked up a picture of Emily off her desk and glanced at it before throwing the rectangle of cardstock back down on the desk. He wondered about that, too, but said nothing. Emily had been coming in and mentoring with Angela for weeks now, but Robbie couldn't help but wonder if the girl possessed other motivations. The picture was article-of-evidence number-one. He turned away.

No, he'd leave her to it with no further preamble. Nothing else would prove healthy. *Professionals—we're professionals. Colleagues. Not colleagues.* He held sway over Angela and should reprimand her for tardiness or counsel her on her responsibilities or ask her what her relationship with Em was. He wouldn't do any of those, so he walked to his own desk and glanced at the map hanging on the plaster wall with gold thumbtacks. The map represented Jerome and the ridge on which it sat. Not much real estate. Just five cascading streets, the narrow blacktop road, the rest nothing save vertical rock face. Maybe a couple extreme hiking trails through small crevices in the rock but not for the average individual.

Sometimes looking at the map made for feelings of claustrophobia. That's how Robbie felt. Some felt different—folks like Harold who were born here in Jerome. The tight confines helped them feel secure and snug. Robbie shivered. All of them being trapped here soon with nothing but snow and each other didn't help him feel secure in the least. He'd best get back on his patrols while he still could navigate the narrow roads. After that, well, he didn't know what he'd do.

Chapter 3

James lay in bed next to Victoria. True to her word, there would be no blue spheres for him. They hung empty yet satisfied, contents voided into a moist plush heaven. How naughty he had felt with Victoria on top, him finishing, then both of them glistening with sweat. They were attempting to stay quiet but failed as they fell into a desperate rhythm while others packed bags, slammed doors, yelled to each other mundane instructions, and otherwise prepared to hit the road. The world of those poor cold souls hadn't existed to him and Vic, filtered through the thick haze of a building climax.

Now, the hotel lay bathed in silence. Everyone on their floor who planned to vacate likely had. Probably already on the switchbacks on the way down to the valley, a herd of sheep following each other down the mountain.

On impulse, James rose from the bed, careful not to disturb Vic because she loved her afternoon naps. He walked the three steps to the French doors, opened one with a quiet turn of the handle, and leaned out onto the narrow balcony. The view, although he'd seen it before, took his breath away. The immediacy of the vertical drop into the valley inspired awe and the feeling of free falling from an aircraft. Once he overcame the vertigo, he allowed his eyes to snake along the lonely road which switch-backed from the valley up several thousand feet to Jerome. As he'd visualized, a silver reflective thread of vehicles made their way downward to beat the weather.

Already, the snow had picked up and now cascaded down with more velocity than before. It wouldn't take long for it to pile up at this rate. And this was just the tip of the iceberg.

Small sleepy snores cascaded from Vic's semi-open mouth as James drew himself back inside. Her eyes fluttered as if in mid-dream. After the fresh air, he could smell the pungent results of their labors and relished it. Soon they'd shower to rid themselves of the sweat and fluids and head down for supper. It would be interesting to see who stayed and who didn't. With any luck, Vic might remain in the mood and allow for some shower-play first. With a swell of emotion, he thought about how much he loved her.

Then a quiet sound broke his reverie. Vic continued to sleep, and he knew the answers to this small mystery would not be found inside their room. He brushed his bare legs against the mattress as he walked by—an uncomfortable mattress with broken springs which made noises of their own but not the noise in question—and strode across the green-carpeted floor. James thought a moment, then padded over to the thin door. He felt sure the noise originated from the hallway beyond. This wouldn't normally hold his attention, but the sound was suspicious. It reminded him not of hotel guests but more of hospitals and cold clinical spaces. He remembered the stories written in the notebook from the coffee table in the lobby. Then he heard it again, nothing much more than a squeak, a rusty hinge perhaps. It reminded him of a gurney in a hospital.

Goose bumps formed on his arms which made James aware of his nakedness. Was he willing to risk a peek into the hall while nude? Risky, yes, but by the time he put on clothes, the source of the noise may elude him. He opened the door just a crack. He didn't believe in ghosts or any other paranormal goings on, yet something told him caution may prove prudent.

The door opened with a small creak after he turned the knob. A waft of fresh air blew in and ruffled his hair as he glanced out into the hall. Just as he looked, a furtive movement captured his attention. James glimpsed a figure in white pushing a cart. Or was it a gurney? It moved out of James' line of sight, but as if the visage wanted one more shot at validity, the wheels of the gurney made a last feeble rolling squeal before the hallway fell silent once again.

The air in the hall felt thick in his throat, and his skin pin-pricked and bathed with static. What had he just experienced? He wanted to rush out and find a logical explanation, but his nakedness prevented this. No rational explanation existed for such a thing. The hotel didn't use nurses or keep gurneys on the premises. A hotel this small would not even harbor a first-aid station, let alone a full-service nurse. These were the things written about in the notebook. He'd seen an apparition. His rational mind wanted to discount this, but he could find zero justification to do so. The dense stillness seemed, if anything, to deepen in the hall. Not a single sound, as if this floor existed in a vacuum. He imagined air pressure building in his ears, although it seemed as real as Vic lying on the bed behind him.

More goose bumps formed, this time not only on his arms but down his ribcage and thighs. He needed to throw on a robe before he walked out into the hallway. James hesitated. He remembered what the lady at the reception desk said about the activity in relation to impending weather, the energy. *And then some!*

A cold wind blew past him as though someone turned on a rather robust fan. No explanation jumped out at him. No air vent existed to accomplish this. No other logical explanation. And then the chilly breeze dissipated, just like that. James remembered ghosts could theoretically make cold spots but couldn't remember the circumstances or why they did it. *Absurd!* James didn't believe in ghosts. But how else could he explain the events of the last several minutes? And the elevator, earlier?

With a quick yet quiet movement, not wishing to wake Victoria, James grabbed the fluffy white hotel robe off a hook in the small bathroom, adjusted it to fit, then stepped out into the hall. He walked with purpose toward the spot where he noticed the figure in white. He refused to let fear dampen his strides. *Probably just a housekeeper with their cart.*

The stairwell where he last saw the figure, sat near the end of the hallway, just down from the elevator. As he passed the possibly possessed contraption, James gave a wide berth for safety's sake. When it didn't spring to life, he hurried on down the green-striped hall. He barely noticed the antiques he passed, curio cabinets of the old hospital equipment, an old piano, a cabinet with information about the old hospital days.

And why did it feel so damn cold out here? Despite the comfort of the plush robe, James placed his arms around his torso. Just what did he hope to accomplish out here, anyway? He felt like an idiot, walking out here in only a hotel robe, looking for...What? An apparition?

When James reached the door to the stairwell with its original-mahogany casings, he leaned in to peek around the corner, just in case. Nothing loomed on the stairs, but the space felt even cooler than the hall. And why did his hair feel as if it stood on end, like a lightweight current of electricity passed through his split-ends? He ran a hand over his dome to make sure it still lay flat to his head.

Unsure what else to do, James took a tentative step into the stairwell but did not descend the staircase. He wouldn't go that far dressed as foolish as this. He didn't wish for anyone to see him in this robe, otherwise nude, and not feeling as clean as he'd prefer the world to see him. Some could just go out in public after sex. James found this difficult.

Ready to head back to the room, having chalked his vision up to an avid imagination, a guest-door directly across the hall from the stairwell burst open. Two children, a boy and a girl, spurt out into the hall, wild-eyed and amped up. They appeared early middle-school. James would know, as he taught tenth-grade American Literature

"Did you see the ghost?" the male child with wild brown hair asked him.

The ghost? James thought. Part of him felt disturbed that the children may know about the worst of the stories. He wondered how the kid knew he'd just seen something out here, whatever it was. Probably a figment of what he read in the lobby, or a trick of the eerie stillness, or even a leftover gas bubble from the burrito he'd filled his pie hole with at the convenience store.

The male child pulled out a device, a multicolored but mostly tan rectangle box with LED lights affixed near the top and a silver antenna poking out like a transistor radio. The lights lit up immediately upon which a hideous series of beeps chimed. The boy read something on a small LCD screen on the front.

The boy said, "Holy shit, Janey! K2 is through the roof and the air temp dropped over ten degrees."

"Told you," she said. A smirk broke out on her face, and James knew she took great pleasure in whatever little game they now played.

Then the boy noticed James again. "Oh, sorry! We get excited about ghosts and shit. Sorry if we're too loud."

"Stop cursing," James said quietly, smirking, "and I can forgive you being loud." He hoped his smile conveyed a light-hearted seriousness. It wouldn't do for the kids to think him a tyrant or heavy-handed. Kids didn't respond well to that kind of thing nowadays. Teachers like that ended up with a classroom full of paper footballs, spit-wads, and thirty to forty beeping and chiming cellphones.

"Yeah, sorry," the boy said. "Sometimes I cuss when I get wound up." The boy wrinkled up his brow. "Why you out here in a robe?"

"Mind your own business," James said.

Janey took a step back. "You some kind of perv?"

James remained patient, however, he also donned an appropriate teacher-like scowl. Tweens could be assholes when not properly parented. He folded his arms and took a step away from her. "Glad to see you're watching out for yourself. Can't be too cautious these days, but you may want to refrain from calling every adult you see in a robe a *perv*. It's disrespectful." James bunched the material together at his neck to cover any exposed flesh and continued, "Anyway, I was about to shower when I thought I heard something out here."

"The ghost!" the boy said. "You saw it, after all!"

"I saw something—" James started.

"Janey here," the boy continued, "is clairvoyant and sensed the ghost and now my Mel Meter says the same thing, so she was right." The kid could go from zero to twenty in about a second. Would probably make a great sports commentator or a politician. Perhaps even a barker for the carnival. James covered his mouth to avoid the child seeing his smile. "We like to confirm our findings that way, a double-whammy, you know." He paused not even long enough for a breath. "Janey got possessed by a demon once." He eyeballed James, testing the waters. "Tracey had to scry and wrap the Ouija board it lived in. Tracey got rid of the thing, but now Janey's a little weird. You understand."

Scry? James thought the term had something to do with the occult and mirrors. It didn't matter. Either the kid was lying or was really messed up. Perhaps he was subjected to too much stimulation or allowed to watch horrible things on Netflix.

"I'm not weird," Janey said, arms folded.

"Just special," the boy agreed.

You're both weird, James thought. "Where are your parents?"

"Why is your aura violet and peach?" Janey asked.

James ignored her.

The boy answered his question, "Ah, they're seeing if the documentary they filmed is gonna make the grade for the Travel channel. You know, the channel with all the ghost shows. They're paranormal investigators and Janey and me, well, we're right behind them in that aspect." The boy lifted his right index finger to his chin but then started to speak again before James could stammer out a response. "Technically, Tracey isn't our mom, but our real mom got killed by the same serial killer who kidnapped me and Janey and made Janey help him open a portal to the spiritual realm."

James rolled his eyes. He wondered for a moment how to handle these blatant lies but decided it wasn't his concern. They weren't his kids, or even his students. Hopefully, he wouldn't run into them again. If he did, he could just ignore them or smile politely and walk on. "You kids possess quite the imagination. No doubt you'll both find careers in the arts."

"Yeah," the boy said. "We're pretty crafty." He didn't seem to catch on that James thought he'd made the whole scenario with his parents up.

"Violet and peach," Janey repeated. "Sometimes Dad has a violet and peach aura first thing in the morning, right after he and Tracey get out of bed. Sometimes, even during the day if they take a nap."

Good Lord! James took great pains to ignore the *innuendo*. He wondered if she understood the implication or was really that unaware. Kids nowadays knew more about sex than a *Kama Sutra* instructor. *Whatever.* "If your parents are touting their ghost documentary," although he doubted the validity of this, "then who are you here with? Certainly, you're not here ghost hunting alone."

"We're here with Auntie Kayla," the boy answered. "She wants to write romance books, I guess. Thought we should come with on account of the hotel having ghosts. Dad and Tracey said that was okay as long as we were sure to film lots for another documentary, you know, and record our evidence like we ought to."

"Ought to?" Kids *ought to* do their homework and make friends with other children. Not run all over tarnation hunting ghosts.

"This," the boy said, holding out the rectangle device, "is a Mel Meter, and it reads ambient K2 electromagnetic frequency, so we know when the field has been disturbed. It also measures air temp and serves as a REM pod or EMF pump."

James had zero idea about what just fell from the kid's mouth. Pumps and pods and…and stuff that sounded like the items his wife picked up from a sex toy party she attended a couple months back. This Auntie Kayla, the romance writer, had her hands full. He hoped she was up for the task of reigning them in and certainly better her than him.

"My name's Miles," the boy said and stuck out his hand.

James, out of habit, grasped the proffered hand and shook. It felt hot and sweaty. James grinned, careful not to laugh out loud. "James Landes," he managed. "Are you children going to run about all day by yourselves?"

"Sure," Miles said. "What else? Auntie Kayla will be in the workshops drooling over that Jack guy, you know, the famous romance writer dude. You know, if he stuck around. So, Janey and me might as well get some good footage."

Footage? James thought about the basement and the poor maintenance man who people thought sometimes showed himself to the unwary. "Perhaps you should skip the basement in your wanderings. It's dangerous, I hear."

Janey looked up at him like he might have said something untoward or, at the very least, dimwitted. Her nose scrunched like she smelled something bad. He remembered Miles had said a demon once possessed her. As disturbing as that sounded, James couldn't help but imagine it was true. She seemed a bit...off, even now. Disturbed or troubled in some way.

"That's especially where we want to try today," Miles exclaimed. "You know, the maintenance dude got his melon squashed down there and sometimes people see stuff. Me and Janey wanna get his splattered head on film."

"Are you serious? Are your parents okay with this?"

"Sure," Miles said, "so long as we get it on a SD card. Like Tracey says, if it's not documented, it never happened." Miles shrugged as if this were as normal as tying his shoe or brushing his teeth. "She's not much for personal experiences. She says nobody ever believes them." Miles placed the Mel Meter in a pouch attached to his waist and withdrew a video camera. James noticed the words *Full Spectrum* on the side of the device. "I can take video or stills with this thing."

James didn't want to know. He really didn't. He wondered if he should try to find Auntie Kayla but realized he didn't have the first clue if she were down in the conference room or elsewhere. He settled for, "Don't you think you should check in with your aunt before wandering about?" James' conservative soul felt firm in its belief tweens shouldn't just wander about unaccompanied, because then he may need to deal with them again.

"Your aura is more violet than peach now," Janey said. "Perhaps you should go shower now. That's what dad does when he turns violet."

"My hygiene is none of your beeswax," James mentioned.

Janey shrugged and then turned her interest toward an antique mirror. She seemed to do nothing but stare at it with a solemn expression. James wondered what she saw in there.

"Don't worry about us," Miles said. "This place is Disneyland compared to some of the places we been."

"Like where?" James asked.

"You know," Miles began, "The Palmer House for one, right in our hometown. Nasty place. Then there's the Killakitchie Murder House, Trans-Allegheny Lunatic Asylum, Bobby Mackay's Music World where there's a portal to hell, not to mention The Demon House, and...crap, can't remember the official name...but, you know, that place Manson talked his followers into offing that movie star."

"Good Lord," James said, but could think of no other response. If this all proved true, that Janey had a demon inside felt accurate. In fact, he would have been more surprised if she hadn't. These kids belonged in school, with kids their own age, not traipsing about in the dark, inside insidious and disease-riddled buildings. "Hasn't anyone ever reported your parents to social services?"

"Naw," Miles said. "The producers helped my dad and Tracey figure everything out so it's legal for us to miss school. No biggie. We're learning more about STEM stuff investigating ghosts than we ever did in school, anyway. School sucks and they don't like ya to learn about anything cool."

"I beg your pardon?"

Janey turned to Miles. Her pupils were almost as big as the color of her eyes. "It's time," she whispered.

Miles nodded. "Nice to meet you, mister. Ghosts are about to go active in the basement. See ya around!" Then they ran down the stairs in a manic frenzy, feet thudding off the steps.

James listened until he couldn't hear them anymore, shook his head, then began the sojourn back to his room...to shower. So, he didn't turn all the way violet.

Chapter 4

The old woman felt the need for expedience. Already, the snow came down like white linen sheets. Within the next couple to three hours, they'd need to prepare themselves. The fortifying ritual needed to happen now, before the rest could begin, but her hands didn't want to cooperate like they had the last time.

The chicken wrenched itself from her grasp at the last moment, so the cleaver in her right hand buried itself in the empty cutting board. It would take her several minutes to wrench it back out. Precious minutes she didn't have at her disposal. They'd waited too long, already.

Her breaths came heavy from ancient lungs as she pried the handle back and forth. Finally, the blade expunged itself from the board, and she lay it down to go in search of the infernal chicken. She could hear it clucking inside the pantry.

She took careful steps as she stalked the chicken because falling now could lead to disastrous consequences. The feathered thing had grown suspicious and found itself in no mood to get caught again. When she dodged left, the quick-footed chicken darted right, leaving her stumbling. She latched onto the food shelves to steady herself, then turned in a careful arc to prepare for another lunge. But the chicken ran from the pantry and, by the sounds of it, through the kitchen door to the freedom of the much-larger front room. The door should have been closed. How she'd missed that detail eluded her. Old age, she supposed.

The woman sighed. "Never catch the chicken out there," she whispered. Goose bumps rippled up her sides and neck, because she understood the consequences of failure. Legs that felt like stilts carried the woman back to the kitchen where she rested a moment to catch her breath, then opened the door to the old propane refrigerator. They left it off, mostly, but when the first call for major snow went out, she'd turned it on in anticipation. At least, she remembered that much.

She remembered the last time, so long ago. The blade arcing through the air, the dull thud, then a gout of blood bursting out onto the floor where it splattered about into a grim artistic endeavor, the chicken flopping about, its head in her much-younger hand.

"Not to be," she mumbled and opened the fridge door. "Plan B." She grabbed a plate of three bloody boneless and skinless chicken breasts off the shelf and plopped them on the countertop. The plate rattled about and a wet strand of watery blood glopped onto the counter.

Four stations complete with supplies sat before her, ready to go. She eyeballed the setup with expert scrutiny, because once she started there would be no stopping. The ritual required perfection, careful consideration, no time overruns, no missed words. Bad enough she'd lost the only live chicken they possessed. No time to worry about that now.

She took a deep breath to stop the trembling in her hands, then pushed a button on the metronome that would tick and tock and give off a chime every two minutes. She knew from experience the two minutes would come quicker than expected.

The ticking and tocking gave speed to her weary hands and arms. She hoisted the first moist chicken breast into the first bowl. The bowl overflowed with a foul-smelling tar mixture, crafted from the sacred mud from the graveyard and chicken blood she'd purchased from the Wiccan over in Spaulding. It stunk to high heaven but would do the trick. Once the breast lay fully coated, she set it aside and grabbed the second.

She must have grown lax, because the breast, just as it touched the mud and tar mixture, flopped from her hand as if alive once more, toppled the bowl, and fell to the floor. *Great!* Most of the sticky mixture now lay on the counter outside the dish and, worse, she could feel the pain in her decrepit hips as she bent to retrieve the wayward breast.

The metronome continued to tick and tock. She imagined the chime and panicked, falling to the floor with the dusty breast of chicken. She picked it up, hefted it, then began the arduous task of picking herself up from her bottom. Joints creaked, and she feared a breakage as her body slowly lifted itself, her arms pulling and her nearly useless legs pushing. Her arms trembled, and the rickety counter shook, but finally the woman made it upright. She rolled the second breast in the mixture on the counter, threw it at the first, then quickly grabbed the third.

The metronome dinged. *Shit!*

The woman scrambled, rolling the last breast in the mixture long enough for a light coating, then brought it to the second station. *Better late than never.* She rolled it in a box of feathers plucked from a suffering live chicken, so the witch told her. These days it was much easier to take some old Wiccan's word for it than do it one's self. She no longer possessed the stomach for it. Just for a moment, she lamented the fact that the youth of today didn't give a rat's bloody ass about the curse. Didn't even believe in it.

With a careful yet quick cadence, she covered all three breasts in the feathers of *the suffered*, just as the metronome dinged again. They looked like chicken breasts that had sat out too long before being put into the fridge. She brought the first over to the next station where—according to the old text—it needed a baptism in blood. The woman dipped into the blood. The feathers flattened and congealed. Then her mind went blank.

The words! She'd forgot the words. *Damn her geriatric brain!* She should have practiced, but she'd been so certain of the words to the ritual. She took a deep breath as the metronome marked the ever-dwindling time. Were the words even important? She'd heard somewhere that intent reigned supreme.

"Okay," she whispered as she held the blood-congealed chicken breast. "Receive this here offering on account of we wanna make it an acceptable sacrifice to it who shall not be named." She hoped this would suffice. No other words came to her, so she plopped the meat next to the fourth and final station and grabbed the second, unsure how much time remained.

The first breast must have lasted longer than she imagined, because the metronome dinged before she was ready. The metronome wanted her to move onto the fourth phase before she'd even gotten to the second breast. She grabbed the other two, drowned them in the blood, looked at them and grimaced. She whispered, "Whatever I said for the other one, same goes for these here." She threw one down and held the other as she moved to the fourth station. *Crap!* She needed to hurry.

In a basket lay pre-cut—just yesterday, in fact—pieces of fabric repurposed from the garments of corpses. Whose corpse, she possessed no clue, and didn't care to. Inside the basket also lay a needle and thread. She yanked a chunk of fabric out, which upset the basket. It spilled off the side of the counter and onto the floor. The spool of thread, as if on greased wheels, escaped and spun off into a dark corner beneath an old rack. At the same moment, the needle clanked, spun, then skittered beneath the damn fridge like a metal cockroach.

God almighty. What else could go wrong? Scratch that! She didn't want to know what else at all. No sense in tempting karma.

As the metronome ticked, she panicked. With a swipe of her flabby toneless arm, she flung all three prepared chunks of meat to the floor with the fabric, which thankfully still lay where landed, then carefully bent down and sprawled next to the whole shittery.

Since she couldn't sew, she grabbed a piece of corpse-garment and wrapped it around a breast as if it was a Christmas present for her great-nephew, Bobby. Thankfully, the chicken breasts were tacky enough to hold the fabric wrap in place without stitching. Patches of fetid moisture leaked through and stained the fabric. Why it needed to be wrapped up all pretty-like eluded her, but the ritual called for it, so she'd do the best she could.

Before she had the second breast wrapped in proper fashion, the metronome dinged again, then set off with a series of shrill alarms. She understood what this meant, so her heart began to thud dangerously in her chest. Good thing for the adrenaline, though. Doubting her ability to get upright, she didn't even try. Instead, with frenzied movements of her hands, she wrapped the other two best she could, scooped them up, and hugged them to her bosom where they made red stains on her skin. She scooted across the linoleum.

When the woman reached the doorway to the front room, the flooring turned to cement, yet she kept scooching her ass-end along the abrasive material. She could feel the pain as the rough cement eroded her pants and scratched the skin of her butt. Yet she scooted until she reached the exterior door. Here, despite the pain, she reached up and turned the latch. The door swung open to expose a slope wooded with junipers and oaks. The snow came down in ropes of white. Already, three to four inches lay on the ground.

The metronome still screeched from the room behind her, reminding her of the clusterfuck she'd made of the ritual. She supposed she'd pay for that, but she had given it the old college try.

Tired now, exhausted beyond measure, she hoped she possessed the strength to perform the tasks which would come next. She couldn't even handle a chicken for goodness sake.

Just then, the live chicken chose that peculiar moment to burst past her in a flurry of wings and out into the storm. It quickly disappeared beyond the veil of falling snow, tracks already filling in. *Speak of the devil*, she thought as she tried to catch her breath. *Asshole.*

After a moment of recovery, wondering what else might go wrong but not really wanting to know, the woman turned to the woods, reared back, then flung the wrapped breasts out into the brush. She sighed, the ritual complete, kind of, but definitely not on time. She hoped it would suffice. On a whim, just before she scooted back inside where she could attempt to stand, she screamed, "Hope you choke!"

Her voice echoed, the only sound save the falling snow against dead brown leaves of the oaks. When she went to close the door, another sound broke the silence. Loud. A scream, something between a hiss and a growl, answered her from up on the slope.

The woman shivered and closed the door.

Chapter 5

Angela needed fresh air. Ironic she now inhaled from the cigarette entrenched in her mouth. She hadn't smoked before but took it up recently. Not that she would recommend it to anyone. She planned to quit soon, but for now it provided her with just enough self-loathing to keep the blinding anger hanging on.

The snow fell in ropes and, with each gust of wind, expanded out into a veil of white. The blanket of powder already covered the toes of her work boots and soon the switchbacks to and from Jerome would become impassable.

Robbie's Jeep crawled a steep grade to the next street, tire-chains churning through the ever-deepening snow. Nice guy. She considered that a true thought. His only issue, or the only one she took exception to, involved how he approached her regarding the miscarriage. Sure, she knew Robbie possessed feelings for her. *If he only knew me better!* Angela didn't blame him for his honest feelings, but when he treated her like a china doll, or worse, like a child, that's where he crossed the definitive line. His pity would never provide her with anything she needed. Pity never fixed a damn thing.

No, she'd buried herself in her work for the last six months and that's what she intended to do for the foreseeable future. Either that or the drinking would consume her. The only thing between herself and a seat in one of the two taverns in town lay inside the building behind her. Alcohol numbed. Work buried her emotions in activity. Smoking kept her busy between times, but nights were the worst. The never-ending periods of darkness which allowed the murky thoughts in and the brooding to begin.

Then she thought of Em and hoped she would see the girl. Another reason Robbie would never get a swing. A warmness pushed some of the winter chill away. Em usually showed up around this time to grill Angela about cop stuff, then she would lure her away for coffee and a donut at the café. Their conversations ranged far and wide, and she would be lying if she said she didn't enjoy them. Angela wondered where things would go with the girl.

Not seeing Em, Angela allowed the vestiges of smoke from her final drag to cascade out over her face, then it disappeared with frightening immediacy into the wintry mix of snow and wind. She threw the filter into the cigarette receptacle because she refused to litter, then walked through downtown to see if tourists were on their way out and if the townies were battening down the hatches.

Not for the first time, she noticed how much newer the Sheriff's office and jail appeared, compared to the quaint shops which surrounded the structure. A nice place to work, sure, but she thanked her lucky stars she didn't work here when the old Yavapai County jailhouse slid down the hill toward the valley. Robbie told her the copper-mine tunnels beneath gave up the ghost and caved, causing the slide. The unstable mines were a constant reminder life could always get worse. *Yes, it could.*

She walked south along Main Street, past Ruby's Country Pantry, Mountain Top Antiques and Curiosities, Lucky Strike Candy Shop, and Lorraine's Bakery & Diner. All were still open, but based on the lack of activity within, they'd soon close and the merchants would make their way home for the duration of the storm.

Several cars passed Angela, families on the skedaddle, those who didn't wish to get stranded up here on the mountain. Even though an exodus never proved fruitful for local commerce, it sure beat a litany of accidents and misadventures because of the snow.

Up the street a block, Harold's squad car sat outside the city maintenance building. Under normal circumstances, that wouldn't cause her alarm, but the way his vehicle sat with the driver's door open piqued her curiosity. *Probably just shooting the shit with Jeb*, Angela thought. But why leave his door open in a heavy snow unless a reason to hurry existed? Maybe he needed help. Angela picked up her pace, in case this wasn't an episode of senior brain-fart. Angela didn't always care for Harold's opinions, but a colleague, especially in police work, needed to know you had their back. She hoped he carried the same sentiment toward her.

Angela picked up her pace to a jog, black hair flailing out behind her. The wind chapped her cheeks, and she supposed her high cheekbones would hold a nice rouge. Despite the smoking habit, Angela kept a decent pace without getting winded. Maybe she would quit now, right after they dug out from the storm, while her health held out. Maybe cut back on the booze, too.

Cautious as she approached, Angela slowed her gait and surveyed the old cruiser. Everything seemed okay if you ignored the open door. Inside, she noticed junk-food wrappers and soda cans. Angela knew Harold held a penchant for the unhealthy and often forgot to clean up after himself, even at the station. But this seemed sloppy beyond even his usual demeanor. Perhaps old age brought an acceleration of degradation to one's bad habits. More reason to quit her own, while only a few stray gray-hairs infiltrated her scalp.

Then she noticed scuff marks in the snow, just now beginning to fill in. *Fresh*. Her instincts told her a struggle may have occurred. Her heart sped up in anticipation and she tensed, muscles ready to react on a moment's notice. Angela looked from the mess of Harold's cruiser and back to the scuff marks that looked like drag marks, if one used their imagination. A scenario began to build in her mind and she placed a hand on the butt of her Glock with little thought. Had someone jumped Harold, pulled him from his squad car, then dragged him inside the city maintenance building? Seemed unlikely in this quiet little town, but one never knew. Angela got paid to trust her instincts.

She followed the scuff—possibly drag—marks to a door that sat just right of the large industrial garage door. The door had been left open a crack. *More carelessness*. Angela opened it the rest of the way on the well-oiled hinges without announcing herself. Through the small crack the partially open door had provided, snow already snuck in and had formed a mini drift just inside. Careful not to disturb the snow, Angela stepped over the small mound and entered the building.

Silence greeted her.

Then a whisper. Just a small let of breath from the backroom, like someone blowing out a candle. Then soft grunts which reminded

Angela of things like exertion, frustration, sex. Angela drew her Glock, raised it with two hands, then continued toward the room in back.

Not much light filtered from back there. The fluorescents were off, so the room looked bathed in inky blackness. Whatever activity presented itself from back there, Angela knew it would prove nefarious. Nobody stood around in the dark and spoke in low tones and made grunting noises for fun. Unless one considered relations of a sexual nature. Angela felt those days well behind Harold at this point in his life. Then again, one never knew. She crept forward.

With a few furtive strides of her long legs, Angela reached the door which led to the darkened room. Like they trained in the Peace Officer Basic Training, she placed her back to the wall, then leaned inward to peer inside. It took her a moment to understand the situation.

Harold stood by a table with his hands on his hips, shoulders drooped in obvious discomfort. He was panting heavily and made little raspy noises as he tried to catch his breath. Jeb, the maintenance guy, stood across the table from Harold and held a rather large and mean-looking knife. He stared at Em Pratt who lay on the desk, tied up, her shirt torn open to expose her bare chest. Someone had taken care to not rip it far enough to expose her breasts.

My God, Em! A flutter began in her own chest as she looked on. Something about Em always appealed to her, had for some time. The girl maintained a positive attitude and hilarious demeanor even during trying times. This spoke to her character yet nothing about her looks, which Angela admitted, ranged well above average. Striking, even. Her heart thumped faster until she needed to remind herself the chick needed saving. Her mind felt fuzzy, struggling for a reason Harold would tie her mentee up on a desk.

Butterflies in her belly, Angela stepped inside with her Glock raised. "Harold, what the hell's going on in here?"

Jeb froze, but the look of intensity in his wide eyes didn't abate. Whatever he was about to do, Jeb took with a serious determination. He tightened the grip on his knife and took a step toward Em, eyes on

Angela. A deep scowl spread across his face, shadows deepening at his mouth and eyes. She'd never known Jeb to get mean, but that's how she would describe him now and how she'd write his demeanor up in the report.

"I mean it, Jeb," Angela said. "Put that knife down and let's talk this out. I'm sure there's a good reason you have Em tied to the desk there." She gestured away from Em with the barrel of her Glock.

Harold didn't appear as sure as Jeb, a sorrowful look in his eyes, like an otherwise good kid talked into jacking a candy bar. His eyes were wide with surprise, bits of sound escaping his mouth that sounded like a bunch of stuttering. She wondered if the beginnings of a stroke were making themselves known. His face turned red as he stammered his nonsense.

Jeb took another step toward Em, shot a withering glance at the stammering Harold, then turned his body enough to point the sharp-edged butcher knife at Angela. He nodded, face still consumed by the mask of anger and shadows. Angela thought he looked like the lead singer for Type O Negative, vampiric yet wolfish in the same stretch of his elongated face.

Angela removed herself from the doorjamb and took a step toward the desk.

"Please stop," Harold said, voice soft and somewhat tender given the circumstance. "I know we have our moments, but I possess no stomach to harm a fellow peace officer. Just turn around and pretend you didn't see any of this. Don't tell Robbie—don't tell anyone and I'll get you through this."

Em trembled on the desk, a tear streaking from her eye. Angela saw a bruise forming high on her cheekbone. Her voice shook when she spoke. "These two asshats tied me up and were about to cut me." She appeared to consider her words while Jeb inched toward her. "Do what he says, Angela. I don't want to see you get hurt." Her eyes pleaded with a sincerity that broke something inside Angela's heart. Em's words would have the opposite effect on her actions whether or not the girl knew this.

Angela scowled. *The voice of an angel.* Then confusion set in. She'd known both Harold and Jeb for years. Sure, they were both old and cranky, almost feeble in their curmudgeonly ways. They definitely held jaundiced views of today's young people, but she'd never known either to have violent tendencies. Perhaps, because of the blizzard, they felt they could get away with murder.

"You better start making some sense, Harold," she warned. Angela took another step forward and felt the tension build as sure as the gauge attached to the old boiler in the maintenance room.

"Offered me a ride like a real gentleman," Em sobbed. She struggled with her bindings. "Real nice guy. Then, instead of driving me home from the pub, he brought me here and hauled me inside where Jeb here tied me down. Now he's gonna cut me." She glanced at Jeb and screeched, "Dickhead!"

Despite her bold words, Angela could see traces of fear in her smudged mascara and down-turned lips. *Brave girl, but not bulletproof. Or knife-proof. Or even dickhead-proof.*

Jeb flinched at Em's words, his face flushed with anger, then turned his dark eyes back to the Glock Angela held in her hand. Jeb would kill her first chance he got. The old man held no love for her— probably didn't understand her. Yet Angela found it hard to believe they would just kill her in cold blood. But here they all were.

"Jeb won't cut on anyone," Angela said. She raised the Glock higher, then turned to Harold, hoping Em felt safer with her here. "Now, what's going on?"

"Just listen," Harold managed. "Hear us out. Once you know the whole story, you might not feel the need to act so hastily. It's for the good of everyone."

"Tying me down and cutting me?" Emily wailed, more tears leaking down her right cheek. She sounded wounded. "That's good for everyone? Thought you were a lawman."

"You'd sure be a sight more important dead than you ever were while breathing...and drinking and whoring," Jeb said, finally breaking the silence.

"I ain't no whore, Jeb Olson! Just because I date lots of guys and gals, don't mean I sleep around. I got a right to make sure I pick the right fella...or gal." She turned to Angela and smiled, tears still leaking.

Angela felt a blush creep up her neck, but ignored the girl's smile for the moment. If she didn't, the situation might slip away from her. She'd always been a business first gal and this was no exception. An innocent life lay in the balance of her actions.

"Don't go and take this personal, Emily," Harold said. "Jeb didn't mean that, did ya, Jeb?"

"I damn well meant it, and I'm gonna butcher her like a pig," Jeb said, voice ice-cold and smooth. Despite the Glock aimed at him, he raised the butcher knife and pointed the tip toward Em's exposed chest-bone.

Harold continued, "Now look, we don't give a cat's backside who you date, even if it's Angela here, but you were there, and the opening ritual already was a going, and we needed the first sacrifice. You understand, don't you?"

"Shut up," Jeb said. White spittle flew from the corners of his mouth. "We've said too much already. Time to end this. And by end this, I mean end Em. Nobody will miss her."

Angela would miss her. She knew this, so she took another step into the gloom.

"Are you on drugs?" Em asked, voice shaky. Angela could tell she was trying to sound brave, perhaps for her sake. "Because you're acting like an asshole and not making a bit of sense." She took the time to glance at Angela, tears ready to burst from the corners of scared eyes.

Angela played along. Perhaps Harold would fuck up, make a mistake, give away his hand, or start some favorable outcome. She smiled as best she could. "Probably senile."

Emily shrugged beneath her harness of rope and attempted to smile but only managed a flicker of levity before it disappeared back into the morass of terror. "Yeah, maybe." Angela appreciated the way the girl conducted herself under duress, despite the tears.

"Never touched drugs," Harold said, looking offended. "And, yeah, I'm sure this all seems strange, but if any of you young ones paid attention to anything that happens around here besides the bottom of a bottle or peering into the bartender's eyes, or each other's, you might just understand a thing or two."

"About what?" Emily choked. Then quieter, an afterthought, "And don't you be cocking off about Adam's eyes. They're that dreamy gray color you almost never see." She smiled at Angela again, her expression bland with fear. "Not so pretty as yours though, babe."

The words stunned Angela, and perhaps, in a different place and a different time, with no snot running from Em's nose and onto her top lip, she would find the sentiment meaningful. She turned to Harold before she could blush. "What are you getting at?"

"You wouldn't understand because you ain't from around these parts," Harold said. "This here isn't any business for outsiders."

"Damn straight!" Jeb gave Harold a stare. "Now, shut up and let's get on with it. Either talk some sense to your deputy or she can die, too. Don't matter much either way to me."

Angela now hated them both. She pointed the Glock straight at Harold's cranium. "You have about one second to explain yourself before I either blow your head from your shoulders or haul you in to see Robbie."

"Now, hold on," Harold said, hands out in front of him. "Okay! Okay. We gotta do this. If we don't, we'll piss off it that shall not be spoken of."

"What shall not be spoken of?" Em sassed, getting into her role of scared motormouth. "That you're a douchebag dickhead?"

"You shut your mouth," Jeb said and raised the knife higher. The tip gleamed in what little light existed. "I'll take pleasure in gutting you, make it hurt extra bad, move the blade around in your innards."

"That goes double for you," Em said, snot bubbles of fear pouring from her nose and littering her full upper lip. Angela noticed how it pooled in her cleft and didn't care for it one bit.

Jeb took a step forward.

Angela swung the Glock toward Jeb who stopped, a foot in the air, eyes locked on the cold metal of the gun. "Slow your role."

While Angela concentrated on Jeb, Harold took a step toward her. His hand went for his own piece and had the gun out of the leather holster before she could react. Then it slipped from his hand, scuttled across the floor, and disappeared beneath an old tool chest.

Everyone froze as if ensconced in blocks of ice. Angela remained confused. Em stared off to where the sidearm disappeared.

Harold mumbled something under his breath and took a step toward the chest.

"Stay where you are," Angela said.

With a faltering step, Harold obeyed. He turned to her with somber eyes. "Leave this be, Angela. I'm begging you—You have no clue what you're messing with here. If we fail, you and Em are dead, anyway."

"You two are about the worst cultists this world has ever seen," Em said. Despite her words, Angela watched her tears gather and spill down her cheeks. A glob of snot elongated and then dripped from her lip to her chin. The bruise on her cheekbone had already become more pronounced. How anyone could stomach hitting Em, Angela didn't know. A slow rage kindled within her, a protective spirit, perhaps something more than just her duty to uphold the law.

Harold dove to the floor, squawked in pain, then crawled toward the cabinet to retrieve his pistol. He made little metallic clanking noises and swore and grumbled a lot as he rummaged about.

While Angela stared at Harold's ass-end, Jeb made his move and lunged, knife out, at Emily. "Die, dammit!" Jeb screamed as he drove the knife downward.

Angela saw the motion as if slowed down just for her. The knife came down, and Em shrieked as if she'd been stabbed, mouth wide with terror. Angela saw the glint in the girl's eye—a changing of the structure and depth, a hardening of sorts—when she made her move.

Em hadn't been tied down near tight enough and rolled to her right as the knife flew downward at her chest.

The metal blade clanged off the table, broke in two, and rattled over by where Harold worked to retrieve his pistol from beneath the cabinet. The handle remained in a confused Jeb's hand. He lifted it to his face as if he couldn't see what happened. Then the black part of his eyes grew pitch-dark like two orbs of polished onyx. He shook his head. "You wanna make this hard, then I'm gonna enjoy myself."

Em's face scrunched in concentration, eyes darting back and forth in a rapid motion. Angela knew the girl couldn't avoid the killing stroke forever and moved forward.

"What's going on?" Harold yelled, now either stuck beneath the cabinet or unable to crawl out with any haste.

"I'll kill you with my bare hands," Jeb hissed and reached for Em's neck. "Gonna feel your windpipe crunch in my hands. Watch the light go out of your eyes, whore."

"No," Harold yelled. "You gotta make the mark first or it that shouldn't get mentioned won't accept the offering!"

Jeb continued, anyway, as if he just knew Angela wouldn't use the Glock in her hand. She hadn't yet and Jeb appeared a desperate man. Despite sounding off his rocker, these two believed in their mission. She believed Jeb would do what he said.

Keeping some distance from Em's thrashing head, he gripped her neck with both hands—her all arms, legs, and screams—and held it like a lover might.

"Feels good," Jeb said. "A shame, really."

Em spit in his face. "Kill me, then. Just stop touching me like that. Nobody gets to touch me like that. Nobody." She struggled beneath his beefy arms.

Jeb didn't bother to wipe the spittle from between his eyes, and he bunched his shoulder muscles to better squeeze and finish the job.

Em let out with a strangled screech and continued to thrash around on the desk. She bucked her butt up and down off the desk trying to dislodge Jeb from her throat.

Angela stalked forward. She'd never shot a person before. It would be hard to live with but she had limited options. Shoot or let Em die. Angela aimed, then shot Jeb in the leg. Blood spurted in a thick rope of liquid red which pooled on the floor and ran for the drain.

Jeb screamed like a banshee and dropped to the floor, hand flat against his thigh to staunch the blood flow.

"Holy shit," Em yelled, "you shot the old dickhead!" She sounded relieved, but Em noticed how she twisted her now-bruised throat in discomfort. She glanced at Angela, eyes soft and moist. She smiled a little. "What took ya so long?"

Angela managed a short, clipped laugh. That's all Em would get, though.

"Stop! Jeb, you okay?" Harold yelled but still couldn't get out from under the cabinet. His legs kicked and bucked, and Angela heard something pop in the man's joints. "Ouch! Sumbitch!"

Jeb, like one of the serial-killers in the old slasher movies who just wouldn't stop, clung to the edge of the table with bloody fingers and lifted himself up. He reached for Emily's throat again, with a growl. Blood leaked from his leg and pattered to the floor and formed a puddle in the low point in the concrete before it could reach the drain.

Time slowed down again. Angela would never reach Em in time or even deliver a bullet.

Em quieted, eyes hard, jaw set in a determined scowl. Angela felt she looked too calm and waited for the girl to launch into whatever plan she had concocted. One she probably used more than once over at the pub. Em waited for Jeb to draw near, the opportune moment, then as the killer grimaced and went for her neck, she drove her forehead into the bridge of Jeb's nose with a savage thrust.

The nose burst like an overripe tomato, a red dot making an ink-blot test of Em's forehead.

Jeb teetered, then fell to the floor, screeching, one hand over the bullet hole, the other over his nose. He bled from both ends as he flailed about.

Angela didn't feel in the particular mood to care. "Nice move," she said.

"Girl learns to take pretty good care of herself around here," Em said, a smirk planted on her lips.

Both men thrashed on the floor a moment before Angela unhooked the walkie from her belt. She raised it to her lips and pressed the long button on the side. "Angela calling Robbie. Come in, Robbie."

"We're all doomed," Harold wailed.

"Robbie here," he answered through a belch of white noise.

"You're all gonna burn in hell," Jeb added.

"You better get over to the maintenance garage. You aren't going to believe this."

Chapter 6

James sat across the table from Vic, menu in his hand. He stared at the back flap as if fearing possession. In a large rectangle at the bottom, it stated, *The ghosts of Jerome Grand Hotel enjoy watching guests as they eat. Imagine that every empty seat harbors a member of the deceased.*

"No, thank you," James whispered to himself. Yet he glanced about furtively in a way that wouldn't bother other guests, checking each empty seat. There were several, but more book folks had stuck around than he'd expected. At least a dozen tables held patrons.

"What was that?" Vic asked, looking up from her own menu where she perused the entrees instead of the ghost information.

"Oh, nothing," James said. He changed the subject, "Looks like some of your colleagues decided to stick things out."

"Yes," Vic said. "Including Jack, thank goodness. Wouldn't be much of a conference without him. Such as it is now."

James nodded, somewhat distracted as his eyes flitted to empty chairs where he didn't notice any apparitions. He wondered if his aura was now thoroughly violet only, or if the last bout of attention in the shower from Vic sent strands of peach racing back into it.

"World to James," Vic murmured.

"Oh," James said and looked into her dark eyes, "sorry. Just thinking about my experience earlier, I guess. You know how it is." He hated to admit this paranormal stuff bothered him. But it kind of did. It just didn't jibe with his sensibilities or world view. He was a man of science, of things he could touch and feel. Now, he could admit, if only to himself, he felt out of his element and the slightest bit discombobulated. He'd always thought it rubbish. But now...

"I thought all that angst would have been drained from you in the shower," Vic said. She batted her eyes.

"Stop," James said, more conservative in public than her. He looked to see if anyone heard. "You just like to embarrass me." He smiled so she knew he held no grudges about the matter. He loved the attention, just not the entire world knowing about it.

"You weren't embarrassed when you fucked me in the shower...from behind," Vic whispered, then winked at him. She glanced around at the others. "No one's paying attention, and even if they were, it'll do them good to witness a healthy sex life. It'll make their writing better, too."

James felt himself turn red. This was a perfect example of what he both loved and sometimes disliked about Vic. Sex talk, even gestures, in public never bothered her in the least. If someone stared, she'd whisper, "They should buy a ticket."

"Anyway," Vic went on. "Before I distracted you in the shower, and you curled my toes in pleasure, you mentioned seeing something in the hall outside our room. A nurse and a gurney, you said?"

He nodded. "Probably just a cleaner and her cart. You know, with all the guests checking out." James wished she would drop it. He couldn't articulate his feelings even to himself, let alone to her.

Vic made a noncommittal little noise deep in her throat. "You're always one to swing things back to the rational." She paused. "What if it was a ghost?"

"Well, there were the children," James said as an afterthought. He hoped this train of conversation wouldn't backfire on him.

"Ghost children?"

"No, no," James said. "These were flesh and blood, without a doubt. They were ghost hunting, so they said. Like playing house, I suppose."

"Oh?" she asked. "You didn't mention that in the shower."

"Well, I was distracted," he said and reached out for her hand and squeezed it. He stared into her bright eyes and saw his forever. After a romantic moment, James continued, "But they were precocious. Made up an outrageous story about their Dad and his girlfriend, Tracey, getting some paranormal documentary over to the Travel channel, and how Janey, the girl, was possessed by a demon after her mother was murdered by a serial killer."

"Good Lord," Vic said. "Sounds like the plot of a horror movie."

"All made up, almost certainly," James said with what he hoped was a reassuring smile. He wanted to drop the matter. Any reasonable person could see the kids possessed quite the imagination. "Anyway, they said they had to get things on film and traipsed off with a video camera to get the maintenance guy's splattered head on film." He laughed with an uncomfortable chortle.

"How, macabre," Vic replied. James could tell the topic fascinated her because of the way her pupils turned black. *Crap.* She scrunched up her eyes and looked past James. "Is that them?"

James turned in his seat. Sure enough, a woman, presumably Auntie Kayla, and the two kids sat at a table across the room. The boy and woman sipped soft drinks, but the girl stared into a mirror on the wall next to her. Her features were slack, and the reflection of her eyes in the mirror looked dull and empty. From this angle, he couldn't tell what the girl stared at so attentively. What a peculiar child, James thought. He found he didn't care for the behavior and felt the pinpricks of unease in his belly. He took a deep breath and tried to not let the kids bother him.

With a sudden movement, the reflection of her eyes in the mirror flickered over to make eye-contact with him, as if she'd sensed him observing her somehow.

He felt a second and stronger jolt of anxiety, so he turned back to their table and his menu. "Yes," he answered, "that's them." He wanted to change the subject because the paranormal nature of the kids creeped him out. Already he could hear the boy's excited voice all the way from his table. More ghost stuff, he assumed. "So, what is recommended on this menu, anyway?"

"Ribs and the garlic mashed potato, according to Jack." But she looked at him funny. "Are you okay? You've turned a ghost-like shade of white."

"I'm fine," he lied, then glanced out the window to avoid her inquisitive stare. He knew she'd demand a better answer than what he gave. He wasn't sure how to explain that the supposed ghosts of the Jerome Grand made him anxious. He focused on the gigantic window cased in original dark oak he and Vic sat next to. It overlooked the valley way down below. Snow came down in thick torrents and already half a foot lay on top of the remaining cars in the small narrow parking lot. The sun hung low in the sky, obscured by a thick blanket of storm clouds. Twilight would begin soon. Then what? That thought also made him nervous. He'd never believed in ghosts but now…well, here they were.

"Except during our frolicking, you've been preoccupied since we got here. If I didn't know better, I'd think you actually believe in ghosts and were afraid of them."

"Nonsense," James said with a flip of his wrist and a quick smile. He glanced once more at the menu. "Ribs and squashed taters it is." Then he wished he hadn't used the word squashed. It reminded him of the maintenance guy the kids wanted to get on video.

Vic nodded. "Some of the other writers want to get together after supper for drinks to discuss the use of proper genre plot devices. Can you entertain yourself?" She set her menu over James' to signal the waiter.

"Of course," James said. "I have plenty of papers to grade just waiting for me upstairs in my briefcase. No worries. Go enjoy yourself." He wanted her to. This week was for her, and ghosts or no ghosts, he would make do.

The waiter showed up and took their food orders. They also ordered another round of Moscato. The waiter smiled and traipsed back to the kitchen, ignoring the table with Auntie Kayla and the two kids even though Kayla held a waving hand in the air. Perhaps the guy had picked up on the strangeness same as James himself had. James felt a rush of vindication.

Before he turned back around, James noticed Janey seemed obsessed with the mirror. He wondered if she'd been possessed again. It wouldn't surprise him, though he didn't believe in such. At least he hadn't. James imagined Tracey, whatever she looked like, wrapping this mirror like she had the other as the story went. *Complete rubbish.* He turned back to Vic who then stood.

"I shall allow you to get acquainted with solitary confinement while I use the bathroom. Try not to bother those kids by staring at them. Thank you." She smiled, then turned and walked away before James could protest.

"I couldn't care less about them," he whispered, then took a sip from his water as he sat forlorn and chastised. He looked out into the growing darkness where night fell faster than usual because of the blizzard and wished the restaurant were better lit. Low lighting made for great romance but poor eyesight conditions. And, for that little butterfly feeling in his stomach. Still watching the storm, he thought he could make out figures, shadows of figures, making their way through the storm. Only his imagination, James supposed.

Just as James was about to take another sip of water, he heard the boy shout, "There, in the mirror!"

Despite his promise to Vic, James turned around.

Vic freshened her lipstick in the mirror. No need to rush. The way James acted, he could use some time alone. *He's jumpy as a cat on a hot roof.* She'd never known him to embrace the supernatural, but he seemed to now. When in Rome, she supposed. The place gave off a certain vibe. She crammed the tube back in her purse, then fluffed her hair which the storm was affecting more than she cared for. She walked toward the door. Just for the briefest of moments, Vic wondered how long they would remain here, snowed in, and decided it didn't matter. James didn't have school for another week, and she could write from anywhere. *And the sex!*

She smiled salaciously at her thoughts before pushing open the heavy oak bathroom door. It slid effortlessly on well-maintained hinges and this made her think of the poor handyman that got…squashed beneath the elevator car. Vic shuddered but her smile never faltered. Life was good.

The door swung closed behind her as she stepped from the white-tiled floor of the bathroom onto the striped two-toned green carpeting of the main hallway. The old-fashioned brass-lantern style votive candles on the wall gave off enough light for comfort, but not much more than that. Vic imagined they contributed to the ghost stories.

Out in the hall, she heard commotion from the dining room, although she remained far enough away she couldn't hear as well as she wanted to. Probably someone told a joke. She hoped with all her heart James wouldn't end up at the center of that fuss. He seemed obsessed with the ghost-hunting children, and Vic could see where that kind of thing could lead to trouble with their aunt. Sometimes James erred on the side of too conservative and took his role as an educator to all new levels. Sometimes he went way too far.

James was the best kind of teacher, but sometimes that also led him to bouts of righteous indignation in which he felt it necessary to intervene and create precious learning moments. These moments were often unwanted, and sometimes unwarranted in Vic's opinion, making him look like a prude.

Just as Vic would have turned down the hall to return to the restaurant, a door slid open in the opposite direction and a head emerged from it. The shroud of white hair surrounding a pale white face looked rumpled. Was that blood on the woman's cheek? *A woman?* Yes, Vic knew. Marion, she thought. The helpful lady from the front desk.

Marion waved a weak arm, her hand fluttering in a slow gesture. The loose skin beneath her bicep swung in lazy arcs. "I need help," the woman said. "Please."

"Of course," Vic said, and walked toward the woman. She felt a sense of dread. Something about the woman's expression. "What's wrong?"

Instead of answering, Marion ducked back inside the room, leaving the door open so Vic could enter. She paused at the doorway because it lay bathed in darkness. No lights were on in the room, and this concerned her. Why would Marion want her inside a darkened room? Perhaps all the bulbs had burned out, and that's what the older woman needed help with. Too frightened to climb a ladder to those twelve-foot heights, she mused. Vic pushed the door open but did not enter.

The light from the hallway entered the room a short way but not far enough to see Marion standing in there. Shadows appeared to crawl and drift about and, for a reason Vic didn't quite understand yet, these shadows made her feel uncomfortable. They looked menacing and cruel.

"Hello?" Vic said.

"Help!" she heard the woman say, voice strained and scratchy, as if something was wrong with her.

"Have you fallen?" Vic asked. "Why are the lights out?" She looked down the main hallway in both directions hoping to see someone else who could help. No such luck. She should go get James. Anything but walk into that room full of shadows.

"Help," Marion repeated from somewhere in the bowels of the inky-dark room. "I'm in here."

"Yes, I know," Vic said, somewhat annoyed with the repetitive nature of the woman's pleas. "But I can't see a thing. It would help if you told me the nature of your emergency. Then I can go get the proper personnel."

The woman moaned. "I'm bleeding."

Vic had seen the blood on Marion's cheek. So, she didn't doubt the woman, but it had looked like very little to fret about, just a shiny smear of crimson across her right cheekbone and jowl. "Okay," Vic said. "I'm stepping inside. Where are you?"

"Here," Marion answered, her voice not much beyond a whisper.

In the darkness, Vic could make out the corner of a made bed, and she thought Marion's voice came from that general direction. She took a step inside but stayed inside the small rectangle of light that pushed in from the hallway sconces. She felt if she stepped out of the light, she would fall into an abyss of darkness and join those shadows. Vic listened and thought she could hear the old woman breathing. "Hello?" Her voice echoed.

"Come here," Marion said, sounding testier than Vic cared for. "There's nothing to be frightened of. The dark is our friend."

"Perhaps," Vic said, although she disagreed. The dark, even as a child, rarely frightened her, but to seek it out seemed another matter. Especially in this situation where she couldn't see to lend assistance. "However, it's not yours if you need my help. I can't see a damn thing." She looked for a switch in case Marion shut the lights off and couldn't turn them back on but didn't see one. "Where's the light-switch?" Vic asked.

"Over here," Marion said. She paused as if considering how to answer this further. "One light is burned out. The other won't turn on." Then she moaned.

"Okay," Vic said, and against better judgement, she took another step inside. She stood at the furthest reaches of the hallway lights. Vic still couldn't see anything except for the corner of the bed. The curtains must be drawn, she thought, because even the outside twilight was brighter than this gloom. She took another step. Finally, Vic reached the corner of the bed and looked around the corner to her right.

At first, she saw nothing. Then a blur of motion, an apparition, came from that direction as if floating across the thick carpet, slow at first, then faster, as if motivated by Vic's proximity. She let out a small screech of surprise.

Vic held out a protective hand, then the blur took shape and looked very much like Marion with a clothing-iron above her head. Marion's hands came down as she approached, and the iron whistled toward Vic's head.

A rush of adrenaline flashed through Vic's system. Was the old woman trying to harm her? The iron glistened as it caught the small bit of light from the hallway, just enough for Vic to track its progress toward her cranium. God, but the old woman moved like a panther. Vic took a step back to prolong the moment of contact. Just as Marion and the iron reached her, Vic sidestepped. With a violent turn of her body, she knocked the iron off course with one hand and shoved the old woman past her with the other. The iron clanked to the floor and rolled away. Marion screeched and stumbled past Vic, arms pinwheeling in a hasty and unbalanced fashion. Vic stepped back into the rectangle of light, her safe place.

"You just tried to murder me," Vic said, her breath coming in heaves from her now-tight chest, unsure of what else to say. She placed her hands on her knees as she searched for Marion in the darkness. Vic knew she should run and seek help but her legs didn't wish to cooperate.

Nothing but heavy breaths for a moment, then, "Come here," Marion croaked.

"I think not," Vic said, who reached around the corner where Marion had just been and flipped the light switch. The room erupted with brightness and now Vic could see the situation in its full glory.

Marion stood by a table on the other side of the bed, one hand on the table to steady herself, the other on her chest. Blood splattered the woman's face and clothes, and there was a darker splotch from her ass-end where some material had worn away to her skin. An abrasion of some sort.

"You're bleeding," Vic said. "Why did you attack me when I only wished to help?"

"I got confused," the old woman said. Vic knew this was a lie. Marion continued, "Sometimes my dementia kicks in and I get goofy, think people are after me. I'm okay now, just come over here."

"Why are you all scraped up?"

"Fell down."

Vic nodded. She didn't believe the old woman. The scrape on her backside, maybe, but a fall wouldn't account for the watered-down blood on her face and clothes. Yes, definitely watered down, not full-on arterial blood by any means. "Whose blood is all over you? Looks watered down, like you tried to clean up."

"Wouldn't you?" the woman asked. "Clean up, I mean." She paused, but when Vic waited, she continued, "I fell, bled, then tried to clean up. I might've hit my head, I think. Things are a bit...fuzzy."

Marion's chest heaved. The woman's story sounded plausible, however unlikely. Then Vic noticed Marion's jaundiced eyes flicker to the fallen clothes-iron, just for a moment. She returned them to Vic almost right away, but Vic had noticed the small transgression. She hurried toward the solid-looking iron. If Marion had been successful in delivering the blow, Vic might very well be on the floor now, writhing in pain, possibly even dead.

At the same time, Marion made a quick move in the iron's direction, intent on reaching it first. The moment Marion transferred weight from her left foot to her right, her leg crumpled and she fell to the floor like a slab of beef and lay unmoving. "My hip," she groaned. She looked up at Vic through rheumy bloodshot eyes.

Just for good measure, even though she knew Marion would never reach the item now, Vic reached down and picked up the iron, then threw it out in the main hallway where it rattled about before coming to rest next to the wall.

"Come down here and let me kill you," Marion hissed through her pain.

"I don't think so," Vic said. *The woman must be insane.*

"Better than what will happen to you later if you don't."

"What do you mean?"

"I mean," Marion said through clenched teeth, "if you don't let me sacrifice you in a nice humane way, you'll die screaming later, along with your husband, those kids, and everyone else."

"Not at your hand, I dare say," Vic quipped. "You broke your hip or worse and will need to recuperate in a home. Not ideal, but that's what one gets when they try to commit murder."

Marion sighed. "Sure was a spat easier thirty years ago," she said "Back then, nobody could keep us from what we needed to do."

"And what's that?"

"Sacrifice seven folks," Marion said. "Then it'll go away and leave the rest of us be."

"I'd say, you failed," Vic said with a triumphant tone, pleased she could end this madness. The other thing the woman mentioned didn't worry her, not yet. Not while this glorious adrenaline pumped through her body. However, a little voice in the back of her mind told her she may need to worry about that more later.

"No, shit," Marion wheezed. She shot Vic a look. "And don't think it's a blessing. You'll see real soon. You'll wish I would have killed you with that iron."

Vic laughed at this. Sour grapes, she knew. "I'll go call the sheriff. He can call you an ambulance. If one can get through in this storm."

"Don't matter," the woman said. "I'm already dead. Or good as, anyway."

"Such a pessimist."

"You're just saying that because you don't know what you're up against." Marion closed her eyes and refused to speak any further.

Vic, somewhat put out by the woman's unwillingness to speak, turned and walked into the hall, determined to get ahold of the sheriff. Something very wrong was happening at the Jerome Grand.

Chapter 7

Against his better judgment, James turned and looked at the table where the boy spouted his wild accusations. The kid stared at the mirror now, along with the girl. Auntie Kayla tried best she could to quiet him, using soft words and a gentle hand on the kid's shoulder. James decided he could be of some help. He was a schoolteacher, after all, trained to handle unruly children and their flights of fancy. He got up and walked over without hesitation.

"What seems to be the matter?" he asked Auntie Kayla. He wished to sound authoritative yet helpful. Useful but not intrusive. Intrusive behavior occasionally got him reprimanded, either by Vic or the dean. The dean, he could handle.

She looked embarrassed. Then a raising of her right eyebrow made James fear she was irritated by his helpfulness. "Oh, you know…kids." She said this slowly, as if trying to feel James out. "Miles says he saw something in the mirror other than Janey and the room. His imagination is quite active." She smiled and turned away from him.

James didn't appreciate the dismissal when he only wished to help. He decided to remain patient and wondered if Auntie Kayla knew about Janey's supposed possession and Tracey's wrapping of the mirror. He supposed not. The kids were probably careful what they said around her out of fear their excursions would end.

"Let's see if I can help," James offered. "I'm a teacher."

Kayla frowned and looked, by the pursing of her lips and sharp intake of air, about to tell James off. But then she must have reconsidered. "Oh," Kayla said. She shrugged and let out a tired sigh. She looked from the kids to James before taking another sip from her wine glass. "If you think you can. Sometimes they have to just run it out of their systems." She paused and a smirk grew on her lips. "In fact, I'm feeling a little bit ill. I think I'll take the back stairs up to my room and grab a nap. The kids have been on their own all day, anyway. They behave better when I'm not around, it seems."

"I don't know about that," James said. He hoped he sounded polite. "I'm sure they enjoy your company. Anyway, I hope you feel better. And don't worry. I'll have a quick chat with them and send them on their way."

"Thank you," Kayla said. "You kids try not to disturb the other guests and be back to the room by nine, okay?"

"Sure," Miles said. A smile blossomed on his face and James figured this was due to the perceived freedom he would now have.

Kayla waved, took a drunken little stumble, then walked toward the back stairs with wine glass in hand.

"She has trouble with a lot of people sometimes," Miles said.

"Crowds aren't her thing?" James asked.

"No," he said. "She'd way rather drink wine and scribble love stories in her notebook."

"Yes, of course," James said. "Some folks just prefer solitude while others crave excitement and stimulation."

"I guess. She worries a lot. Not about Janey and me so much, but about bad things happening and stuff. Sometimes she just kind of zones out, especially when we talk about ghosts. She really freaks when our dad and Tracey try to get her involved with the documentaries. She drinks liquor a lot too."

"Speaking of ghosts," James said, glad to change the subject from Kayla and her liquor to their wild claims. "What have we here?" He pointed at Janey and the mirror. "More spooks for your video camera?" He tried for his best condescending smile to properly convey his disbelief in the paranormal. But did he disbelieve? He tried not to think about it and concentrated on Miles.

Miles smiled his enthusiasm for the subject.

James laughed in a way he hoped would calm the child down. "What an imagination, you have."

"You saw a ghost," Miles pointed out.

James glanced around to make sure nobody overheard that little gem of information. He felt a lump of concern in his throat when a couple people turned to look in his direction.

He laughed again, to show a proper measure of skepticism to the closest. "Just a cleaner and her cart out in the hall," James said. "Nothing of any paranormal significance, I can assure you. Not that the paranormal exists at all, mind you." It wouldn't do to have a grown adult think he believed in things like this. That would shoot his credibility to hell and back. Yet, that little voice in the back of his mind told him something else.

That's when Janey turned away from the mirror. "It wants to kill us all," she said in a soft tone.

"Holy shit!" Miles exclaimed. "Hear that? It wants to off us...all of us! The thing I saw in the mirror. Janey's been talking to it."

People from adjoining tables stared at them as if they were the Manson family. One table even left, but not before casting an ugly glance in their direction.

James blushed. Screaming and cursing kids just wouldn't do. He contemplated what to say for a moment, reaching deep into his bag of useful tools before addressing Janey. "It's not appropriate to make up stories such as that. Death is never a laughing matter." He turned to Miles. "Please watch your mouth."

Janey stared at him in her eerie way, eyes dark, forehead creased, then turned back to the mirror. James could see her reflection, and she looked sleepy or bored.

"Who's laughing, and who's making stuff up, Mister?" Miles asked. "I saw something in there. The mirror turned all dark, then there was this face full of teeth, it looked like. Then it just disappeared. And Janey doesn't lie. Sure, she's weird, but if she says the face with teeth wants to kill us all, well, I think we better believe her."

Janey didn't turn around, but said, "I'm not weird."

Yes, you are, James thought. *Good Lord.* If he lived another day, another century, James knew he would never meet kids as weird as these two. They ranged so far off the charts he couldn't even find a suitable malady to label them with.

"Eccentric," Miles countered. "That's what Tracey says."

Janey shrugged, perhaps more comfortable with this label than the other. She continued to stare into the mirror as if her favorite YouTube video played inside.

"Six of one, half a dozen of the other, I'm sure," James said. "All the same, you kids, even if you're not outright fibbing, you need not frighten the other dinner guests. They deserve to eat in peace."

"So, you don't think they'd want to know if something wants to off them?" Miles asked. "I would, just saying."

Janey began to hum to herself, as if to some music nobody else could here. Then the hum turned into a repetition of consonants. It sounded to James as if she was repeating the letter C over and over under her breath.

"Sometimes she does that when she Scrys," Miles said. "Repeats words that spirits give her."

"Is she frightened?" James asked. He knew she must be, or she wouldn't be chattering like that. If she'd experienced half the things Miles claimed, it would be no surprise to see her crumpled into a bawling mess on the floor. These kids didn't act like any he had ever encountered. "What exactly is this scrying business?"

"She loves scrying. You know, divining information by talking to spirits through a mirror. Tracey says spirits can use old antique mirrors as a portal to and from the spirit realms. Only the old ones with silver backing, though. Not the new worthless ones. They're just trash. And naw. Janey doesn't get scared." Miles shook his head back and forth in emphasis.

Oh, God, James thought. *Here we are again.* The kid could tell stories like no other. It's no wonder Janey acted so strangely with a brother and the parentage she had at her disposal.

"Janey," Miles continued, "says the mirrors here are all old ones, and the spirits are really active. They been trying to warn her about some bad thing about to go down. Probably got to do with the thing that wants to off everyone."

James was about to try and argue his doubts about Janey's assessment when from the back of the restaurant, "James," Vic shouted. She waved her arms at him as if he could have missed her. Then she turned, pointing to the cellphone in her hand, and asked something of the bartender.

He stared hard in her direction, trying to determine the problem. She looked harried, and that usually took some doing. Vic almost always proved stalwart and calm under fire, if not a bit of a smartass and demanding when it came to her own personal well-being.

James watched as the bartender picked up the bar phone, dialed a number, let it ring, then hung up. He said something to Vic, then shrugged an apology.

Vic nodded, then turned and nearly sprinted toward James and the others. When she neared, she said, "James, that old crone, Marion, tried to bludgeon me with one of those old heavy clothes irons. But she's incapacitated now, maybe worse."

"Holy fucking shit," Miles said. "She tried to off ya. Just like Janey said."

Janey kept on staring into the mirror.

James put an arm on Vic's shoulder. "My God, are you okay?" He looked back toward the bar to make sure the woman wasn't sneaking up on them.

"She lured me in there, James," Vic said. "Lured me in with the explicit intent of sacrificing me so that some abomination, a creature by the sounds of it, wouldn't come murder everyone else. She's gone insane."

Janey turned to Vic with dilated pupils. She didn't even blink.

James thought the entire world had gone mad, lost its center. Nothing made a lick of sense. The world he knew rained down around him as fast as the falling snow outside.

Vic waited for a response but James felt tongue tied and that anything he said would prove ineffectual. He was a schoolteacher, not a criminal investigator or a ghost hunter.

"My dad writes horror," Miles spouted. "Wrote a novel about his childhood and some chick named Jewel. That's the name of the book.

Anyway, it sold over ten-thousand copies, which might not sound like a lot, but it's not bad for a small press sale."

This, about Miles' father, didn't faze James. *The man writes horror. Makes all the sense in the world.*

Vic continued, "I dialed 911 and I got forwarded to the State police. They forwarded me to the sheriff who didn't answer. Apparently, Jerome only has a clinic with one on-call nurse practitioner who probably went home. That woman, despite her atrocities, deserves medical attention."

"Can I go look?" Miles asked, excited as always.

"For the sheriff?" James asked the boy. "No, it's a blizzard out there." That's all they needed was for the kids to go racing through the winter wonderland outside. Enough problems existed without heaping that onto the pile.

"Naw," Miles said, "at the dead old lady. I wanna get some footage for Tracey on the video camera. Her ghost is probably still lurking about, especially since it sounds like she has plenty to say."

What? He wondered for the first time if his world would ever return. Vic jabbered into one ear, Miles the other, but he didn't hear either. They canceled each other out.

"It wants to kill us," Janey repeated.

This James heard. "Why?" he nearly screamed. *And what?* He didn't wish for the answers and wanted nothing more than to take Vic to their room and get a good night's sleep, then get out of here in the morning.

Janey shrugged. "You know, the ritual failed." She said this as if every person on the planet should already know.

"Who wants to kill us?" Vic asked. "Someone besides Marion?"

"Not a who, I don't think," Janey said. "Probably an *it*."

"What kind of *it*?" James asked. "You mean like that clown from the movie?" He didn't wish an answer to this. He meant it rhetorically, but supposed he would get an answer, because that's just how the night was shaping up.

Janey turned back to the mirror to find the answer.

Miles laughed at this. "The clown wasn't named *IT*, just the movie. The clown with the big teeth was Pennywise. He liked to kill kids."

"Whatever," James whispered, but couldn't help but glance into the mirror, into Janey's half-lidded eyes. *It wants to kill us all. And the kid is giggling about it.*

"What are we gonna do about *it*?" Vic demanded.

James shook his head. He needed time to think somewhere quiet. Very quiet.

Writer Jack hollered from over by the bar, "Hey, the receptionist is laying in a room over here. I think she's dead." The bartender pointed to the phone and probably explained, for the second time in a minute, that nobody answered at the constable when the State police transferred the call.

Vic waved to him. "I know all about it," she hollered back. "We're just discussing it."

James didn't care for how calm Jack appeared. If a normal person found a corpse, wouldn't they freak out, at least a little? What kind of man took death as calmly as this?

As Jack approached, Vic said, "She tried to kill me with a clothes iron and hurt herself. Karma, if you ask me."

"Indeed," Jack said. "My gosh, are you okay?"

"Yes, yes," she said. "I'm just fine, but I'd feel better if we could reach the sheriff or the clinic." Then she glanced at the kids, nodded, and turned back to Jack. "I don't know if there's anything to it, but both Marion and Janey here mentioned we may still be in danger from someone who wants everyone dead."

"You don't say," Jack said. "All of us?"

"So, she said," Vic mentioned and shrugged.

"My goodness," Jack said, then glanced out the window into the snowy night. He looked at James. "Well, the town's pretty small. What say we go find the man? Anything less than a four-wheel-drive won't get us there, so might as well use good old-fashioned foot power."

"You sure that's wise?" James asked. "Maybe we should all stay together."

"We'll be fine," Jack said. "It'll help us both to wear off supper. Besides, we can do some good. If that woman's not dead, she's at the very least, injured."

"But I didn't even get to eat my meal," James said.

"Please, yes," Vic said. She winked at James. "I'll make it up to you."

"Fine," James said as he felt his stomach rumble. But he wondered how she would make it up to him. They'd already performed almost every maneuver in their repertoire. Perhaps her luggage contained a sex swing and a whip. Maybe an anal plug. The thought made him blush.

"Can I go?" Miles asked. "It sounds like fun. More fun than watching Janey stare into the mirror and mumble shit. And I don't think Vic will let me look at the dead old woman like I want to."

"No," James and Vic said at the same time.

"Let the squirt come," Jack said with a grin. "The more the merrier. Safety in numbers, am I right?"

"Yes!" Miles shouted.

Janey turned to them. "It's out there," she whispered. "By itself. In the wind and the cold and the snow. It waits. It waits to kill."

"What's out there, darling?" Jack asked.

"The thing," she answered, as if this were common knowledge. "The thing caught between worlds. It laments through the mirrors but only I can hear it."

"See what I mean about weird?" Miles said. "Let's go."

"Such an active imagination," James mumbled but didn't address anyone in particular. "Such a precocious child. A future in the entertainment industry, I wouldn't wonder." When he looked back up and past Janey, the mirror appeared to turn slate black, no reflections. When nobody else appeared to notice this anomaly, he said, "Let's get our jackets. We won't find the sheriff having dinner here." Anywhere was better than here.

Then Janey grinned—with a crooked toothy smile—at him like they shared a terrible secret. Her eyes bored into his.

"For now, it waits," Janey repeated. "But it wants to kill. Soon."

Chapter 8

"You are one stupid motherfucker," Robbie hollered at Harold as he stuffed him into the jail cell. "I could see Jeb doing something like this, but not you. You were the damn sheriff once upon a time."

Harold stumbled and caught himself on the bunk, then turned and scowled at Robbie.

Jeb hollered from the other cell. "I'm still telling ya! You got this all wrong. It's them two women tried to kill us. Look at my leg; she done shot a hole clean through it."

"I've shot targets with Angela enough to know," Robbie shouted, "if she wanted you dead, there'd be a hole right betwixt your stupid eyeballs."

"You gonna believe that drunkard whore over me?" Jeb asked.

At least Harold had the sense to keep quiet.

"Stop being a douchebag dickhead, Jeb!" Emily shouted from the reception area. "I'm no whore. I just date lots. Don't mean I put out, because I don't." Angela watched her calm herself by closing her beautiful eyes. "Just own up to your bullshit and take personal responsibility for it. Tell him about the ritual and shit."

"I was talking about Angela," Jeb said. "But if the shoe fits."

Angela listened but ignored all these exchanges, a headache mounting in her cranium while she filled out the proper forms. Penance for shooting that bastard Jeb in the leg. *Should've just shot center-mass by the sounds of things.* She sure could use a drink.

"Don't say nothing, Jeb!" Harold said. "It might not be too late. We can fix this."

"It's over, Harold," Jeb lamented. "It's gonna rip us from limb to limb, then kill off everyone else, too. Should've known this would happen one day. None of the young, strong folks would join us, and we done got too old to get the job done."

"What are you two old asshats flapping your gums about?" Robbie asked. "What ritual? What thing? And what's this about killing everyone? Spit it out. I ain't got all night. In case you haven't noticed, we're in the middle of a massive storm. Be lucky to get under three feet."

"Course we noticed," Harold whined. "Or else we wouldn't be worried about this at all. We'd be at home, sipping a nice Irish coffee."

"Like hell you would," Robbie shouted. "You'd be out on patrol, making sure the citizenry is safe. Now, clue me in, Harold. Why did I just lose a third of my workforce?"

Harold moaned a little but otherwise held his tongue, likely debating the wisdom of a tell-all monologue versus keeping his mouth shut.

Angela almost hoped he chose the latter, so she didn't have to hear him blather on about things which made little sense. Jeb alluded to something, a specific something, which he felt endangered his life. He believed this to the point of attempting to butcher an innocent female. Sure, Em could come across as annoying on occasion. Perhaps she would spill her entire life story to the wrong folks a bit too often, or maybe embellishes a wee bit, but she didn't deserve a knife to the heart.

Angela let out a breath and scribbled the last of what she'd witnessed down on the government form. She didn't enjoy the form, but knew it stopped officers of the law from just blowing people away whenever the thought crossed their minds. Angela supposed she would eventually have to justify the discharge of her firearm to some board or another, but not until after they opened the roads again. Who knew when that would occur?

"Just tell him, Harold," Jeb pleaded. "Maybe he'll let us out."

"Unlikely," Robbie said, jaw set and rigid.

"Don't be so sure," Jeb said in a cryptic tone. "We's the only ones with even a hope and a prayer of stopping this thing. You'll see. Tell him, Harold."

"Fine," Harold grumbled. "It's all over, anyway. We'll all be dead by the time they get the roads cleared, so what difference does it make?"

Angela didn't care for Harold's tone. It wasn't like him to roll over and give up. Then she felt, more than saw, Em perk up and pay close attention. Nothing exciting ever happened here. Hell, it'd been a few years since anyone even got lost in the old mine shafts or needed rescue from the deep rugged Cleopatra Hill wilderness. Now, Harold and Jeb just tried to murder Em and were talking about all kinds of nonsense. Only, Angela didn't feel like they were lying; she didn't get that vibe at all. Harold and Jeb seemed serious and believed the things they said were the truth.

"Whole thing started for us some sixty years ago," Harold said. "Me and Jeb here weren't but seven. Just trainees back then. But we think it'd been going on for way longer than us."

"Way longer," Jeb added. "Maybe centuries."

Angela watched Robbie run a hand through his dark hair. She noticed the gray that sprouted in a couple key locations and found the color suited him. He said, "What's been going on?" His jaw clenched and the little muscle at the corners bulged with the stress.

"Might's well tell him, Harold," Jeb said.

"Fine," Harold sighed. "We're all dead-flesh walking. So, every thirty years we get paid a little visit. When the big snows come."

The little tingle roaming up and down Angela's spine grew intense. Harold's words sounded like magic as they floated from his mouth.

Em placed a delicate hand on Angela's left wrist, and she knew the girl felt nervous and needed comfort. Angela also knew Em could sense the energy in Harold's words, same as she could. And she couldn't help but feel Harold would now pass a torch, give the responsibility to someone else. Whatever that responsibility turned out to represent.

"From who?" Robbie asked. "Someone's been visiting us every thirty years since you two were seven? I find that—"

"Don't matter much how you find that, sheriff," Harold said. "Truth is truth, whether you believe in it or not. When the big snow comes like clockwork, it comes a calling, looking for the fresh blood and skin due it."

Robbie's eyes popped open. "Blood and skin? Explain."

"Sacrifice," Harold whispered. Angela needed to listen closely to hear him. "It asks us to sacrifice seven of our own to save the rest. I'm sure that little tidbit will turn you a might salty, but just think about the situation a minute. Seven versus hundreds."

"What?" Robbie said, breaking with the sanctity of the hushed moment before. "You mean to tell me every thirty years you two old fools have killed seven people because you think something out there," he pointed at the door now, worked up, "wants you to do it? Did it somehow communicate this to you? Are you insane?"

"Figured you'd get salty," Harold said. "No, it never has communicated with us. Never needed to. We've always got the job done. The sacrifice ritual has been passed down from generation to generation, from the old families, for a long time. Way before me and Jeb. We just continued it. But now…"

"But now we busted your sorry asses before you could murder seven more," Robbie said, enraged. He shook his head. "You've as much as admitted to enthusiastically witnessing seven murders and committing seven yourselves. I can't nail you on things that happened when you were kids, but we got you on the seven you committed as adults thirty years ago and now attempted murder." He glanced at Angela with a frown, then turned back to Harold. "You and Jeb the only ones involved in this insanity?"

"Yep," Jeb said, before Harold could answer. Probably to change the subject, Angela figured. He continued, "My leg hurts. I know the nurse from the clinic disinfected it and all, patched it up, but it aches something fierce. Maybe you should get me to the hospital down in Prescott."

"Too late," Robbie said. "They already closed the switchbacks. Can't even get a snowmobile through the pass. You're stuck here with the rest of us until the snow stops and the county gets the plows out." Robbie pointed at Jeb. "So, for the sake of argument, let's say what you two are blabbing about is true. What are we stuck up here with?"

Angela wished Robbie hadn't dropped the line of questioning which involved accomplices. Her gut told her they didn't have all the parties involved in custody. She almost laughed. Thinking of Jeb and Harold as murderers sounded funny until you thought about what they'd done over the years. Sure, now they were bumbling old fools. Back thirty years ago, they were strong and capable as they sacrificed their terrified victims. And more, dare she say cultists, may exist out there, cutting up victims while the Jerome sheriff's force sat around here and screwed around with these two old windbags. Suddenly, Angela felt angry and a little scared.

A glance out the window told Angela darkness had descended for the evening.

"Can't rightly say," Harold said. "Never seen it. But it's always taken the sacrifices, and the footprints leading away from the pile of flesh out in the woods were a good size bigger than both of yours put together."

"I heard it once," Jeb said, "roaring around out there in the blizzard. That was enough to keep me vested in the ritual work at hand."

"So, you're willing to murder people—people you know—sight unseen? For an it that may not even exist, just because some others, like you two old coots, told you about it." Robbie shook his head. "For all you two know, the others could have fashioned those tracks to fool you. Bigfoot tracks get faked all the time. And the sounds could have been the wind playing on your imagination, Jeb." Robbie scrunched his eyes and nodded. "The more I think about it, the more I'm inclined to believe what I just said. A reasonable explanation exists, and that makes you two murderers. Killed a bunch of folks just because you're both superstitious old fools."

"We'll see who lives through the night and who doesn't," Harold snapped.

"Don't get cocky," Jeb said. "We're no safer than anyone else, Harold. The ritual failed. We're locked up and can't finish it."

"Ain't over…" Harold started, then thought better of it.

Too late, Angela thought.

"Shit," Jeb whispered.

"What's not over?" Robbie asked.

Bingo, Angela thought.

"Nothing," Harold muttered. "It's all over, and we're all dead flesh-bags walking. You just don't believe it yet, is all."

"No, you're right, I don't believe you," Robbie said. "I think there's more of you out there and you two know exactly who they are and what they're up to. Spill your guts or you're both gonna rot in a prison cell for the rest of your life."

"Better than the beast's belly," Harold said.

"Oh, God," Em croaked. She squeezed Angela's wrist even harder, then laid her head on her forearm for further comfort. "I'm getting kinda scared." She peered up at Angela's face, bangs over her wet blue eyes. She looked like a child, but not so much Angela couldn't see the beauty of the woman. *A looker*, Angela thought. The reason why single guys, and some of the married ones, chased her around like their lives depended on it.

For a reason she didn't fully understand, Angela reached down and ran her fingers through the frightened woman's hair. "It'll end up all right. Stay strong."

Em smiled. Her eyes shone like pieces of glass in the bright lighting of the jailhouse. The smile and the eyes seemed tied together with a thread of emotion Angela couldn't quite place but felt some broken part of her should understand. Goose bumps rose on Angela's arms she couldn't attribute to Harold and Jeb's story.

"You don't even know there is a beast," Robbie said. "Even if there was at one time, how could the same beast still roam these hills and mountains for centuries?"

"How should we know?" Harold said. "Maybe there's a whole clan of them. Or maybe the thing is magic. Who knows? Both scenarios seem likely."

"Both scenarios seem like bullshit," Robbie said. "A clan of beasts big enough to drag seven bodies off would have likely been discovered years ago. Dead bodies would turn up, piles of excrement, dwellings.

And, in today's day and age, with all the trail cameras that the hunters and other wildlife enthusiasts like to use out there? Shit! So many pictures would exist it'd make your head spin off your shoulders."

"Good points," Harold said, sarcastic. "Magic, then. Probably feeds off the energy of the ritual. Makes sense."

"It doesn't make a lick of sense," Robbie said.

For the record, Angela didn't think so either, but felt like Robbie could try a little harder. Ghosts and ghouls didn't set well in the craw of law enforcement, yet facts were facts. Smoke and fire and all that jazz. As she listened to Robbie's scrutiny of Harold, a subtle pressure began to build in her ear canals. It felt as though she was riding in an airplane or skiing at over ten-thousand feet. As always, the thought of skiing stirred mixed emotions within her, ever since the incident. She would try not to think about it.

Without warning, the pressure built faster, and two things happened. First, glass shattered in an explosion of small fragments and then the vocal-cord-ripping scream of pain and excruciating terror blasted through the enclosed space. One may have happened right before the other, but Angela couldn't tell which.

Jeb continued to scream but his voice sounded wet and distorted, as if trying to speak without his tongue.

Em latched on harder as Angela attempted to stand. "Please don't leave me," Em hissed. Her gaze looked intense and Angela could see the palpable fear. But something more than fear lived there, inside those two blue torches of light. Angela thought she also read concern and something else, perhaps.

Robbie had already leapt forward, Glock drawn, and now wiggled the key back and forth in the lock of Jeb's cell. He finally got it open and stumbled inside. "Oh my God! Jeb, what have you done?"

Harold screamed unintelligible things from his cell—things that sounded a little like madness and a lot like fear. "It's here," he babbled.

What's here? Angela thought.

"Call the nurse," Robbie screamed. "Jeb…the mirror…the walls…there's blood everywhere in here."

Angela looked at the girl next to her. "Em, I need you to call the clinic. The nurse practitioner should still be on call."

Em nodded, bangs bouncing around her heart-shaped face, eyes filled with both fear and the eagerness to please Angela.

Once she knew the girl would follow through, Angela drew her own Glock and made to join Robbie at Jeb's cell. As Angela passed by, she noticed Harold had crawled beneath his bunk and placed a pillow over his head. A yellow puddle of piss ran from his middle to the drain in the gray-tiled floor. "Don't let it at me," Harold said. "Please."

Seeing nothing but a fearful Harold, Angela continued toward where she could hear Robbie cursing and gagging. When she arrived, Angela could only stare.

The gray tile of the floor and concrete wall beneath Jeb's mirror lay bathed in his blood. Long, narrow shards of glass from the mirror protruded from the man's eyes and throat. His head looked like a porcupine with glass quills. The frame of the mirror looked like a jagged portal to hell. It looked to Angela as if something had grabbed ahold of Jeb and repeatedly smashed him into the mirror.

Jeb, silent now, twitched a couple times, then lay still. Even with eyes destroyed, the look of terror on his face could not go misinterpreted, not by a long stretch. His mouth, stuck open in a rictus grin of terror, made Jeb look like a perpetual scream would, from now on, spill from the bloody orifice as a warning. Angela almost gagged when she noticed bits of glass were stuck between the man's teeth, piercing and shredding his gumline.

"Suicide?" Angela asked, though she doubted any human could do this much damage to themselves in such a short amount of time. The pain alone should have proven enough to stop a grizzly bear.

"No glass pieces in his hands," Robbie said. "He would have had to bash his own face into the mirror. Over and over."

"Weren't no suicide," Harold screamed, too loud in the small space. "The beast got him."

"The clinic sent everyone home because of the storm," Em said as she ran over. When she noticed Jeb, she placed both hands over her mouth.

Angela placed a well-toned arm over the girl's shoulders and brought her in close. "It's okay," she whispered into the girl's ear. But she wasn't so sure herself.

"It's coming for us," Harold babbled. "Because we failed it. Then it'll come for all of you!"

"How did it get in here, if it was this creature you speak of?" Robbie asked. It sounded rhetorical to Angela. "Where is it?" Robbie swiveled about, Glock out, dark eyes searching.

"Magic," Harold whispered. "Just like the old stories of failure foretold. You all ain't seen nothing yet."

Then Angela heard glass breaking inside Harold's cell. The same power that just claimed Jeb was now trying to get Harold. But she heard no screams, no sounds of carnage. She hurried away from Jeb and stood before Harold's cage. Mirror glass lay all over his floor. Harold sat on the only bunk, sullen, but glanced at her as she stood there. Angela knew he'd broken the mirror as a preemptive strike.

"Ain't gonna get me," Harold whispered.

Angela needed a drink.

Chapter 9

The mirror before her turned black as if someone, or something, placed a muddy film over the smooth glass. Her own reflection and that of the room behind her faded. She pulled her hands away so she wouldn't have to feel what must, even now, represent the demise of a dear friend.

She knew they had taken Jeb and Harold into custody. That left her and Marion. *Dear Marion.* It had to be Marion in anguish, because Robbie wouldn't allow the beast access to the jail. Certainly, not. But what did any of them know of the creature's power? Maybe it could shape-shift or travel through the electrical lines. Maybe it used pure brute strength and ripped doors off their hinges. Then something occurred to her, and she backed away from the mirror. One couldn't be too careful, she thought.

Nothing had gone as planned this time. Marion's ritual proved inadequate and Jeb and Harold botched the ceremony with barfly Emily. But she wasn't ready to give up just yet, mostly because she wanted nothing to do with the beast's wrath. She'd heard stories about the penalties of failure from the elders—stories she desperately wished not to relive in the flesh.

No, perhaps Marion's half-ass ritual could still prove okay if she offered all seven sacrifices to the beast. Time still existed to accomplish what needed doing; she just needed to set her mind to things, proper like. Not like the kids today where they half-assed their way through a meaningless and worthless life. *Just sit around and watch TV and shoot each other's asses off on those stupid ass video game contraptions.* Most didn't even go outside when the weather was nice. No wonder they couldn't recruit anyone new to join them. Nobody believed in magic anymore. Times were changing, and she wondered what the beast would do to compensate for this. Perhaps it would forgive the cult this one transgression of failure because of unforeseen circumstances: the demise of the nation's youth.

She supposed not. So, that meant things now lay in her lap. If she didn't succeed, everyone would die. *Painfully, at that.* Tomorrow she would set things right. Yes, tomorrow. First, she had to live through the night.

One didn't reach this ripe old age without learning about protections, so she took a long wooden match and lit both a white and black candle. The smoke from each met in the middle, intertwined, then rose together in a helix pattern toward the tiled ceiling. Strange that the black candle cast a reflection in the darkened mirror but the white remained unseen. *Unusual times.*

Then the old woman took a necklace from the jewelry box to her left and placed it over her head. It lay just above where her breasts once hung before gravity put them through their paces. Somewhere between the brightness of the black candle and the complete obscurity of the white, she could make out the amulet against her ruddy chest. It should offer some protection against evil. As would the contrast between the white and black candles. Everyone possessed the culpability of evil and capability for good, and the candles represented such human frailties. This would benefit her.

As she stared into the darkened mirror and thought about what forces could cause such a phenomenon, she planned for the morrow. Her place of employment would provide her with ample opportunity. Sure, she didn't have the luxury of hand picking and choosing anymore, but this no longer mattered. The ritual needed tending and she would tend it, with whoever graced her with their presence. Let God or the beast decide who died. That, in all actuality, took a lot of the pressure off her.

She smiled and found she could see her teeth shine like bright Chiclet orbs in the mirror's gloom. And then, she thought she could make out something else.

Chapter 10

"I don't know why I had to stay here," Miles whined. "You won't even let me go see the dead lady."

"We don't know that she's dead," Vic said. "That's morbid, by the way, wanting to see…her." She didn't wish to call it a corpse in front of the boy whether the woman was dead or not.

"Dang it," Miles said, then held out his EMF detector to get a reading. He held a voice-recorder in the other hand. The rest of his equipment lay within a black carpenter's apron tied around his waist.

"I should go check on the woman," Vic responded. If still alive, she wanted to help the woman despite her trying to brain her. "From the doorway, it looked like she might still be breathing, but I didn't dare get any closer." When Miles looked to her with hope, she added hastily, "And no, you can't come with."

Miles rolled his eyes and let out a breath. "Let's go together. At least I can run for help if she makes a play for you again." After a moment of silence in which Vic refused to answer, he added, "I won't even look at her."

"What about Janey?" Vic asked. "Your Aunt went to your room and there's nobody else now to watch over her."

"She'll sit in front of that mirror for hours."

Vic couldn't help but smile at the kid's tenaciousness.

"Yeah," Miles said, "let's go. If she's dead, I'll try to communicate with her ghost. If she's alive, I'll grill her about why she tried to off ya. Then, when the sheriff gets here, I can tell him all about it."

Vic wondered what would have to happen in a child's life to lead them to this kind of reaction to such sordid circumstances. "You will stay behind me…and please, let's show some respect. She may have tried to *off me* as you say, but she's elderly and hurt."

Miles checked his device. "Sure," he said. "If the old lady was nice, like Grandma Hylden, then I'd feel bad." He shrugged. "But this lady tried to brain you with a rusty old iron." He shook his head. "I'll take the chance and place my bets on the side of not caring too much."

"You're weird," Vic said. She made sure to smile.

"Not that weird," Miles said as he pointed toward Janey.

Vic agreed with the kid's assessment. *She rarely speaks and just stares into the mirror.*

The girl stood, both hands on the mirror before her. In the reflection, which Vic thought looked diminished somehow, not as clear as it appeared earlier, Janey mouthed words Vic couldn't hear. Vic walked around dinner tables, some full of patrons yet, some not, and approached the girl.

Some guests watched the little girl with looks on their faces which suggested Janey may need assistance.

As Vic approached, she heard Janey mumble, "It's beginning. It's angry now. The center couldn't hold." She shouted, "It's your fault, cunt!" She banged her head off the glass of the mirror, causing the rectangle to swing on its hook.

Miles giggled.

"Oh, hey," Vic said. She wondered where the girl picked up that foul language and why she chose this moment to scream it. "Watch your mouth or we'll go find your aunt."

The table of people seated next to Janey stared at the girl. Vic smiled at a man dressed in a suit coat and held her palms out before turning back to Janey. She hoped the diners had enough to worry about with the storm and herself being attacked to worry much about Janey.

Just when Vic felt the worst was over, Janey screamed again. "It is too your fault, you old bitch...cunt!"

Vic let out a breath and couldn't seem to catch another. She laid a hand on Janey's shoulder to show support. She also hoped it would relax the child and quiet her.

The table of folks led by the man in the suit jacket got up. Vic assumed they were only in here because they had nowhere else to go and going back to their rooms wouldn't be a hardship for them. Who could eat under these circumstances?

"Janey," Miles said, "quiet down. People are leaving because of you. You sound like a dipshit."

Janey took a moment from her tirade to turn and glance at Miles. "I do not." She turned back to the mirror and murmured, "It's killing now." She said this a few times.

Miles turned back to Vic. "Ever since she got herself possessed, it's like this every time she gets in a good scry. It's C-bomb city." He smirked at Janey who still faced the mirror. "She has C-bomb Tourette's on account of psychic residue."

Vic doubted the validity of this statement, but who knew? Right now, she would believe just about anything.

Janey looked from the mirror and glared at Miles, eyes hooded. She whispered, "I don't have Tourette's."

Vic, needing to feel useful, rubbed Janey's shoulder. She wanted for her to stop saying vulgar things in public, wanted her to quit staring into that infernal mirror where Vic couldn't see anything but the girl's dead eyes and the room beyond.

"Leave me be," Janey snapped and tugged her shoulder back so she could continue to stare into the mirror. After a moment, she went back to, "It's killing now. Blood. There's blood. So much blood." Quiet for a minute. Then, "It's dark now. It's back in the dark places."

"What is, honey?" Vic asked. "What's in the dark?"

Janey turned toward Vic. "The beast from the snow, don't ya know? It wants all of us, but first things first."

"What things?" Vic asked. She wished, immediately, to take the words back. Sometimes not knowing was so much better.

A loud crash boomed from outside the restaurant, probably down the main hall in the vicinity of the reception desk. The few remaining diners looked up in concern. The bartender exited the bar and took a couple tentative steps before stopping and staring down the hall.

"Those things," Janey whispered.

Vic could feel the pitter-pat of her heart racing, the lightheadedness of her blood pressure rising. What was happening? It sounded like a herd of elephants stampeding down the hall.

"Holy crap!" Miles yelled. "Sounded like windows breaking."

Before Vic could get a hand on his collar, he bounded for the exit, jumped a couple chairs, one with an older man still in it, and then rounded the corner out into the main hall. Vic figured he would make a fantastic running back, but he also didn't seem like the sort of kid who bothered with sports. She watched as Miles' paranormal equipment bounced and clattered on his waist as he ran.

"Just great," Vic said to Janey. "The hotel is probably caving in and Miles feels the need to put himself in the middle of it."

Janey turned back to the mirror.

Vic decided to follow him. "Janey, please stay right here at the table, okay? I'll be just a few minutes and then we'll go find your aunt."

When Janey didn't respond, Vic started after Miles. The girl seemed content to sit and stare into the mirror.

Just as Vic took her first few steps after Miles, she heard Janey whisper, "It's the beast. It's mad because the cunt failed it. Now we'll all pay."

Oh boy. Vic hurried toward the exit. The looks on the other patrons' faces, and their nervous banter, told her they were anxious. Between the blizzard, an attempted murder, unruly kids, and a thunderous crack that sounded like hell descending, things were well beyond Janey making a scene. She couldn't worry about that.

As she passed by the bar and the open-mouthed bartender, the main hall appeared empty. But she noticed the door to the room where the old woman lay stood wide open. Pieces of glass lay strewn on the floor outside the room, shining like diamonds by the light of the small chandeliers mounted on the ceiling. The lights swung back and forth on their narrow tethers, as if a slight ghostly wind now rushed through the hall.

The smell of ozone, like after a thunderstorm, filled the air. About to leap over the broken glass and enter the room, Vic noticed a blur of motion from down the hall before she could do so. *Oh God*, she thought. Vic covered her mouth with a trembling hand. This couldn't be—shouldn't be. A pressure built in her ears.

Down the hall by the elevator carriage, a woman in a white nurse's uniform pushed a gurney with a body on it. The nurse stared at Vic as if to communicate with her.

Vic knew this thing represented a once living person, but no more. She remembered James prattling on about the specter of a nurse with a gurney as they showered together before dinner. Vic's ears felt filled with cotton, yet she heard when the apparition spoke, either with her diminished hearing or in her mind. Perhaps, both.

"Beware the beast," it said.

Just as Vic was about to respond—granted, it took her some time to regain her composure—the image of the nurse before her flickered, disappeared, reappeared, then vanished in dramatic fashion for the final time. *A warning, then.*

Time stood still for a moment, probably more to do with Vic's shock than any mystical strange doings. She lived a normal life, somewhat sheltered. Sure, a little more excitement would be nice on occasion. She wrote, James taught school. They ate out a couple times a week, perhaps three. Sometimes, in the winter, they traveled to places with a beach and palm trees for a week. There was the occasional tryst of cunnilingus or a quickie in the odd place or time they enjoyed. Just your typical middle-class fare. Normal stuff. So, when confronted with such things as the paranormal, it took Vic a moment to reconcile the circumstances between her satisfying yet mundane life and the spectacular.

Like thunder, the world rushed back full force to Vic. A giant tidal wave of sound and light. Miles screamed at her from inside the room where wind and snow whistled through the broken window. Pieces of jagged glass, covered in blood, hair and sinew, stuck out of the window-casing like razors.

How had she not noticed this mayhem moments ago, when she approached, and the apparition appeared to communicate with her about the beast? A snow beast, if Janey possessed the correct data.

"Holy Jesus on a crutch," Miles yelled over the din of the wind, which had reached gale-force. "The old lady must have got dragged out the window. Look at her guts!" He pointed at the mess caught on the glass, then stuck his head outside.

The mother inside Vic—even though she and James never conceived—wanted to rush over and drag the kid back in before he could jump out. Because, he would. With tentative steps, Vic made her way to the boy, until she noticed a rather long portion of the old woman's intestines hanging on like a streamer, attached precariously to a jagged chunk of glass. Then, for the first time, the scent of offal hit her, and without preamble, she retched in violent fashion onto the floor between her black Louis Vuitton's.

Shit, they're ruined!

Miles went on despite Vic's shock, "That beast Janey keeps gibbering about must've got her. Probably munching on her liver by now, out there in the woods." He pointed out the window as if it never occurred to him that said beast could grab him, too, if it were looking for another victim.

"Just stop," Vic said, probably not loud enough for Miles to hear over the wind.

"I'd say we go after her, but..." He pointed at the length of glistening-wet small intestine hanging in the window frame "...but nobody can live too long without that much gut."

"Normally?" Vic managed.

"Sure," he said. "I saw a dude who got himself butchered out in Buck Hill Swamp. He lost so much gut they looked like wings spread out around him on account he was hanging up in the brush. And the ants found the guts, so they looked all fuzzy like feathers, if you know what I mean."

"Your dad let you see that?" Vic squinted into the wind and shook her head. What was wrong with people? She was no prude, not by a long stretch, but good Lord. How old could Miles be…twelve, thirteen? And he reacted to a length of intestine as if it were old hat.

"Naw," he said. "I snuck a peek."

"Your dad's a cop?" She hoped not, because that would mean no hope existed in the world. If a cop's kids acted like this then what of everyone else? She shook her head.

"Naw," Miles said, a bit annoyed with the fifth degree, Vic supposed. "He and Tracey investigate paranormal matters, like I said. Sometimes they help when the police can't explain something. You know, like ghost stuff. With the butchered dude, it was cult stuff."

Vic shook her head again. And people wondered why she and James had yet to reproduce. "Well, whatever," she said, "but yes, let's not go after her. We'll let the sheriff figure things out. Come on, let's get back to your aunt and Janey."

Vic didn't know if a beast really took the old woman or if she threw herself out the window in some fit of rage. If she did it to herself, she must have crawled off into the night or else they would have noticed her laying outside the window in the snow. At least she'd make a decent sized bump. In a bout of questionable decision making, Vic looked. When she noticed the large footprints quickly disappearing beneath a layer of snow, she wished she hadn't.

"Must be big," Miles said when he noticed her looking. He used a camera pulled from his pouch and took a picture of the almost non-existent footprints before Vic could pull her head away.

"There," Miles said. "Wanted to capture the evidence on full-spectrum for the sheriff before the snow got rid of it completely." He scrunched up his eyes in thought. "Guess he'll see the blood and guts well enough for himself."

"Yes," Vic said, "let's leave the rest for him and his deputies. We don't want to be here if it comes back."

"Speak for yourself," Miles said. "Can you imagine the footage of that thing?" He shook his head and smiled. "Our documentary would be on every network in the world and our YouTube channel would get millions of hits. We'd get rich in a hurry."

Vic turned and walked, hand stretched back, hoping he would grab it and they could stumble out of the room together. Briefly, she imagined James and Jack walking out in the blizzard, looking for the sheriff. She hoped they were okay. *Good Lord, could anything else go wrong?* When Miles didn't take her hand, Vic stopped and looked back over her shoulder, expecting to find Miles with his camera. Instead, she saw a bunch of nothing. Just a broken window, wind gusting through, and clumps of bloody guts stuck to the jagged shards around the edges.

Miles no longer stood with his head out the window, gone now from her view altogether. Against her better judgement, heart palpitating, Vic ran to the window and peered out into the blizzard. Next to the quickly filling prints of the beast, a set of much smaller prints followed them out into the darkness.

Vic stood in the window, wondering what to do. She could follow the tracks, but even in her stupor, she understood the folly of running off into nearly a foot of snow in a pair of flats. Her feet would freeze within minutes. She tried to remember what Miles wore on his feet and recalled a pair of rugged hiking boots clonking off the floor when the kid ran. Yes, his feet would be fine. But what would she tell Aunt Kayla? "Sorry, but I lost Miles?" *Shit!*

Not daring to get too close to the window, Vic yelled, "Miles!"

Nothing answered but wind through the window.

Then, a terrible feeling set in. Vic knew if she didn't leave the room immediately, she would see something untoward, something outside the realm of her experience. Something dangerous. Mind made up, Vic turned to return to Janey. The sheriff would arrive soon enough, and he could go look for Miles. A large part of her felt guilty for not jumping out the window and following but she didn't have a death wish. She hoped the sheriff showed up soon.

Chapter 11

James walked beside Dowling, working hard to match the man stride for stride in the deepening snow. A half hour from now their footprints may not even be visible. Apparently, Jack Dowling exercised vigorously and often, and the guy waited for no lesser man. James sometimes felt his years as a teacher gave him visage as an armchair psychologist, and he would have bet his last marble the guy was overcompensating for some shade lain upon him in youth. Weren't they all? James wondered what anyone would find beneath the man's physical traits and the fiction he wrought, the man behind the image, the one in the mirror. James continued to stumble through the snow.

The sun had dropped below the horizon and, with the heavy cloud cover, night descended in rapid fashion. Even the streetlights, which James deemed too few, appeared subdued and inadequate for anything but a casual stroll. *The maintenance team in this village ought to hear about this!*

"This is the kind of night that lets a man know he's alive and kicking," Jack said. "Sure beats sitting in a small room with poor lighting, punching away at a keyboard. Man's gotta get out and kick the tires now and again."

James wasn't sure the double analogy made any sense but kept that fact to himself. No sense in irritating the writer when James only wished to get to a constable, then get back to Vic. He imagined what they may get up to upon his return. Perhaps a flashback to earlier days and then a quickie in the elevator. They could put on a show for that poor deceased maintenance man. The thought gave renewed energy to his legs.

"Agreed," James answered. "Nothing like a bout of exercise to get the old blood moving through the veins." He huffed and puffed. "Have probably missed a few workouts lately. You know how a vacation goes."

"Sure," Jack said, chest puffed out. The writer sniffed in a large lungful of snowy air. "As for me, I try to keep on it. If I didn't, well, I'd never get a decent workout in, not with my schedule. On the road every other week, it seems. The spoils of victory."

James rubbed his hands together and blew out a plume of breath. He figured the man meant his writing success but decided not to encourage any egotistical or esoteric rants. Vic enjoyed hearing such drivel and circumstance, but James did not. He would begrudge no human their small victories, however, a fine line existed between humble consideration and pomp.

Jack went on, "Even carry my own dumbbell set with me. A pain for the bellman, I suspect, but keeps them fit as a fiddle with the exertion." The man laughed at this, a hardy blast of air that made his lips move in a fashion which displeased James on some level.

Arrogant, James thought. He'd prove difficult to deal with on the occasion he became indignant or quarrelsome. *Probably at the drop of a hat*. He was sure the guy ran his critics through the proverbial wringer, a professional writer by day, a horrid lout by night, when he sat too long reading his own material and thinking it grand. James worked on a conservative premise, a strict regimen of critical-eye thinking, one's own worst critic and all that jazz. Nobody was harder on themselves than Vic. *As things should turn out with it being her art, her career*. Makes one a better artist. He rubbed his hands together again. *It's too cold for this shit*.

"Strong body, stronger mind," Dowling went on saying. "It always helps to live up to one's reputation when sitting at the signing table. When women read romance, they imagine a male writer as one of his protagonists. You know, an Apollo. So, if one wishes to sell and sign his wares, one does what they can."

A regular blowhard. Social media would tear this man apart if it caught even a whiff of what this man really thought. *Good Lord! An Apollo*. The man held himself in such high regard. Did a man become this way because of the fruits of his labor or the other way?

"What do you do for work again?" Dowling asked. "I'm sure you said, but you know." He pointed at his head. "When you have so many characters and narratives and plot lines roaming around in there, something has to suffer. You understand."

"Of course," James said. *What a cocksure bastard.* "I'm a schoolteacher. American Literature. A couple of my students, I'm proud to say, have moved on to journalistic careers. One has even published a book of rather perverse poetry."

"Most poetry is," Dowling lamented. "Anyway, good for you, man. We need excellent people shaping our youth. We need more writers who can spin a yarn with an uncanny knack for not stooping to over-dramatization. Too many Salingers and not enough Wildes, if you catch my drift."

James didn't but left it at that.

When James refused to answer, Jack grinned as if he'd won a victory. "I hope you won't stand in the way of Victoria. You know what I mean, don't you?"

"I wouldn't think of it," James said. "She is talented and entitled to her occupation of choice. Not like she sits around all day eating bonbons and watching afternoon dramas. She works hard and has sold several stories now."

"Good," Dowling said. "With her talent, she can almost write her own ticket, so to speak. She doesn't need a butt-hurt husband." After letting a gout of fog from his mouth, he smiled. "I get a lot of action but I stay single for a reason."

Was this man warning him about infidelity, if he didn't grow accustomed to men throwing accolades at Vic's feet?

Dowling kicked snow with his boots but gazed at James from the corner of his eye.

James felt himself about to say something he may regret later, which might even affect his chances of a blowjob in the elevator, as he'd imagined. But once started, he'd slug this lout right in the mouth, and they'd see just how much the ladies fancied him with no front teeth.

Dowling glared at James as if he knew what to expect, as if he found himself in this kind of situation regularly. He moved toward James aggressively.

James bristled.

Then a scream disrupted the relative quiet of the snowy evening. Not just a scream, James thought, but an opportune one. It sounded like a female in distress or like a cross between a woman and a wild mountain animal. It ranged from a low guttural force to an octave so high James questioned how much her vocal cords could take before rupturing. She sounded close, just off in the darkness of Cleopatra Hill above them.

James tried to remember what the terrain comprised. Dwarfed pines and oaks, some brush, and the occasional grouping of high-desert cactus.

Dowling stared into the darkness when an odor appeared to offend him. Now James smelled the foul stench too, filling him as if with sand. He wanted to expel the odor back out of his nose, as if it were a physical presence.

"Good night," Dowling said, placing his nose and mouth inside his jacket. "What on Earth is that stench?"

Indeed, what? Perhaps an amalgamation of death and rot mixed with fish guts and excrement. Yes, definitely a hint of the outhouse in there somewhere. How all these odors could exist at once eluded him.

"Smells like someone took a shit in an open grave after they ate raw tuna," Dowling said in a way James thought sounded entirely unlike an author.

Whoever lurked up above screeched like a banshee, much closer, as if the woman in distress had noticed them and was moving in their direction. He envisioned a lady who looked like Vic, stumbling through ten inches of snow.

The scent grew stronger and James fought not to disgorge his fine meal, hand over mouth, throat convulsing.

Mouth still inserted in his winter jacket, Dowling took steps toward the darkness of the hillside, until a series of loud knocks rang through the night.

The knocks sounded hardcore, like someone large and bulging swung a wooden bat into an oak tree, over and over.

"Do you think she is trying to get our attention?" Dowling mumbled through his jacket. "Maybe she can't go on, perhaps about to freeze to death?"

The aggression behind the knocks didn't sound like that of a dying person. "I really wouldn't know," James said through the stench. Fear crept in and James wouldn't be so pig-headed as to not admit such an obvious thing.

"I'm gonna go have a look," Dowling said. "You stay here in case I need you to get medical personnel. Sounds like someone might be hurt."

James knew what Dowling wanted: the label of hero, and to hear more accolades concerning his bravery and know-how heaped like a cherry on top of his literary prowess.

Dowling marched uphill in his snow-boots until he disappeared into the gloom. Only the stench remained with James. No more screams ripped through the night and for this, he felt gratitude. They unhinged him on some psychological level. He thought this was how nature intended things, a man's reaction to a female in distress.

No word from Dowling yet. Just his diminishing tracks leading up into the darkness. The woman had sounded close, so James found it hard to fathom this long of a wait. He figured the pompous man would waste no time barking out commands. Yet, here James stood beneath the weak light of a street-bulb, waiting for orders like a good soldier. He stomped his feet. Snow cascaded down around him like streamers of white rope.

Quiet—too much quiet. Not even a breath of wind ruffled the dead leaves of the stunted oaks. Only the stench plagued him like an unwanted guest, a lingering negative presence. He wondered what they were dealing with here and what Dowling had found. Out of all the horrible things, the knocks bothered him most. James imagined a baseball soaring out of the old ballpark on a sunny weekend afternoon.

James wrapped his arms around his torso and wondered if he should just trundle down to find the sheriff as originally planned. Not like he owed Dowling anything. If the woman was hurt, she would need medical assistance. *Probably won't get it tonight.*

He took his first downhill step when something tumbled through the top of one of the taller trees beside the road. It sounded heavy, like a large raccoon, or a basketball as it crashed downward, branch to branch.

James squinted to see better and felt something wet and warm splatter his face. He wiped at the moisture with a long narrow hand. It came away streaked with crimson.

The pinball up in the oak continued to descend and hit every branch on the way down, until something round and significant fell from the lower branches and into the snow. James approached carefully as if the item fell from space. He remembered a short story by Stephen King where fungus grew all over a man after he touched a meteor. The guy ended up with his mouth full of a shotgun barrel as James recalled. Not ideal.

James looked down at the sphere. It consisted of stringy gray hair, moist with blood. He nudged the sphere with his right foot. It rocked and fell back in place. James kicked a bit harder and turned the sphere over in its bed of snow. *Good Lord!* James stumbled back, mouth open, hand quick to cover it.

Marion's head lay before him, wide open mouth and eyeless sockets quickly filling with snow. His brain tried desperately to come up with an explanation for this heinous act of violence. The stench returned even stronger and James stumbled back, out onto the snow-laden asphalt road. He turned to run, because it seemed the obvious thing to do. If the scream had come from Marion, she was beyond his help. He doubted such a forceful noise could have ever come from the old woman's withered lungs and the very thought of the woman beating on a tree to gather their attention sounded absurd.

He considered Dowling for a moment, then decided the best thing he could do for the man was run and get the sheriff. James turned to his right to leave and stopped in his tracks. He considered the writer a second time. No avoiding the subject now.

James held his breath until his lungs ached and he kept his mouth open for so long the snow and cool air stung his tongue. Just for a moment, he thought the fleshy object hanging from a tree branch above only resembled the author. *No such luck.*

From a skinny, leafless oak branch hung the facial skin of Jack Dowling. It sagged in on itself and the lack of eyeballs lent a certain fear-factor to eye sockets filled with nothing but inky darkness. His hair ruffled about in the slight breeze and James could still see the part on the left side where Dowling preferred it.

Good Lord! James couldn't get his feet to move properly, more like peg-legs on a hardwood deck. From up on the slope, the woman's scream pounded his eardrums. James looked from the dark hillside back to Dowling's face. Motor skills returning, James found his footing and headed full speed down the road. The sheriff was paid to deal with things like this.

Chapter 12

Angela raised the shot glass to her lips and tipped it back. The bourbon scorched the back of her mouth, then produced that old faithful burn down her throat. *An ounce of liquid heaven.* After what she witnessed in Jeb's cell, she needed the fortification.

Next to her, Em performed the same act, grimaced, then returned her attention to Angela. Angela hoped the booze would do her some good too. Calm her. Angela tried to shield her from the worst, but Em understood enough.

"Hit the spot," Angela said, because she couldn't think of anything more profound to say—and because she couldn't read the girl's eyes. She smiled softly and felt a swell of gratitude for Robbie who knew enough to cut her loose for the evening. There was no way to patrol in this weather anyway. First thing in the morning, he wanted Angela at the library researching the things Jeb and Harold revealed. Had this thing really happened every thirty years? Were they serial killers? She thought of Jeb lying dead in his cell and that line of thinking dried up. Supernatural possibilities invaded her mind and Angela knew she'd have a hard time with sleep. Yes, the liquor would help. It always did.

"You okay?" Em asked. "Suicide is never pretty."

"You sure that's what it was?"

Em tipped her head sideways and smiled. "You believe Harold? I mean, it's fine if you do."

"I don't know," Angela whispered.

Em rubbed her hand up Angela's arm. Angela didn't stop her. The touch felt great, the physical attention, and she wondered why, considering the fact it came from another female. It felt less like comfort and more like pure closeness.

You've just had a long day, is all.

When Em moved her attention to the small spaces between Angela's knuckles, Angela realized it could be something more.

"That feel good?" Em asked. Her eyes shone in the poorly lit bar like jewels. Concern and tenderness etched her face. "I don't want to make you uncomfortable, if you don't like it."

Angela couldn't get any words out. A tight wedge of warmth had inserted itself in her chest and throat. She felt tears leak from her dark eyes.

"Babe?" Em asked. Sincerity laced her voice like silk on velvet.

The way Em said the word "Babe" produced more tears from Angela, sliding down her cheeks. She thought her tears all dried up, spent, but here they were. Angela fought a bout of confusion she couldn't express. She realized it wasn't the words that elicited this reaction. It was the emotion in Em's voice as those words had sprung from her mouth. The concern, the caring, perhaps just a hint of longing thrown in.

"Talk to me, Angela," Em whispered. "You can trust me with anything you have to say, no matter if it's the case of what…what happened in the past, or…or, you know." She continued to rub the area between Angela's knuckles on her right hand.

Angela, in need of another drink, lifted her left hand—God no, not her right—and indicated such. "One for Em here too. On me." She brought her attention back to Em. The girl stared her in the eyes, unafraid to broach difficult emotions.

Angela and Em looked down where their arms touched at the same time, then smiled at each other. Angela noticed the goose bumps on Em's arms, noticed her chest rise and fall with emotion.

"Angela?" Em whispered. The girl continued to stare at Angela's arm as if it were a life-vest to a drowning woman.

"Yeah?" Angela whispered, afraid to speak louder and break the spell. She felt on the verge of a profound revelation. She could hear Em's heavy breaths. She felt the events of the last several hours fade a little.

Em shook her head, unable to speak and continued to rub Angela's right hand. She never broke eye-contact. A tear dripped from her left eye and streaked her high cheekbone until finally dripping off her jawline. "I…" She didn't finish and took a deep breath. Finally, "I…I know I could never replace the baby you lost. I'm sorry."

Angela stared at Em, felt something inside her crumble down and erode. Her turn to shake her head. "I don't know what—"

"Yes, you do," Em said. She sounded more confident now. "You know. You can feel it, same as me. All those times I dropped by the station house."

Angela smiled. "You mean you weren't really interested in becoming a cop?"

"Not true," Em said in a soft tone. "I do enjoy sleuthing about. Probably why Jeb and Harold knew they could grab me for the sacrifice or whatever they called it." She leaned forward. "But you noticed I never went to Harold or Robbie for career advice."

"I noticed," Angela said. "Never thought much about it until this moment. Had no reason to. So, you have your fill of stupid men or what?"

Em shrugged. "Guess I have. Something I've given a lot of thought to lately. How I feel. How I've always felt since I was a little girl. So, I need a life change, to follow my heart, so figured getting close to you could kill two birds."

"Oh, yeah?" Angela asked. She didn't feel uncomfortable in the least with the direction of their conversation. She felt something for Em. The only thing that confused her was the timing. Why now, after all these years, was she figuring out her sexuality? Best not to overthink it.

Em nodded. Then she blurted things she must have kept bottled up, because they poured from her beautiful red lips. "Ever since that bastard left you for no good reason, you know, just because you skied while pregnant then lost the baby, I started thinking about things. Thinking about the real reason I felt close to you, why you seemed to enjoy my company."

Angela couldn't deny this. She enjoyed Em's company, could see the mature woman through the immature front she put on for everyone else. They'd been visiting almost every day for a year. Mostly about the rigors of POST and the physical tests. But also about failed relationships. And about their dreams and hopes. Their pasts. She nodded.

Em took a deep breath and another tear spread down her cheek. "Relationships should be about love and understanding, not control and convenience. I guess what I'm trying to say is…" Another wash of tears.

With a trembling left hand, Angela reached up and wiped the tears away from Em's eye, stroked her right cheekbone with her thumb in a gentle back-and-forth motion.

The bartender clunked both shots down on the stained handcrafted bar and said, "Ladies. I'm closing because of the blizzard. Best drink up." He looked at them both, but knew enough, or sensed enough, to say nothing further. He gave them their privacy.

Angela smiled at Em, then motioned toward the glasses. "Maybe this will help."

"Can't hurt." Em picked up her shot-glass at the same time as Angela.

They slugged the brown liquid back, then both women slammed their glasses down at the edge of the bar. Angela thought the can-lights above the bar seemed to waver, as did the colored lights behind the bottles of booze on the shelf across. *That's the stuff*, Angela thought as the last of the liquor slid down her throat. Angela shook her head and blew out a breath.

Em reached over, grabbed Angela by the collar and pulled her until they sat face to face.

Angela could feel Em's breath on her lips, butterflies in her own stomach, and imagined forever in the depths of Em's eyes. Those eyes morphed into pools through her own tears, and she wished now to dive in and never get out. How could it have taken her so long to realize how she felt, when Em must have felt this way the whole time?

She thought Em would kiss her, and it felt like the most natural thing in the entire world. Except it didn't happen. They remained close. Angela imagined the softness of Em's lips, the tenderness of her touch, the softness of her words, and realized this is how love should feel. Not as that hard, prickly, cold existence she'd endured for five long years.

Angela's life felt like a rather large puzzle she'd been looking at from the wrong perspective. Now that the puzzle had turned on its axis, a few pieces fell into place. The failed relationships, the fights, the utter devastation of a marriage. A marriage dead long before the incident which sent it hurdling off the cliff and into the abyss.

Em broke away first but maintained eye contact. She whispered, "I care about you…and I'm not ashamed to admit it or show you, even in public."

Angela, not usually one for public affection, save for handholding and hugs on the occasion, slid her lips up to Em's ear. "Yeah," she whispered. "Me, too."

Em held her and pressed her forehead into her neck. Angela felt like she'd just met her other half. Despite the blizzard and Jeb's death and the attack on Em, she'd found her life again, and someone to share it with. That's all that mattered. Sure, some things didn't last forever, but this felt like it could. Either way, Em had opened her eyes to possibilities.

And that's when she looked up and noticed a man run by the large plate-glass window of the bar like hell was pursuing him. His arms and legs flailed in a way that reminded her of Ichabod Crane. Looked like he was heading to the jail. Perhaps she'd best get Em out of here before whatever was chasing him also came to pay them a visit. Or before Robbie decided he needed her back on duty.

Perhaps, a date with Em at the library tonight would be exactly what she needed. The library was only a couple blocks away and they had nothing better to do. *Time for a little detective action.*

Robbie cleaned up Jeb and his jail cell best he could. He'd leave the rest for the usual housecleaning outfit if they could get here. He'd call in the morning. They'd have to red-bag all the rags and towels, all saturated with Jeb's blood. Blood-cleanup protocol dictated such with bloodborne pathogens and all.

He washed his hands with disinfecting soap and felt as exhausted as Angela and Em had looked when he allowed them to leave. He didn't plan on sleeping. Once Harold was calm, he would go out on patrol with his Jeep and make sure the town weathered the storm. He only hoped the weird stuff would end. Maybe Jeb killed himself or maybe not, but Robbie hoped this concluded the bloodletting. *That on top of my deputy and his buddy trying to sacrifice Em!*

Approaching footsteps echoed outside the jailhouse door. The doorknob turned and a rather excited man stumbled inside, bringing with him a gust of wind and swirling snowflakes. His eyes were bloodshot, and he was unable to string an intelligible sentence together.

"Hold on," Robbie said. "Calm down so I can understand you."

The man pointed back the way he'd come. He said, "Screaming, horrible, and blood! The face is still hanging from the tree. And the old woman's head is the worst! It's just lying out there in the snow."

So much for wishful thinking. He regretted letting Angela go. He may need her yet. But she'd looked dead tired and stressed. "You need to calm down and start making some sense."

The tall, gangly man rubbed his face as if to wash it clean, then took a deep breath. He looked back at Robbie and made eye contact. "Okay, look, I know how this sounds. But the writer from the conference, Dowling, we were on our way to see you. A woman is dead up at the hotel. Same woman whose head is now getting buried in the snow right up the road." He pointed back the way he came again.

"So, someone killed a woman, so you came to find me, but on the way, you found that woman's head in the snow?" Robbie wanted to ask how it'd gotten from her shoulders out into the snow, but realized it was the wrong way to go about his questioning. If the man knew that, he wouldn't be babbling.

"I bet it was Marion!" Harold shouted. His voice shook with fear and sounded squeaky. "We're dropping like flies!"

"Yes," the stranger said, "Marion."

"The receptionist up at the hotel?" Robbie asked.

The man nodded with emphatic thrusts of his head. "Yes! She tried to murder my wife, hurt herself while at it, then someone, or something, got to her."

What the hell is going on around here? First Harold and Jeb, now Marion.

"At least she tried to carry on," Harold sobbed, emotional over the woman's death. "In a short while, you're gonna wish she'd succeeded, wish we all had."

"Pretty sure Jack Dowling didn't care who carried on as his face got skinned off his head," the stranger said.

"See!" Harold screamed.

Robbie shook his head but extended his arm. "I'm Robbie, the sheriff." He wished he had taken that job in Kansas. Anywhere but here in this raging blizzard, trapped with people who babbled on about things that made no sense. He was a cop, not a ghost hunter or an FBI profiler.

The man accepted the handshake and mentioned his name was James Landes. He went on, "Dowling went up the hill into the dark to check on the screams we heard. He never came back…unless you count his face skin. Then something threw the old woman's head at me."

The man couldn't be serious. He'd most likely misunderstood what he saw. "You know anything about taxidermy? Even the most skilled taxidermist would take hours, not minutes, to accomplish a face skinning. And that's on a thick-skinned animal." He better just have the man show him.

James shrugged. "I told you the truth. I can't tell it any different."

"Don't be obtuse, Robbie," Harold said. "You won't find a rational explanation for this. I tried to warn ya. Best thing you can do now is go lock yourself up and hope the beast doesn't already have a mind to get after you."

"I can't do that, Harold," Robbie said. "Got a job to do, just like you used to." He turned to James. "Show me."

"Who's that?" James asked. "In the cell. Seems like he knows a thing or two about this stuff."

"I do," Harold said. "Been helping keep this thing at bay for nigh on sixty years. Marion, too! Along with others."

"What others?" Robbie asked. His instincts had told him the two men were holding back. Now he had proof.

Harold seemed to catch himself. "You know…Jeb."

"You said others, not just Jeb," Robbie said. Harold was covering things up. If other murderers existed, he needed to keep them from sacrificing people. "Spill your guts."

"I said too much already. If I say any more, it'll come for me for sure. Already got Jeb!" Harold sounded close to hysterics.

"Who's this Jeb?" James asked. "Someone else got murdered tonight?"

"Yes!" Harold said.

"Maybe," Robbie countered. He didn't wish to divulge too much information until he understood this man's motives and level of accuracy. "Might have killed himself with the glass from the mirror in his cell. You would have had to see him…"

"No thanks," James said. "I've seen enough. Can you stop up to the hotel? I know the old lady isn't there anymore, but we may have other problems."

"No more than anyone else, bub," Harold said. "Get in line."

"Seems bossy," James said.

"Sure does," Robbie said, loud enough for Harold to hear. He decided to continue holding pieces of information confidential. "He broke the law this evening and needs to stay in his cell and quiet down."

Harold harrumphed deep in his throat. "We needed seven sacrifices to stop the thing that killed Jeb and Marion and skinned that writer guy," Harold said. "Now it'll kill us all."

"Shut it," Robbie said.

"That true?" James asked Robbie.

"I have no idea, but I better work on the premise that it is. The part about murder. I'm not sure about the other parts." He didn't want to think about the other stuff. His cop instincts wanted to grasp onto the logical and explainable, not all this heebie jeebie hobgoblin bullshit.

"Can we get the army up here?" James asked. "The thing sounded tough. And the way it threw that old woman's head speaks to its strength and determination."

"Afraid we're on our own until the storm ends, and the roads get cleared." He tried to imagine speaking on the phone to a National Guard sergeant and attempting to explain why he needed his help. The military, and any other peace-keeping personnel, would laugh him off the planet.

"That's why it waits for the curse to provide the thirty-year blizzard," Harold said.

"Let's get you back to the hotel before there's too much snow," Robbie said. "I'll give the place a good search, make sure you and the others are safe."

"Take me with," Harold said. "Ya can't leave me in here with a corpse!"

"No," Robbie said. "You broke the law. You wait here. You're probably safer here, behind bars. Think about what ya did."

"Steel bars won't stop shit," Harold grumbled.

"Let's go," Robbie said. He plopped his sheriff's hat on his head, adjusted his gun belt, and walked for the door. He couldn't imagine how things could get any worse, but he feared they would. He could do only one thing about any of this, try to make good decisions and keep folks safe.

Chapter 13

The Jeep's tires spun in the snow, then bucked like a bronco when the chains caught traction. James felt motion sickness setting in, so he concentrated on the view straight ahead. White sheets of snow fell in a continuous blur of motion, having added an inch since James ran through it on his way to the jailhouse.

Chains churned uphill, the Jeep's bumper already pushing snow ahead until the white stuff slipped around and fell behind.

"Won't be long until the only way to get around is a pair of snowshoes," Robbie said. "Unless I can figure out how to work the plow truck in the morning." He answered James' question before he could ask. "Now that Jeb's gone."

A mighty smart beast, James thought. *Or a lucky coincidence to take out the only plow driver.*

"Suppose I could get on it myself, figure things out in the morning. But tonight, I better stick to what I do best and keep the peace."

"And how does one…keep the peace against something like this?" James asked, not meaning to sound sarcastic but supposed he did. He didn't want to disparage the sheriff, but this whole thing seemed outside of their collective experiences.

"Depends on if we're dealing with flesh and blood killers or something like Harold described. Personally, I'm on the fence about it. Could go either way, although the realist in me has a tough time believing in monsters and ghosts."

"I can assure you," James said, "what I witnessed with Dowling, no man could have accomplished. Not in that amount of time." James remembered the author's face dangling there like an old dishtowel, the darkness of the eye-sockets, the full head of hair blowing in the fierce wind. It had looked like something Dahmer would wear around.

"You sure the face was real; Dowling's, I mean?" Robbie asked. "They make some pretty realistic fake stuff in the movie-monster labs these days."

"I suppose anything is possible," James said, but he didn't enjoy being second-guessed. "But that would only lead us down an equally unbelievable chain of logic. That would assume Dowling had a hand in faking his own death."

Robbie stared at him a moment before the Jeep struck an object beneath the snow, canted to the left, stealing the man's attention.

James placed a steadying hand on the dash and continued. "Then there's also the fact that said conspirators would have needed to murder poor Marion and fling her head into the oaks using a catapult." He paused. "Or, using your logic, they may have planted a replica in the tree ahead of time, then released the synthetic bundle of joy as it suited their plans." He hoped his sarcasm shone through like a beacon of reason.

"Well, since you put it that way, no, it doesn't sound likely," Robbie said. "I'll need to study the evidence myself, of course, to come up with a logical explanation or lack thereof."

"Well then, here we are." James pointed toward the side of the road. He could see the deflated sphere of flesh swinging in the breeze, and the lump of snow which represented Marion's head. His stomach roiled, and he felt a tightness in his chest. Seeing all this a second time didn't feel any better than the first.

Robbie pulled to the side of the road and looked past James into the night. James followed his gaze and received another close-up view of Dowling's face. The smallest of mercies, the flesh had frozen and lost its slimy elastic look. He was reminded of a frozen playground ball, half deflated.

"Lookit those tracks, both sets!"

James looked beneath the swinging face and noticed one gargantuan set of prints, size twenty at least. Next to the giant's, with a bit less snow accumulated within, lay a set of much smaller prints. James thought of the kids from the hotel and felt something watching from the darkness.

"What could make a track that big?" the sheriff whispered, then moved his left hand to the door handle. "The other looks like a kid's. I better check it out."

"There are a couple of children staying at the hotel," James said. "Outspoken children, always speaking of unsavory things."

"What kind of unsavory things?"

"Well, you know, ghosts, serial killers. One of them, the girl child, claims to have been possessed."

"I think we better get you back up there. And I'll see if one of the kids is missing." He continued to stare into the darkness. "If they are, I'll come back out for them."

"Sounds good," James said, not wishing for the sheriff to leave the Jeep. He didn't even know if he could sufficiently operate the vehicle in this much snow and walking seemed like it was getting more difficult by the minute. Scanning the darkness, he still felt eyes upon them, and something told him they may both die if the sheriff looked closer.

Thankfully, Robbie threw the Jeep back in gear and continued the slow chug up Cleopatra Hill toward the hotel. After a couple more switch-backed turns than James remembered, the lights of the Jerome Grand flashed into view and they pushed snow the final hundred feet. Robbie parked out front and got out.

James followed and entered the hotel lobby behind him. He welcomed the heat after riding in the drafty Wrangler. James stomped the excess snow off his feet and onto the rubber welcome mat. He looked around the lobby, half expecting the elevator to spring to life in greeting.

Nobody sat behind the reception desk—Marion's old post she would never attend to again in this lifetime—and James figured the hotel management who probably lived in the valley below couldn't find anyone else on this short of notice. At least, not before morning.

"Where is everyone?" Robbie asked. "I hear a number of people decided to stay."

"The restaurant, last I knew."

Robbie turned the corner down the main hall, and James followed. He slipped quickly past the unopened elevator in case it delivered an undesirable payload of ghosts. James continued to follow down the hall until they came across a splotch of glass fragments outside a guest room. The fragments shone like diamonds in the light.

"What the Sam Hill?" Robbie turned to investigate the still-lit room. "Damn! Someone has busted out the large window. And what's all that hanging from the shards?" The sheriff turned to James with a palm outstretched. "Stay back." He placed a hand on the butt of his Glock and entered.

James peered past the sheriff and noticed the guts on the window. *Not here, too.* He felt the desire to find Vic. "This was the room where Marion tried to murder Vic and ended up hurting herself." He hoped this latest development had nothing to do with Vic and her well-being.

"Well, she's not here now."

James shrugged. "I know right where her head is. But, as for the rest of her…" James didn't want to finish the sentence as he felt a surge of guilt for not retrieving the poor woman's head from beneath the pile of snow. She tried to kill Vic but she was still a human being.

Robbie nodded his understanding. He scanned the room as if a perp may be lurking in the shadows. His eyes roved back and forth.

A cascade of voices came from the dining room. "Not to tell you your job, but you might interview the others. Perhaps they can throw some light on the situation." He wished to go find Vic, and then go to their room and get away from all this.

"In a minute," Robbie said. He took one last look at the broken window and whatever substance clung to it. Then he peered out into the storm and ran a hand over his stubbled jaw. He turned and walked swiftly. "Let's go."

James followed as they entered the dining area and noticed a couple small groups sitting at the bar as their members spoke quietly. When they noticed the sheriff's uniform, they perked up with anticipation.

"Sheriff, are we safe?" a woman in a blue dinner-dress asked. "There's been an attempted murder and we hear the perpetrator is missing."

"Quite safe," Robbie said, then followed James past them into the dining area.

James noticed Vic right away and felt immediate relief. If anything had happened to her, he would never have forgiven himself. "Vic!" James said. She looked okay, uninjured, and turned to him with a smile.

Just as Vic headed toward him, the girl turned from the giant mirror and screamed, "She's real nice, but the cunt failed, so the thing will devour her, too. And Miles is out there…".

James cringed at the outburst.

"One of the kids you spoke about?" Robbie asked. He approached her.

"One of the two, yes," James said. "You can hear for yourself what I meant about them being outspoken." He sped over to Vic and grabbed her hand. "Vic, thank God you're okay!"

Vic wrapped her arms around his shoulders. He'd be a liar if he said it didn't feel exceptional to lose himself in his wife's arms. There was a moment out there in the blizzard when he was unsure he'd ever get back to her.

"I hear Marion tried to murder one of you," Robbie said.

James put an arm around Vic's shoulder to show his support.

"Yes," Vic said. "That's me. I'm fine, but now her body's gone, and I'm afraid Miles went after it, out into the blizzard. He jumped out the window." She pointed back toward the exit.

That explains the footprints, James thought. *The kid's out there with that thing.*

Robbie nodded. "Dammit," he said and shook his head. "Yeah, we saw his prints in the snow. Now I wish I'd gone after him." James noticed a wave of guilt flood over the sheriff's face. "I'll go fetch him here in a minute, soon as I make sure everything's under control here."

Vic turned and looked toward Janey, who sat in front of the mirror. "We've been getting the play-by-play from Janey. She claims to have a connection to what's going on. She uses the mirror. I think we should listen to her."

Janey turned. "It's all true." Then she turned back to the mirror, both hands and forehead pressed against the glass.

"What's she doing?" Robbie asked.

"Scrying," Vic said, "according to her." She sighed. "Miles explained that it's a way in which she can communicate with the dead."

Janey turned. "Not just the dead. Not all spirits were once alive." She turned back.

The sheriff folded his arms over his chest and stared at Janey's back.

"Say, where's Jack Dowling? Isn't he with you?" Vic asked.

Oh boy. James wasn't sure there was a way to deliver this news tactfully.

The sheriff cleared his throat and put on a sorrowful frown. "Dead, we assume," Robbie said. "I'm sorry to be the bearer of bad news."

Good Lord!

"What?" Vic asked. She didn't cry, and for this James felt grateful, but her lower lip quivered like she may.

"No need for every detail," James said to Robbie. He stared at the sheriff, trying to convey a sentiment he felt every man should already understand.

Robbie nodded.

James turned to Vic, who stared at him as if he himself may have murdered the man. "So," he began, but then wondered how exactly to explain this in a tactful fashion. He started over. "Dowling and I heard a scream, so he went to investigate. He never returned."

"First," Vic said, "how do you know he is dead, if he never returned? Second, why did you let him traipse off alone?" She shook her head. "Now we need to find Miles and Jack Dowling."

James noticed the moment in which the sheriff decided on a blunt approach. "I'm very sorry, ma'am. We have physical evidence of his demise," he said.

Vic placed a hand over her mouth. "Oh no," she whispered.

James wished there was another way to deliver this news, to spare Vic the brutal details. He rubbed her shoulder, but she shrugged him away. Sometimes she just needed to be left alone.

"Sorry for your loss," Robbie said, "but we have no time for word games and suppositions. The woman who tried to murder..."

Janey cut him off without turning around. "The cunt who failed," she corrected. "Her head lays next to the face of the writer man on the branch. Buried in the snow."

"And just how do you know that?" Robbie asked. James thought he looked like a doe in the headlights, staring as if someone else knowing what he knew was an impossibility.

James watched as Vic's face paled. Through a trembling hand that poorly masked her emotions, Vic said, "She uses the mirror." Her voice sounded thick with emotion.

"I happen to know she's correct," Robbie said. "So, I repeat, how do you know? How does the mirror help?" He placed a hand on his hip.

Janey turned, staring at Robbie from the tops of her eye sockets. "I've seen it in the mirror." Her voice sounded tired and mixed with gravel, and if James was being truly honest, a bit creepy.

Before Robbie could follow up, Janey added, "It wants us all."

"What does?" Robbie asked. "If you know what's happening, then please tell me what I'm dealing with."

James could tell the sheriff was trying to sound pleasant.

"It's become a spoiled brat," Janey whispered into the mirror. "The cunt never failed it before, nor any of the one's previous. This is a first, and it wants to kill."

"What is it?" Robbie asked. "And how do I stop it?"

"You can't," Janey said. "Only its own rage can stop it now."

"What's that mean?" Robbie asked. "Your information seems either a bit too much or not enough. Now please tell me what you see in there."

"I only get what I get," Janey whispered, her small ponytail shifting as she shook her head, hands still on the mirror.

James allowed Vic to bury her head in his shoulder as he watched Robbie and Janey. He wondered what the sheriff would get from the girl that made any sense. He wasn't sure if he or Vic could take much more of this.

"Convenient," Robbie said. James could tell the man was frustrated. Robbie ran a hand through hair that remained dark but mixed with grays. "When we first walked in you said something about someone being nice, but they'd die anyway. Because someone failed."

"The cunt that failed," Janey said.

"*Who* failed," James corrected with a compulsive flash of teacherly alteration. He immediately regretted opening his mouth when Vic pounded him in the ribs with her elbow.

"Whatever," Janey said. She looked right at James. "...cunt."

"You and the C-bomb," Robbie said, facial features showing his exasperation.

"Psychic residue," Vic explained. "The missing boy, Miles, said she was possessed once, and the psychic residue causes her to use unsavory language from time to time." She looked apologetic.

"Possessed once?" Robbie asked, but didn't say anything further, which James felt sure would have caused a stirring if not a full-blown argument with the child. Robbie continued in a soft patient voice, "Cunt, fine, whatever. *Who's* in danger?"

Janey remained quiet a moment. "The nice one. The one you like but who can never like you back."

"Who?" Robbie asked. But James saw the gears turning behind the sheriff's eyes and wondered what Janey had divined that the sheriff didn't think anyone else knew about.

"It's better if you try to not take what she says personally," James explained. He'd already learned this lesson the hard way and hoped to avoid any further outbursts.

"You love her, but she loves someone else," Janey went on. "She just found out not so very long ago."

"You mean since I gave her the rest of the night off?" Robbie asked. His eyes were soft and shiny with moisture.

James found the tone a mix of wonder and grief. Even Vic was pulled from the cold dark place where she must be imagining Dowling's face hanging from a branch. It sounded like Janey and Robbie were speaking of someone the rest of them didn't know.

Janey seemed to get off track. "It never lived, you know."

"What didn't?" Robbie asked, still confused. James could see all the man's unanswered questions in his soft eyes.

"It," Janey mentioned.

As James observed the sheriff and tried to comprehend what Janey was talking about, a woman in the bar area kicked her chair over and backed away. She pointed down the hall toward the lobby. "A ghost!" she shrieked. "A man with no head on his shoulders! It's looking…it's looking at us!"

"Now what?" Robbie said, but continued to stare at the back of Janey's head waiting for answers. He slowly turned toward the pandemonium.

James looked over the top of Vic's head, still holding her as the lady and a couple other people pointed and chattered. He'd heard the words *headless* and *ghost* and this reminded him of the poor maintenance man who purportedly haunted the elevator and surrounding areas of the hotel. Vic sniffed, then shifted her head to look in that direction. He wondered if the ghost would wander right in and present itself to the crowd. His mind balked at the idea, as if this whole thing would just end up being a bad nightmare. He held Vic tighter.

The sheriff stood, hand on the butt of his Glock.

Glass exploded out of a window halfway to the bar and a lump of flesh followed and skidded to a stop. It looked skinless and headless.

James couldn't find his voice. Vic tensed in his arms and stopped breathing. The sheriff took a few steps forward and stopped, his eyes intense but his mouth open.

After a gulp of air, Vic shrieked at Jack Dowling's remains, the parts which hadn't hung in the tree. James could feel her quiver against him. He felt he should say something, but every time he tried, nothing came to him.

James didn't know what to do. He felt he should shriek along with Vic or vomit or run from the room, but current events seemed to have left him desensitized to death. Either that or shock had set in. He felt bad for Dowling. Sure, the man was annoying, but his reduction to a quivering mass of red gelatin fell into the realm of overkill. It also occurred to him that someone, or something, from down below must have heaved the corpse up here.

The woman who saw the ghost and most of the remaining guests ran toward the hallway, the apparition long forgotten. James supposed they would head for their rooms. *Not such a bad move.*

"The cunt failed, big time," Janey whispered. She turned to James with a smirk. "Who..."

Part of James' psyche—the part not actively panicking—appreciated the girl's effort at proper grammar. That was until Vic pulled him to her so tight he thought he'd not be able to breathe.

Sheriff Robbie stared at the partially skinned corpse and the glass and the snow that blew in behind it. He drew his piece and James watched him stride toward the broken window. He peered out into the storm, his hair blowing back from the wind as he shielded his eyes from the lights to better see.

"It'll feed off fear, first," Janey whispered. "Then the flesh. Rage. So says the conduit." Then Janey turned to James with a little smirk. "All violet, no peach."

Good Lord! James wondered what kid could face this kind of terror and still crack an ongoing inside joke. Her demeanor appeared un-kid like, and he wondered if her psychic residue had temporarily taken complete control.

Janey, eyes having turned pure obsidian, took a step toward the corpse, and James thought she looked mad enough—or possessed enough—to take a bite out of it.

Chapter 14

"I didn't expect you to take me home after our first date," Em said. "But I definitely didn't expect breaking and entering. Good one. Original."

"I aim to please," Angela said as she trudged the last few steps through the snow. She realized this would be one of Em's endearing qualities, sarcasm amid chaos. "We need a better understanding of what we're dealing with. I don't plan to die in this town. I never wanted to, but now that I know how you feel…how I feel…"

"Aw," Em said, her voice sweet. "I make you happy. You make me happy."

"Good," Angela said, keeping her voice soft. She stopped at the door to the library and removed the keyring with the key on it. The key turned noiselessly in the lock and the mechanism clicked, and the door swung open on well-oiled hinges. Darkness spilled out like a physical presence.

"In we go," Angela said, then wondered how she'd justify this midnight excursion with Em to Robbie. She could have, perhaps should have, waited until morning. But morning could become a complete catastrophe if Harold's claims held even a margin of truth. She drew her Glock—why, she wasn't sure—and entered the darkness.

The smell of old books hit Angela and brought back memories of story-time and carefree summers. Days with her mother, evenings with her father when he finished his shift at the copper mine. Life registered well on the good-bad meter often, until she met Ron. Then came all the bad things. His hypersensitivity to other guys, his blaming—blaming her for the miscarriage, even though the doctor told him it had nothing to do with the skiing accident. He hated her after, but not for the reasons he enjoyed telling others. No, he hated the fact she could find fun without him.

"So, you gonna blast some books, kapow some comics, mangle a magazine," Em joked. "I mean, a gun in a library seems a wee bit overkill, even for you."

"An overabundance of caution," Angela whispered. "Help me find the local section."

"It's over by the reference desk," Em said. "I used to restock books in the summers. Best job of my life."

Angela turned to her. "I remember."

"You noticed me?" Em asked.

"Maybe," Angela said, smiling. When she felt uncomfortable with the silence and Em's huge grin and the fact she should show some emotion, Angela continued, "Now help me find books on local history and folklore. Anything that might explain what Harold told us about the ongoing sacrifices every thirty years. Maybe we'll luck out and learn something about when the rituals fail."

"I think I remember a book about local legends," Em said. She perused the stacks, using the light from the headlamp Angela gave her. "It included Jerome among other parts of the Mogollon Ridge." Her hands worked over the titles until she found the book she wanted. Angela noticed her long thin fingers and royal blue fingernails. "Here it is! I'm surprised it's still here after all this time. Thought Penny might've sold it at the annual purge."

"Let's bring it to a table," Angela said. She couldn't stop staring at the book, as if it may hold the key to everything. It seemed like a longshot, but longshots sometimes panned out in police work. No stone left unturned.

They picked a rectangle table adjacent to the local stacks and Angela cleared some space, pushing away some pamphlets on proper book care and a few bookmarks. Em hauled over another chair to compliment the one already there. Both women sat and opened the book to the table of contents.

They found a chapter on ghost stories from the Jerome Grand Hotel, but nothing else definitively Jerome. Then something caught Angela's eye.

"What's that chapter about the Mogollon Monster?" she asked.

Em turned the pages with a delicate hand, careful not to bend a page or crease the spine. When they reached the correct page, both women leaned in until their shoulders touched, and Em laid her head on Angela's shoulder.

She's so petite. Her own body held an athletic frame, built on the slopes of the Rocky Mountains. As a kid, she and her friends would ski all day for fun on the weekends, then ski all week for the team. She'd missed the Olympics by one measly run back in nineteen ninety-eight. Then she'd become a cop and thoroughly enjoyed roughing up the guys at the POST academy.

"This is nice," Em said. "I'm a cuddler."

"It is nice," Angela agreed and made sure to lean her head against Em's. Truth was, she didn't always like to cuddle, only sometimes, only when all her work lay in the old outbox. But this felt good and right, and she wouldn't ruin the moment by insisting on waiting for a better time. The library felt warm and cozy and private, the perfect atmosphere to enjoy each other's company.

"Here," Em said. She pointed at the page. "Says here there have been sightings in the Grand Canyon, the Mogollon Ridge from Williams to Clifton, and here in Jerome…in the Prescott National Forest."

"Yeah," Angela said. "Interesting. Here it says some believe it's a Bigfoot type creature, some large primate."

"And here," Em continued, "it speaks of an old Native American legend. It says that as far back as the Anasazi, the Native Americans drew cave drawings of a creature that could take a physical form and a spirit form." Em tapped her finger at the beginning of another sentence. "Later, the legend was continued by the Apache. Their legend claims the creature is the spirit of an old chief. He killed his entire tribe during a blizzard because they betrayed the old mystical ways."

Em ran a long skinny finger over a few sentences until she found something else of interest. "Says here he used a poison found within a local plant and finished by killing himself. Legend says his ghost, monster-sized, makes an appearance every thirty years and brings the big snow with it." Em remained quiet, then, "I paraphrased that, just saying."

Angela nodded but remained quiet, trying to think. That was a lot to digest. The similarities between what Harold and Jeb told them and the book were too alike to be a coincidence. Angela didn't believe in coincidences. Either Jeb and Harold read the book and were using it as a cover story or it was the truth.

Angela looked up at Em. "Yeah, great job on the paraphrasing. But how could the same creature live from the time of the Anasazi all the way to the Apache?" Angela asked. "That's a span of hundreds of years, maybe thousands. Is the creature the reason the Anasazi disappeared?"

Em shrugged. "The book doesn't speculate, just that there are similarities to the creature talked about by the Apache." She smiled. "There's pictures!"

Angela leaned into Em and closer to the book. She scanned the paragraphs from such proximity she could smell the dust from the book's yellowing pages. "Yes, you're right," she whispered. "The author attempts to portray both legends in a similar light." She studied the pictographs from both cultures and could see the similarities. She remained skeptical because it was her job to do so. "I don't want to sound like an asshole, but a lot of the ancient Native legends have similarities."

"More reason to believe them?" Em suggested. "Personally, I think Native Americans have a lot of things figured out better than the rest of us immigrants."

"Maybe..." Angela started. Generally, she agreed with this sentiment but also realized some of their stories were largely symbolic and ambiguous.

"Better start believing a might stronger than that," a voice said from behind them. "Because you're about to find out, firsthand. Put that pistol down, Angela."

Angela turned her head, still leaning on Em, and looked behind her. How could she have been so engrossed as to not hear someone sneak up on them? *Some cop you are.*

"Stay still," Angela whispered. Behind them stood Penny Erickson, the old librarian, and she held a shotgun in her shaky arms. Despite the trembling, Angela couldn't tell if the woman could shoot or not, and she didn't want to risk Em getting hurt.

"Drop it," Penny repeated.

"No, you drop the shotgun, Penny," Angela said. She attempted to keep her voice low and authoritative. "I don't know what this is all about, but you don't want to go to jail."

"Sounds like you know exactly what this is about," Penny said. Her voice sounded scratchy with emotion. "I heard you reading from the book. It doesn't get it exactly right, but closer than one would imagine." She mumbled, "I should've thrown that old text out a long time ago."

Angela tried another tact. She wanted to keep Penny preoccupied until she could formulate a concrete plan of action. Angela decided to play along. "Okay, suppose there is a creature roaming these mountains around Jerome, and it does bring the big snows with it. Harold says it's too late, the ritual failed. So, we need to all get out of here—all of us are in danger."

"Harold is an old fool," Penny croaked. "And gives up a might too easy. I think Marion's opening ritual took just fine, and it's not too late to get our seven sacrifices in. The two of you will make a mighty fine dent in the thing, especially since Emily should already be dead. Hell, even if I fail, the beast will see I tried and spare me."

"I wouldn't count on it," Angela said. She needed to keep Penny talking and preoccupied until she could take action. "Jeb's already dead. It got him in the jail."

"I don't believe you," Penny said. "Folks tell all kinds of lies when they get desperate. I've seen it before." She cackled at the memory. "One gal even said she'd give me a thousand dollars every month for the rest of my life just before I slit her a new, much bigger, smile beneath her old one." She stared at Angela. "There's something 'bout the feel of a blade making its way through live flesh."

Geez. How could the librarian be so off her rocker without any of them noticing? She remembered back to her youth, listening to Penny read at Summer Storytime. Angela shuddered at the thought and said the first thing that came to her. "We can work together and get off the side of this cliff. It's not too late. Robbie is already working on a plan. Harold and Jeb told us everything."

"First mistake, you're working off the premise I want to escape," Penny said. "Second, I know you're a lying sack of shit, because if Harold and Jeb told you everything, then you wouldn't be here. But make no bones about it, I'm glad you showed up. Was about to go hunt folks down as they stumbled out of the bar. Nothing like drunk barflies when it comes to a good butchering. They never know what hits them, drunk as they are. By the time they realize what's what, their blood is already on the way out of their necks."

"Follow my lead," Angela whispered, only loud enough for Em to hear. The chances of talking their way out of this were slim to nil.

Em nodded enough Angela knew she understood.

"Now, drop that pistol, Angela," Penny said. "Personally, I like both you gals. Remember you both from when you were kids. Why, Emily, you even worked for me awhile. But this business is what it is, and my fond memories won't stop me from doing what I gotta do. I've ritually sacrificed people closer to me than the two of you."

"Last time was thirty years ago," Angela said, to keep the older woman talking. "Seems like the whole lot of you have lost a little something since. I see that shotgun shaking, Penny. Better hope you kill me or you're gonna take a nine-millimeter slug to the chest. Count on it."

"Protecting your own there, I see," Penny countered. "I get it—yes, even an old lady gets it. You love Em, she loves you. It's plain. So I'll make this quick, despite how feeble you think I've become. True love may even make the ritual count for more in the eyes of the beast."

"You sound like a wicked witch from the fairytales," Em said. "Been working in the kids' section here in the library too many years."

Angela nudged her in the ribs with her elbow. "Shut it," Angela hissed into her ear. There was a time for biting sarcasm and a time to zip lips.

"Trust me," Em whispered back, then turned and brushed her lips against Angela's.

Angela hoped the girl knew what she was doing.

"Nice try, dear," Penny said. "But this is no fairy tale. However, this can have a happy ending for everyone else if you two and five others will stand up and provide flesh for the sacrifice."

"I know how that must sound in your head," Em said. "Probably pretty good. But not so good when you're on the receiving end. Don't take it personal if we don't oblige."

"Nobody ever does," Penny said. She took a step closer.

Angela began a slow course of action, moving her hand upward millimeter by millimeter. She hoped Penny would think the subtle movement only a trick of the shadows. If she could just get a shot off, even if it only nicked Penny, she and Em could dive behind the stacks before the older woman recovered.

Penny took another step and raised the shotgun to her shoulder. A huge butcher knife glinted at her side.

"And here I was just having a good hair-day," Em said, head still on Angela's shoulder. Angela could feel Em's muscles quiver, stressed tight, ready for action.

"Enough chit-chat," Penny said and pumped a round into the chamber. An empty casing rattled to the floor and Angela caught a whiff of old gunpowder. The older woman took another step and squinted down the barrel as if she couldn't see well.

Angela moved her pistol again, just a bit, trying to get a decent shot off. Her muscles quivered with the exertion of moving so slowly and the Glock wasn't exactly lightweight. A bead of sweat trickled from her hairline all the way to her jaw. She felt Em shiver next to her and wondered how the girl would react when shit hit the fan. *No time to worry about that.* Angela figured only seconds remained until Penny pulled the trigger.

A knock came at the door and all their eyes darted in that direction. Penny kept the shotgun poised and ready.

"Hello?" a voice said. Sounded like a kid, Angela thought. *What's a kid doing outside on a night like this?*

"Could anything else possibly go wrong, tonight?" Penny said. "I swear, this is a clusterfuck of epic proportions."

"Everyone gets older," Em said, voice high like a child. "It's not your fault. Like Vince Neil said, 'If we gotta blame something, then let's blame it on the rain.' Or the snow. You know."

"No, I don't know," Penny said. She whispered, "Kids now days." The shotgun never wavered, aimed at Angela, ready to deal a death blow.

Another knock. "Hello? Anyone in there?" Then the knob began to turn.

Angela thought she remembered from one of the paranormal shows, demons could use the voice of kids to trick people.

"Shit," Penny whispered. Her eyes glanced at the door, but the shotgun remained steady.

One pull of the trigger. She knew most people thought about their past in situations like this, but Angela could only think about her future with Em and how it would never happen if they lay bleeding out on the library floor.

The door creaked open and a small shadow stood, backlit by the somewhat lighter rectangle. An easy target, Angela thought. "Who's here?" the shadow asked. "I saw a light. I know you're here." Then the kid, or whatever it was, must have noticed Penny and the shotgun. "Hey, put that down."

"Get in here and shut the damn door," Penny said. "You born in a barn?"

The kid complied. When he shut the door, a blanket of darkness returned to the library.

Just as the inky darkness obscured Penny, Angela squeezed her finger and fired a round. It sounded like a cannon in the enclosed space. She grabbed Em, and both women tumbled to the floor and half-rolled, half-scurried to the stacks.

Penny pulled the trigger and staggered back from the kick when the shotgun went off. A cloud of torn paper and debris floated down and around Angela's shoulders. *Way too close!*

"Stay down," Angela hissed to Em.

"Yes, my warrior goddess," Em said in Angela's ear. "You're sexy as sin when you get in a firefight."

Angela wanted to turn and smile at Em. She couldn't allow herself to be distracted, so she kept a close eye on the space she knew Penny would attack from. Time for flirting would come later, after they were safe and sound. She felt Em rub her shoulder.

"Hey," the kid said. He sounded far away, like he found a place to hide. "Stop shooting up the library! That's low, ma'am. I can forgive a lot of stuff, but books are sacred territory."

"Get out of here, kid," Angela said. "The psycho with the shotgun is looking to murder seven people and she won't discriminate. Get out!"

The shotgun blasted with a bright tongue of flame, this time from a dark corner of the large room. More books disintegrated above Angela's head. Debris fell and shot across the floor behind her and Em. Angela raised her Glock and fired three shots into the corner.

Silence, except for the ringing in Angela's ears, so she couldn't be sure if the room remained silent or if she'd just gone deaf.

"Holy shit," the kid yelled from his hiding spot, "it's like the gunfight at the O.K. Corral in here!"

"I told you to get out, kid," Angela said. What the hell was wrong with him? First, he'd been wandering around in the blizzard, all alone. Second, he seemed to possess no fear of death.

"Not any safer out there," the kid explained. "Found some poor dude's face hanging from a branch up by the hotel. And the front-desk lady's head. I'll take my chances in here, thanks."

A wheezing, bronchial, sound resonated from the dark corner. Then a shaky voice said, "Was—was it Marion's head?"

"Yeah," the kid said with a sad tone. "The not-so-nice lady from the reception desk. Somebody cut her head off and left it lay in the snow. Took her eyes, too, like taking her body wasn't enough. Course, she did try to murder someone."

A choked sob from the corner. "I loved that old bat."

"Well," Em started, "this is what you get when you murder people. You can't tell me you didn't suspect something like this could happen, especially at your age."

A bright tongue of orange light licked out of the barrel and more books exploded off the shelves. Lead BBs ricocheted off walls and floors and tore through paper. One stray pellet streaked across Angela's left forearm. It stung like crazy and she pulled her arm close to her body.

Ignoring the pain, Angela covered Em's head with her body and wrapped her arms around her shoulders. She felt the overwhelming desire to protect this girl.

Shotgun leveled waist high, Penny stumbled out of the dark corner. A bullet wound in her abdomen leaked crimson down her blouse. She didn't bother to cover it or try to stop the bleeding. The shotgun shook. From what Angela could see of her eyes, they looked glazed. In shock, Angela knew.

"Drop the shotgun, Penny," Angela shouted. "Let me help you."

"You can't help me," Penny rasped. "Nobody can help me, even God." She stumbled toward Angela and Em, as if she wanted her last act on this Earth to be murder.

"I'd stop right there, Lady," the kid said from beneath a table. Angela could barely make him out under there, amid the shadows. "You're already in miserable shape. Just saying."

"This doesn't have to turn out like in the movies," Em said. "It's not too late to see your errors and correct them."

Penny raised the shotgun with shaking arms.

Angela squeezed the trigger, because she would not leave Em's or the kid's odds of survival to chance.

Penny's head snapped back, a gout of red and white liquid chunks propelling out the back and onto the floor. Penny wobbled, then her body fell to the hardwood like a bag of flour. The shotgun bounced once, then laid still.

"Holy cow!" the kid shouted as he cautiously climbed out from beneath the table. "You wasted her!"

Chapter 15

Harold sat on a bunk inside the miserable holding cell and tried to feel safe. Tough to do when your buddy's corpse lay in the next cell over. At least he'd broken the mirror so the beast couldn't get at him through that avenue.

He wondered about Penny, if she'd fared any better than he and Jeb and Marion. *Couldn't have done any worse.* He doubted if she would succeed in securing all seven sacrifices on her own. They'd all grown feeble over the years, and their failure to acquire younger recruits had come back to hamstring them. He also wondered about Jeb's soul. If the beast got him, did it just kill his sorry old ass, or did it drag his soul kicking and screaming off with it into the abyss?

Harold shivered. These were things you didn't worry about when you were younger and full of piss and vinegar. Death felt a long way off back then, but now it was waving at him from right around the corner. Even if the beast didn't steal his soul, what would become of it? He didn't wish for his consciousness to spend eternity in some claustrophobic burning hell. No, non-existence would prove a far better option. He imagined staring out from behind the beast's eyes, a sliver of his consciousness trapped along with a headful of other poor souls jockeying for position.

At least Robbie left one light on for me. The dim bulb threw enough light outside the cell to form inky shadows within the building's corners. He imagined Jeb's spirit standing in one of those corners staring in at him. This creeped him out, so he placed his hands on his forehead, leaned down and studied the painted-cement floor.

He allowed his mind to wander over the last sixty years. Where had it all gone? At seven, the elders mentored him and allowed him to watch them conduct the sacrifices and perform the rituals with joy in their hearts. He remembered those first experiences and relished them. Not an ounce of fear or hesitation back then, and the elders found no problems in convincing him and others of the need to continue tradition.

Harold remembered his thirty-seventh year, when the curse brought the snows again. A little wiser, the group planned their efforts meticulously. No elders remained young enough to lead them and so they led themselves. It'd gone without a hitch, and with no one suspecting they committed the murders. The beast had appeared, accepted the offerings, and disappeared for another thirty years.

But now it'd come back, and they'd failed, too old to make it work. And young people today either didn't believe in the beast or remained unafraid—unafraid because they'd never seen it. *All the kids look at nowadays is the damn internet. Instead of engaging in real experiences. We played with an old bike rim and a stick, sometimes an old can.* He shook his head.

The light outside the cell dimmed as if an unholy twilight had arrived. Harold looked up, a twinge of fear worming up his spine. The corners of the room steeped in darkness, so devoid of light Harold couldn't see the brick wall. Anything could stand in those shadows and remain obscured for as long as it wished to. Goose bumps raised on the crepe-papered mottled skin of his arms and neck.

The light bulb dimmed until only a pinprick orb of light remained in the center, then blossomed bright as a super nova. Harold found the need to shade his eyes from the glare. Little noises of discontent pinged from the bulb until it finally exploded in a hail of glass and bathed the jail in complete darkness.

Shit, Harold thought. *Damn fine time for that thing to blow.* Now he would have to sit here in the dark for the night, unless Robbie came back to check on him. He doubted this very much, because it'd be just like Robbie to let him suffer. No respect for those who came before him. *Asshole.*

While Harold sat in the dark, a stench like cooked cabbage mixed with excrement and rot filled the air. He wondered if Jeb's body had vacated its bowels and filled the dead man's undershorts. If so, Harold didn't want to know what he'd eaten in the past twenty-four hours.

Harold's eyes watered. The odor took over his sinuses like a physical presence, plugging them, forcing him to become a mouth-breather. He'd always detested mouth-breathers and hated the fact he'd been reduced to this. *Insult to injury.*

A sound like whispers caught his attention. With rapid blinks, Harold fought through his tears to scan the area outside the bars. Harold brought a hand to his chest. Just outside the cell, a humanoid patch of dark—darker than the surrounding gloom—stood and studied him.

He stared harder, sure this would prove an illusion, a trick of his eyes in the darkness. When the anomaly failed to dissipate, a cold spike of fear shot up from his bowels to his chest like he'd been skewered by an icicle from ass-end to brain.

Twin pinpricks of red erupted from the humanoid shadow's head, then grew in both size and intensity. They fell upon Harold like twin lasers.

"No," Harold wheezed, because now he understood. "We did our best. We tried. But we're old, and the young ones don't give two fucks. Go kill them, not me. Please!" The cold skewer inside him grew larger and colder until Harold felt like he'd freeze solid and explode into several frozen and bloody chunks.

The beast approached the bars, the stench preceding it like an invisible fog. It wove its way through the iron bars as if they didn't exist, until it stood before Harold like an overlord.

Harold fell to his knees, tears spilling down his cheeks. "Please," he begged. "I don't wanna die. I don't wanna spend eternity with you. No! I'll make things right. Let me go. I'll find Penny and we'll get you what you want. Please!"

A disapproving growl burst forth from just below the red eyes.

"I mean, some dead bodies for you is better than none, right?" Louder, "Right? You don't wanna kill 'em your own self."

The beast turned its head sideways as if considering. It stayed this way until two shadowy appendages shot out of its dark bulk. What felt like cold hands gripped Harold's shoulders in an icy twin-vice and lifted him off the cot. The pinch and cold of the hands felt like talons piercing his flesh.

The beast lifted Harold until they were face-to-face, its red eyes boring into his. Hot piss dribbled from the saturated seat of his pants onto the floor. For the first time in his life, Harold screamed in terror. His throat throbbed in pain from the effort.

In his last moments, he considered the kids he never had, grandkids he'd never hold, and for God's sake, he'd only copulated and writhed between the legs of Marion and Penny. He'd barely lived his life, yet. It didn't seem fair. He would've liked to get on top of Angela, but that would never happen whether he lived or died.

Harold felt his skin rub across the cement floor as the beast dragged him toward the metal bars. The shadow creature slipped right through, but Harold clanked against the metal.

"Ouch, you stupid asshole," Harold shouted. "You are one stupid motherfucker." The cussing felt good but only for a moment. The beast upended him, grabbed his foot and pulled his legs through the opening between the bars. Then his ribs caught, but the creature kept pulling until they cracked. Harold's mouth worked open and closed like a fish. He couldn't catch enough air to feed his burning lungs.

Harold saw spots and felt one last agonizing tug when his compressed and broken ribs finally passed through the metal bars. Air rushed back into his lungs with a painful flurry. Just as that relief came, his head caught. His classmates in school always teased him about his oversized dome. He'd heard their taunts, "Big Head Harold, Big Head Harold…" A fiery remembrance enveloped him at this memory, as if the beast knew all about it and would subject him to this psychological torture on top of the physical torment.

"Fuck you," Harold wheezed. His ribs must have punctured a lung. With all the pain, it remained difficult to pinpoint where exactly on his torso this may have occurred. He felt blood on his lips, tasted it on his tongue.

Harold's head remained caught between the two bars as the beast pull him by the legs. An incredible pain, worse than his ribs, erupted in his neck. White flashes of light arched in his peripheral vison. Another tug, then all the pain went away, and all Harold could feel was a rubbery stretching sensation around the base of his head. The image of a headless corpse dimmed until his consciousness remained but a pinprick of light. And then nothing.

Chapter 16

Robbie stared out the window into the darkness of the wooded slopes. Large tracks led away across a good foot of snow. Flakes continued to fall in continuous ropes of white until they hit the wind and scattered into obscuring sheets.

It'd take more than a bear to heave Dowling's body up and through the window. A good face tear or decapitation, sure, but not this. He couldn't imagine what else could accomplish this. Robbie supposed he should take Harold at face value. Something unexplainable stalked his town, and he possessed no better explanation than rituals and monsters. Even the little girl with her face plastered to the mirror seemed in agreement.

The kid mentioned someone he loved stood a chance of death. She must have meant Angela, but he couldn't concern himself with that now. He needed to trust in the fact Angela could damn well take care of herself.

Robbie sighed out of frustration. He needed to do something soon. What he really wanted was to fire his Glock blindly out into the night. At least the people in here would see him attempt something. He knew he needed to take charge before folks went ape shit on him.

Like a magician but not nearly as smooth, Robbie pulled a tablecloth out from beneath a couple plates and an unlit candle. The plates bounced and one chipped, the smaller chunk bounding for the floor and coming to rest beside the bloody corpse. The candle tipped sideways and rolled to the edge of the table, then dropped and rolled toward the wall. Robbie took the tablecloth and, out of a modicum of decency, spread it out over Dowling's desecrated body. It sure made him feel a whole lot calmer not to have to stare at the man's pulpy red muscle and exposed white lesions of fat.

James and Vic stared at the covered body and then at him.

"Listen up, folks," he said to the few people still gawking. "I need you all to go to your rooms and lock the doors. I don't think we have anything to worry about inside, but we'll adhere to an overabundance of caution and get you all secure as possible."

"But we need to find Miles," Vic said. "He's out in the storm. We can't just leave him out there."

Robbie glanced at James just as the man looked his way. He wondered if turning her attention to the kid was the woman's way of dealing with the loss of Dowling. The sheriff nodded. "Look, I get it. He's a kid. But let me get this situation under control first. I have three bodies and don't plan on more." He grabbed a cellphone from his pocket and shook his head. "Tower's down."

"That happen often?" James asked.

"More than I care for," Robbie said. "Doesn't matter. Nobody's getting in or out of here until the snow stops."

James nodded. "We're on our own. As for Miles, he wouldn't hesitate to chase a mystery like this if he thought he could get whatever is guilty of this on film." He nodded toward the body.

"Strange kids," Robbie mumbled. *One glued to a mirror, the other running about in a blizzard with a camera.*

"One minute," Vic said, "he was in the room with Marion's body, the next…gone. I only turned my back for a moment. He jumped out the window." She continued to eyeball Dowling as if he might rise from the dead.

Great, Robbie thought. "So, how did Marion get outside? That have something to do with the broken window and the boy?"

"In a way," Vic said. "She tried to murder me, so I went for help. By the time I got back with Miles, something had dragged her out the window and into the night." She eyeballed the sheet again. Robbie knew she thought the two events related. How could she not? "The boy, I'm sure, followed the tracks."

"You brought the boy to see Marion's corpse?" Robbie asked. He tried not to sound judgmental but found it difficult. He scanned the room and noticed most everyone else had vacated the room.

Vic shrugged, unable to adequately explain why she'd done it. "He—he's a very convincing…and adventurous kid. His dad allows him to do about anything as long as he gets his adventures on film."

"It makes them money," Janey mumbled from the mirror where she still sat with her forehead pressed against it.

"Okay," Robbie said. He thought he was getting a better read on the kids. By all indications, they were handling themselves better than the adults. "Although I don't feel great about it, I need to make a choice. I'm not gonna worry about him for now. He chose to head out into the blizzard, and he has experience with risky situations. I just hope he has the sense to come back in out of the blizzard before he freezes." He looked around. "Let's get you folks to your rooms. I'll make sure the place is locked up. We'll wait out the storm and then get you off this mountain. But until then, stay inside your rooms and don't come out until I tell you. I can't guarantee your safety if you don't."

James nodded and put a hand on Vic's back to guide her. She shrugged him off and this made Robbie smile. *Tough lady.*

Janey turned. "Can you, anyway? Keep us safe, I mean?"

"I know what you meant," Robbie replied without looking at her. "And I hope so." A ripple of unease sliced up his spine. He did hope so, but he had such little intel to go on. Monsters. Ghosts. Sacrifices. What he knew and understood about such matters he could cram into the eye of a needle. He did not know if he could keep people safe from things like that—things he didn't even really believe in. He'd try, because it was his job to try.

"It'll take them to the mine shaft where it sleeps," the girl said.

"Take who there?"

"The cunt *who* failed," and here she glared with her black eyes at James, "and the others. It'll keep their souls there...locked away...forever, if it can. Until someone appeases its rage."

"Jeb and Harold?" Robbie asked, seeing the pattern.

"And others," Janey explained.

"The one I love?" Robbie thought he was beginning to catch onto her little game.

"Perhaps."

Robbie sighed. "I'm sure I really don't want to know, but how did you come across this information?"

"I told you," James said. "She's clairvoyant or a clever liar."

Janey and Vic glared at James.

"Well," James back-peddled, "perhaps liar is a bit strong for the circumstances."

"Cunt," Janey whispered and turned back to the mirror. Instead of slapping her palms to the glass, she pointed with both index fingers. "The spirits tell me things even when I don't want to know. It's not my fault. I can't make them stop."

Robbie felt the need to move Janey away from the mirror and to safety. Her sitting there like a possessed guardian wouldn't help keep them safe from the likes of what threw Dowling through the window. On the other hand, he required more information to do his job. "Where are these mine shafts you spoke about?" Robbie asked. "Where can I look?"

"Beneath the city," Janey said. "Beneath the hotel. Everywhere."

"I know that much," Robbie said. He used to explore the ones beneath the old sheriff's office. Even the kids did, but they never ran into anything like this. "I guess what I'm trying to ask is, where do I find the entrance closest to where this thing will put the people?"

"The corpses," Janey corrected.

"Only corpses?" Robbie asked. Maybe he should go look for Angela right this minute. He couldn't afford to lose his last deputy. Someone he loved.

"I don't know," Janey said.

"You seem to know everything else," Robbie said, then thought he was being unfair. She was only a kid despite the fact she had spirits communicating with her.

Janey shrugged.

"Then where is the entrance?" Robbie asked.

Janey shrugged again. "You could ask the spirits. There are so many here. They know. They know everything. They know about its rage."

Robbie didn't know if he believed in ghosts. Then again, until today he also hadn't believed in creatures powerful enough to throw a man through a second-story window from below. What a shit-show this had all become. He tried to remember why he came here but found his memory cloudy. Just so hell-bent on becoming a sheriff he would have taken a job on the moon, Robbie supposed. Harold hadn't proved hard to beat. He reflected on this. Yes, it could have all ended up different. He imagined himself in Kansas, leading a thirty-person force, visiting his folks every Sunday for dinner. Probably would have settled in and procreated and popped out several offspring. Besides Angela, nobody else on this Godforsaken ledge of a city interested him enough to even get a hard on, let alone have kids with. Anywhere not on the leading edge of a mountain would have better suited him. But here he was, entertaining ghosts and creatures and clairvoyants and God knew what else.

Robbie let out a breath and turned to Janey. "You don't happen to know where Miles is, do you, Janey?"

"He's alive," she said.

"Alive where?" Why did it seem like he had to pry information out of everyone? Couldn't one damn person string together more than a sentence in response to his inquiries? He also knew this attitude stemmed from his frustration with the unknown. He needed to stay patient.

Janey shrugged. "I know what I get told, nothing more." She continued to stare into the mirror. "It's getting hard to hold it back."

"Hold what back?" Vic asked, but it came out with a cracked, squeaky voice.

"It," Janey said. "It likes this mirror and wants to come through it." She whispered, "Over my dead body."

Robbie hoped not.

As if she sat in front of an open window, Janey's hair blew back from her shoulders, away from the mirror. She leaned harder into her work. A stench of death, more pronounced than could come from the still-frozen Dowling, entered the room.

"Get back," Janey screamed. "I won't allow you to enter. So says the conduit. Cunt."

Vic ran up to Janey. "Are you okay?"

"Don't touch me!" Janey said.

Robbie felt disappointed the girl hadn't added the expletive to the end, cheated somehow, as if only the girl screaming the word cunt at the top of her lungs would sate his need for strangeness and inopportune phrasing. It was as if the girl had turned the word into a beautiful verbal-tapestry. Then Robbie felt overtaken with a sudden course of action and felt a need to protect the kid.

"Get back," he shouted. "Get her away from that mirror."

Vic stared hard at the sheriff, but when she noticed how serious he looked, she grabbed the girl by the shoulders and turned her away.

"No!" Janey said. "It's here!"

The moment the girl's palms and forehead left the mirror, dark shadow arms sprouted out of it. The metaphysical winds whistled through and tossed Robbie's bangs, sent napkins spinning off tables. The death and excrement stench built, a presence billowing in like a physical manifestation. A growl pulsed through and Robbie didn't know if he sensed or heard the noise. The chandeliers hanging from the ceiling swung back and forth in a tight formation.

Vic held on to a struggling Janey, and James wrapped his arms around a stunned Vic and pulled them both backwards to a safer distance.

"Stay back!" Robbie said. When they stood safely behind him, Robbie fired three times. The spiritual arms disappeared when Jagged chunks of mirror fell away and nothing remained but a frame and a portion of wall with three bullet holes in the plaster. He didn't realize he'd been screaming as he shot until his throat hurt.

"Now it's really mad," Janey whispered, but looked more relaxed in Vic's arms. More like a little girl. Perhaps this lessened her perceived responsibilities, Robbie thought.

But mine have only escalated.

Chapter 17

"Don't sound so excited about it," Angela said. She walked toward Penny's body with an unsteady gait. She felt off-balance. When she extended an arm to stabilize herself, she noticed the Glock still in her hand. Her whole arm shook. She'd killed someone. She mumbled, "People aren't supposed to sound that excited when people die."

"Take it easy, babe," Em said. She glanced at Angela with concern; Angela sensed it. When Em didn't continue, she figured Em got the hint she needed to be alone for a moment. Thank God! Then Em talked to the kid, probably to distract him from the corpse. "Hey, kid, you from around here?"

"Naw," he said. "I'm from Minnesota. I'm here with my aunt. She's at that Romance convention up at the Jerome Grand."

"How the hell you end up here with that blizzard raging?" Angela asked. She'd stopped between the kid and Penny. She didn't want him seeing this kind of thing. He would probably have nightmares as things stood. And that was her fault. She'd discharged her weapon and killed a woman right in front of him.

"I jumped out a window, followed some big ass tracks, found a face and a head, then saw some lights on in here. Thought I'd warm up before I lit out on the tracks again."

Angela shook her head because she didn't know how much to believe. If the kid really witnessed this carnage he should be crying, wigging out, begging for her to help him. What kid took things in stride? What kid jumped out a window into a blizzard to follow tracks and held a casual conversation after witnessing a woman get her brains blown out of her head? To clear her mind, she turned to Em.

"You okay?" she asked, voice soft. She looked Em over. Em didn't look like she'd been hit. No blood, no limping, just those beautiful eyes.

"Fine," Em said, even softer than Angela. "No bullet holes. But your concern makes me all gooshy inside." She walked over and hugged Angela.

Angela tried to shield Em from the worst of the carnage. Nobody should have to see things like that.

"You two are lovers," Miles whispered. His face held a pleasant smile.

"Yeah," Angela acknowledged, although she wasn't sure about that. She and Emily hadn't exactly made love yet. On the other hand, they were well on the way to falling in love. She was positive Em would say she loved her. "What's it to ya, kid?" She stared into his eyes, dared him to tease them.

"My name's Miles," he said. He seemed to search for the words he wanted. "Tracey says women who love other women make the best women. Not catty and all that. My mom was catty, but she got offed by a serial killer." His eyes swept the floor as if this still pained him to discuss.

When Em lifted her head to glance at Miles, Angela shook her head. The kid had been through enough crap for ten lifetimes.

"Your mom what?" Em asked. Her eyes looked big and wet as if she might shed a tear. "Miles, I am so sorry. That must have sucked royally." She disengaged from Angela and took steps toward him, her arms out like she'd hug him.

"It's okay," Miles said. "It is what it is. My sister Janey had a tougher time, but she's adjusting. That's what Tracey says."

"Who is this Tracey?" Angela asked. Her cop-mind desired concrete facts and she personally wanted reasons for the kid's calm demeanor despite his life events.

"My dad's girlfriend," Miles said. "She's real cool, taught me how to investigate the paranormal. Not catty at all, by the way, 'cept she's not a lesbian. You know, since she's banging my old man."

"Could swing both ways," Em said and nodded.

Angela swung her head toward Em. *Jesus! He's just a kid.*

"What's that mean?" Miles asked. He looked interested in the answer but smiled like he already knew. Angela wouldn't be surprised.

But it certainly wasn't their job to help the kid figure out his orientation.

Before Em could divulge any further facts, Angela said, "Never mind, it's not important." What was important was the corpse on the floor. Angela needed to decide what to do with Penny's body. She walked over to the woman she'd just killed and felt a pang of guilt in her gut. It twisted around in there, but she accepted this as a good sign. Not all her humanity had leaked out with the librarian's blood. Angela took a deep breath and then fell to her knees.

Both Em and Miles walked up to Angela. "Hey, you okay?" Miles asked. Em put a hand on her shoulder.

The comfort more than the corpse broke Angela down. A tear streaked down her cheek and she swiped it away with a trembling fist.

"Don't cry," Miles said.

"You had to," Em whispered in her ear. "Her or us, babe. Self-defense. Had to be done or we'd all be dead, and she'd be off to slaughter some other people."

"Yeah," Angela whispered. "I—I just never killed anyone before. Sure, I shot Jeb, but he didn't die from the gunshot wound."

"You shot someone else today?" Miles asked. When Angela nodded, he said, "That's rough." He patted her shoulder as if to encourage her, to indicate she wasn't to blame. "But you're a cop. Gotta do what ya gotta do." He gave her an apologetic look, complete with sad eyes and a twist of his head. "I have this sneaky feeling you might need to do some more shooting before the night's out. I mean, something is running around here ripping the faces and heads off folks. Not to sound hardcore...just saying." He told them what he knew about what happened up at the hotel.

Angela stood, ready to act. She needed to get herself under control and then the situation. She'd shown enough emotion.

"Oh my God," Em said, hand over mouth. "I'm so sorry you had to go through all that."

"Don't be," Miles said. "I'm just sorry I didn't get anything on film except for the face and the head. And everyone will think we staged those. Tracey always tells me that if it isn't on film as it happens, it *never* happened."

"You are hardcore, kid," Angela said. She wiped her final bout of tears and snot on the sleeve of her uniform. They needed to start thinking about their own safety. If what Penny spoke about was correct, some elders with a vendetta may prove the least of their worries. By the sound of Mile's story, things had already begun to ramp up. She wondered if she should bring the kid and Em up to the hotel and see what's what.

"I've been through a lot," Miles said. "That's what some shrink said about it when the social workers made me go…you know, after my mom got offed. I enjoyed talking to him, but he got more freaked out from hearing it than I ever did living through it. Kind of a wuss, truth be told."

Em clapped a hand over her mouth and giggled. "It's not funny, about your mom and such," she said. "But you sure are." Then she turned to Angela. "I'm sorry. I shouldn't be laughing."

"That's what they tell me," Miles said with a quirky smile. "They also tell me I'm morbid and a bit less sensitive to scary stimulus than I ought to be at my age." He shrugged. "Oh well."

"Everyone's different," Em agreed. She added, "I like you, Miles. If I needed a kid to have my back, I'd want that kid to be you. You're solid."

Angela watched Miles blush and fidget and mumble, probably unsure how to react to kind words from a pretty girl. Her pretty girl. Angela stood. She had responsibilities. "Let's get a move on." She wrestled her attention away from both Miles and Penny to take in the storm outside.

The wind was picking up out there, howling across the eaves of the library and the adjacent tree branches. The howl of the wind sounded a lot like that of a beast, low and visceral. Angela scanned the large windows but noticed nothing out of place, only the wavering giant oaks and their shadows. Her right hand, with an instinct born from practice, moved back to the butt of her Glock.

"Easy," Em said. "Just the wind, I think."

Miles nodded but stayed silent and Angela noticed the kid stare out into the night. She knew he'd seen enough to realize the danger. He'd seen what this thing could do; she hadn't. Not yet, unless she counted Jeb's possible suicide. And she hoped to skip that part—hoped they could just wait out the storm and then get off this cliff face. If the cult had failed, and this thing really was out there killing people, then they were in trouble. How could you fight something like that except with magic—magic she knew nothing of?

"Okay," Angela started, "before we all get freaked, maybe we should go find Robbie. He's probably still at the jail. Maybe he knows something."

"What are you guys doing here?" Miles asked.

Em smiled, reached over, and tucked a wayward tuft of the kid's hair behind his ear. "We were trying to find information about what this thing is that hurt those people." She explained.

"You mean, *killed* them," Miles said. "Anyway, that's like what happened at the hotel. Marion went nuts and tried to kill a lady with a clothes iron. The beast got her after she hurt herself and couldn't get up."

Angela shook her head. Maybe Robbie needed her at the jailhouse. She took her cellphone from her pocket and found it had no signal. *Great*. And she'd left her radio at the jail.

Something banged against the outside of the library and scraped along the outer wall. Then all went silent.

All three stared at the windows. All Angela could see were tree branches and the white of falling snow.

"Probably only a broken tree branch," Em suggested. She didn't sound like she believed that. The girl's eyes roved back and forth looking for another explanation.

Angela drew her Glock.

"That make you feel better?" Miles asked. He nodded at the pistol.

"Yep." She turned her attention back outside. The already weak streetlight gave even less illumination, obscured by the raging blizzard.

Something thudded across the roof above the vaulted library ceiling. Something heavy. The footsteps started at one end of the roof and ended at the other—the one farthest from them. A louder thump outside sounded a lot like something huge jumping from the roofline to the ground.

"More branches?" Miles asked. He stared at the ceiling and then out the patio doors. He looked nervous because of the tick on the right side of his mouth. Like he was trying to smile but couldn't manage the needed levity.

"Sure?" Em answered. She sounded subdued and quiet. She also stared out the doors into the snowy night.

Angela brought the Glock up and braced her shooting hand with the other. She squinted down the sight and took a step toward the sliding glass patio door, ready to protect the two behind her. Angela felt ill-prepared, uneasy, and more than a little foolish. What if this turned out to be a squirrel or a branch or a pinecone? *It was too loud for any of those things.*

"You two stay behind me," she said. "We can't be too careful." Angela sidestepped Penny's corpse taking pains not to glance at it this time.

"Won't we all laugh when this turns out to be nothing but our active imaginations," Em suggested.

"Yeah, ha ha," Miles said, sarcastically.

"Quiet," Angela hissed. She took another step toward the large plate glass rectangles. Nothing was visible save for trees and snow. "I can't hear with you two chattering."

Another howl of the wind, but this time it sounded different. The tone reminded her of a definite growl, low and guttural, like a mama bear protecting her young. The hairs on her arms stood at attention, raised by the gooseflesh beneath. Her heart pounded behind her ribs and sweat saturated her pits. Nervous, she knew. Yes, Angela could admit that. But she knew how to handle such things—knew how to make them work for her. Never again would she remain a slave to such emotions. She took another step toward the patio, no quiver whatsoever in aiming her Glock. She mentally counted the bullets she had expended: *one on that worthless asshole, Jeb, and four on Penny. Three hits out of five. Not good.* That only left her with ten shots and she'd left her extra clip at the office.

"Sounds like an angry animal," Em whispered. She sounded far away now, as if backpedaling as she spoke. This was good. Angela wanted Em out of harm's way.

"Or a monster," Miles said. This Angela didn't need to hear, but at least the volume of Miles' voice indicated he'd also retreated.

When Angela looked back, she confirmed they were both a few steps farther away. Em had grabbed a hold of Miles, holding him close to her in a protective gesture. *What a great gal.* Angela wasn't the only one with a protective spirit. Maybe they could never have kids of their own, but Angela could envision a scenario in which they would adopt children and have a whole houseful of laughter and joy.

Another thud from outside erased Angela's thin smile. She turned her attention back to the sliding door. The growling wind had gone silent for the moment which made her nervous. *The calm before the storm.* It was like she could feel the tension building inside her, a rubber band about to release. Her ears filled with a pressure Angela couldn't explain away as natural.

As if shot from a cannon, a sphere punched through the plate glass of the outside patio, hit the hardwood, then wobbled to Angela's feet. Rather than stare down at the lopsided sphere—even though she wished to kick it back like a playground ball—Angela studied the dark world outside. Something out there was playing cat-and-mouse with them, and it would strike the moment Angela lost concentration.

Em let out a small whimper as the last of the glass shards came to rest at their feet.

"Holy shit," Miles whispered. "Look at that."

Em didn't respond and this unnerved Angela more than the sphere itself. This meant Em knew what the item was. She was probably back there, quiet as a mouse, hands covering her mouth to stave off a scream.

Keeping an eye on the patio door, Angela glanced down at the sphere. The base of the thing had leaked a thick fluid on the floor. It took a moment to understand this was blood as seen in the underlit room. She also noticed the quill-like shards of glass still sticking from the sphere. Sure, some of them broke off during the impact with the glass, but she could still see them, even in the poor light. *Jeb*. And if the beast had taken Jeb, where the hell was Robbie? How this thing could have gotten Jeb out of the cell without a key and without Robbie's knowledge eluded her. His baleful deflated eyes looked up at her as if pleading for help. But he was beyond their help now, in the hands of whatever deity Jeb worshipped.

"Stay back," Angela said. "If this thing gets in here, I don't want either of you between me and it. Understand? I need a clear shot."

"Understood," Em said. She sounded frightened.

"You got it," Miles said. He sounded less scared, but Angela recognized the apprehension in the kid's voice. She imagined the nervous tick his lips produced.

Angela slowed her breathing and dried her sweaty shooting hand on her pants.

The beast growled a harsh warning. That sound rumbled and pierced Angela's chest and grabbed hold of her beating heart and shook it. Something dark moved like a twister outside the patio door. As the dark mass approached the glass, it morphed from a patch of darkness into a humanoid shape. The figure wore a large headdress of feathers and a tomahawk around its waist. As it spun, these items moved with the creature, whirling about like debris around a tornado.

Angela heard feet on hardwood as Em and Miles took a few steps backward.

Just when Angela thought the creature would smash through the glass, it glided in like a wraith and stood before her. A growl rumbled deep in its chest, its red eyes seeking them. Angela took a shaky breath and fought the urge to bolt. This thing wasn't natural, but she understood its intent. Angela squeezed off a solitary shot, center mass. Nothing happened. Her heart sank with the realization she lacked the expertise to deal with such a thing. If they weren't having a group hallucination, they were in some serious trouble. She took a step backward.

The beast laughed an ungodly, inhuman chortle. Dead cornstalks in a stout breeze. The apparition morphed from the Native guise to an amorphous shadow and then back as if it lacked the power to stay formed.

"Stay back," Angela warned. She'd meant the warning for the beast, for what little good it did, but hoped Em and Miles would heed it also. She didn't think she could kill this thing, so they needed to run. She kept the Glock trained on the thing as it mocked her.

"Go on!" Miles said. "Get out of here. We don't belong to you, so you got no power over us!"

This quieted the beast and it appeared to ponder what the boy said. It turned its head toward Miles and tilted it sideways. The boy had captured its undivided attention, and Angela wondered what she could do while it remained preoccupied. Nothing came to mind.

"You heard me," Miles continued. "We aren't scared of you. Go on, get out of here!"

The beast laughed with those dry scraping bursts, but they sounded less confident, a little unsure. Perhaps nobody had ever stood up to it like this before. Angela remembered from one of the ghost shows, demons—if this was a demon—fed off fear. Perhaps Miles' bravery would give the thing pause.

It took a step forward despite Miles' boldness and the footfall sounded like a log hitting the ground. It growled. The beast's red eyes flickered in and out as if physical eyelids obscured them intermittently. *That stench alone could knock out a bull.* The odor of rotten vegetables and spoiled meat wafted about them. *Smells like an open grave.*

"Did the ritual fail?" Miles asked. He sounded calm. Too calm, Angela thought. Not like a kid but an adult stuffed inside a kid's body. "That why you're so sore—why you're ripping off heads and faces and such?

Em gasped as if Miles' words scared her. She took another step toward the door, a hand on Miles' shoulder.

Angela couldn't help a small smile. She noticed he held a video-camera in his hands and the red light illuminated the hardwood in front of him. Like her Glock, the camera never shook, rock steady in his small hands. Whoever trained him, did it well.

The creature rumbled a deep growl but stood its ground. It continued to study this child who dared defy it. The headdress continued to morph in and out of the top of the black mass and its red eyes, like lasers, continued to blink at them.

"Back up slow," Angela said. She knew this bout of curiosity and inactivity wouldn't hold. They needed to act while they still could. "Steady movements, nothing sudden, show no fear. Back toward the door where we came in." She kept her voice low and calm. She walked backwards, one foot after the other, careful not to stumble. Her aim needed to remain true.

Miles and Em must have followed suit, because she didn't run into them. They had already covered three-quarters of the distance. *Keep moving. Slow and steady*. They might just make it out of this library yet, but then what? Where did one go to get away from an apparition who could travel anywhere and wasn't hindered by solid walls?

Angela estimated they should have reached the doorway, so she shouted, "Run! Out the door!" She heard the other two scramble over hardwood. She shuffled backwards until she reached the threshold. *Good, the others must already be out in the snow*. A small comfort.

The beast came out of its trance and lost its mind. It howled, enraged, and it sounded like the wind. The headdress and tomahawk disappeared and nothing remained but an amorphous black shadow and the red piercing eyes. It raced toward Angela on legs that emerged and disappeared from the black mass of its gigantic body. The footfalls sounded like death.

Chapter 18

James thought Janey looked lost without her mirror. *Like a teenager without a cellphone.* The girl wandered behind the sheriff without any other sense of direction. This disturbed James because he was beginning to have a change of heart about the girl. His gut told him she may have answers the rest of them didn't. Sure, there might be ghosts in this building, but he felt sure they would prove innocent of any killing or throwing of corpses. He felt like Janey would know for sure.

The sheriff led them like cattle through the bar area and into the main hallway until Janey stopped and turned toward the dark bedroom. James noticed a melting pile of snow had already accumulated beneath the window.

Janey stared at the glassless window, wind whipping her ponytail. She whispered, "It doesn't belong here, has no real power. No ritual, no intent, then no power. It lives off our fear and its rage."

James wished her words weren't so fierce and that she didn't remain so calm while saying them. He wanted badly to believe she made them up but knew she didn't, the girl guided by the residue within her.

The curtains billowed with a gust of wind, and James thought he might need to grab Vic and run for his life. When nothing appeared out of the darkness, he relaxed. He glanced at Vic. Her eyes looked sunken with deep shadows. Vic needed sleep after what she'd seen and been through.

"Keep moving," the sheriff said. "Let's get you folks to your rooms so I can handle this situation."

James remained skeptical about the sheriff's methods. He doubted if the sheriff understood what plagued them, let alone possessed the ability to find an adequate solution. His money remained on Janey. But how could he convince the hard-nosed sheriff of this? Perhaps he could reason with the man.

He decided on, "Perhaps we should allow Janey to help us."

"Help us what?" Robbie asked.

"Help us stay alive," James said. He tried to look serious with only a note of placid self-assurance. This expression often worked wonders with his students. "Always a good idea, in my humble opinion."

"I have a firearm," Robbie said. "You'll all stay plenty safe. No killer I ever heard about could take a slug to the chest and keep on killing."

"You saw Dowling's corpse come smashing through the window and those arms come out of the mirror," James said.

"And my bullets put an end to the thing."

"Are you an idiot?" Janey asked. She no longer sounded like a little girl.

Good Lord, James thought. If the sheriff didn't trust the girl before, he certainly wouldn't after she said that. He would go it on his own, and that would ruin them all.

James held his breath, ready for Robbie to take charge and dismiss the one person who may understand what's going on. He was all for respecting authority, but sometimes authority needed to respect folks with answers.

Robbie frowned, then shook his head. He let out a long breath as if to calm himself, then smiled. "What do you mean, Janey? Tell me what I'm missing."

"You really think you can kill a shadow?" Janey asked. "It's spirit form, flesh and blood and spirit, choosing whichever manifestation best suits its needs."

James knew the sheriff was still thinking about those black appendages reaching out of the mirror. Perhaps he'd already chalked them up to a trick of the light or his imagination, group hallucination, something. James noticed when the realization this would prove something more than that settled in like sand into the bottom of an hourglass. *A perfect analogy*. James thought about the hourglass that sat on his desk at school, given to him by his principal when he achieved tenure. He desperately wished he were there to see it.

"You can't kill it," Janey continued. "Your bullets only closed the portal it used. It will return for vengeance."

"You mentioned something about flesh and blood," Robbie said. He looked at her with an expectant gaze.

"Maybe then," Janey said. "But good luck. The only place you'll find it vulnerable enough for that is near it's vessel."

"It's what?" Robbie asked.

New territory. Miles had explained about Janey's psychic residue and James guessed it was working some serious overtime to deliver this kind of information.

"*Vessel of the Diablo Si,*" Janey said. "Where it lives when not accepting sacrifices or killing. Where it slumbers for thirty years."

"And you know this how?" Robbie asked.

Janey shrugged as if the how didn't matter.

"I understand your reluctance," James said to Robbie. He rubbed the stubble and nodded with a solemn shake of his head. He strove for his lecture tone, which he enjoyed breaking out when all else failed. "As an educator, I have seen my fill of kids and their robust imaginations. But, in this case, I think we've all seen enough to understand the girl's ideas may have merit."

"Yeah," Robbie whispered. He swiped a hand over his face as if to wash it. "Look, I know this place is supposed to be haunted and relies on that for tourism. And yes, I saw what came out of that mirror, same as everyone else. I may buy into ghosts. But some spirit form thing, as Janey described, going around killing folks? I don't know."

"Suit yourself," James said. "I saw that face hanging from the tree while it was still fresh. I watched Marion's head sail through the treetops, then Dowling's body after it was flung through the window. I believe something supernatural is doing this."

Janey whistled with a low tone, sounding appreciative of James' attitude.

Robbie took a deep breath and exhaled. "Okay," he said. "But whatever this is, I can't guarantee safety to any of you outside your rooms. I suggest…"

"Again, is it in your power to guarantee anything, at all?" the child said.

James thought she sounded mature beyond her years—well beyond. *Psychic residue.*

The sheriff stared into the darkness outside. James wondered what kind of thoughts coursed through the sheriff's mind.

"I have no idea what's going on here," Robbie finally said. He shook his head. "But no way we get down off this mountain until daylight. We gotta make it through until then. Best way is to keep as many walls as possible between us and…whoever or whatever is outside. That's the only plan I can come up with."

"Shouldn't we stay together?" James asked.

The sheriff wiped at his face, something James noticed he did often when confronted with a tough decision. Robbie looked up at James, eyes red with stress. "Yes," he said. Robbie rubbed the stubble on his chin. "Okay, we stay together in the hotel. But stay away from windows and doors. We've seen what this thing can do."

"Your plan will fail just as the cunt's did," Janey whispered. She walked past the sheriff and headed down the middle of the hallway, her little body swaying to the rhythm of her ponytail as if all her life energy emanated from her hair.

James wondered how far she would walk. He imagined her walking down the hall, through the lobby, and out into the snowy night.

"Where's she going?" Robbie asked.

Vic took a step toward the girl. "Janey, where are you going?"

Janey didn't turn, just kept moving down the hall. When she reached the elevator, Janey waved them forward with a movement of her arm.

"What does she mean for us to do?" Vic asked.

James put an arm around her. Vic put on a strong front, but when things got to be too much, she'd sometimes withdraw into herself. She hadn't done this since her mother passed away some years ago. That's when she took up writing, found she possessed a knack for it, then began to sell some work. Only short fiction and a lone novella, but it was a start. Now, he feared a setback.

"Would going back to the room to write help take your mind off things?" James asked.

"Are you kidding?" Vic said. "You want me to write a horror story? I just saw my mentor—my literary hero—without his skin, James! Try and make some sense."

Janey turned toward the lobby where Marion used to work and then turned once more to peer into the dark elevator again. "He says we should follow him down."

"Who is him and down where?" Vic asked.

"The old fixer-upper guy," Janey answered. "He wants us down there." She pointed at the floor, but James knew the girl meant the basement beneath them.

"Can you see him?" James asked.

"Of course."

Robbie sneezed into the crook of his elbow and looked away. James thought he was trying to hide the fact he didn't believe the girl.

"He's kind of a mess, bloody and stuff," she explained. "But he doesn't seem to mind. Wants me to follow him, really bad."

"Does he frighten you?" James asked. He walked up to her and found nothing inside the elevator but shadows. His eyes darted back and forth, from dark corner to dark corner.

"No," she said. "He can't hurt us. Wouldn't if he could. Just a person without a body."

"Is the thing…the thing outside a person without a body?" James asked.

"No," Janey said. "Part of it was human once, but not anymore."

"Then what is it?" James asked. He felt the girl was withholding pertinent information.

"Stop asking the wrong questions," Vic said. She turned to Robbie who pretended to rummage through papers on the reception desk like they may harbor a clue. "Sheriff, I think the spirit inside Janey is trying to lead us to something specific."

"I don't know," Janey said in answer to James, ignoring Vic. She nodded to someone nobody could see but her and added, "Inhuman." She stepped toward the elevator and then looked up, nodded in confirmation to someone James couldn't see and stepped back out. She headed toward the stairwell.

"You want me to ask her how to keep us safe?" Robbie asked. "I told you all to get to your rooms. That's how you stay safe."

The lights dimmed as if the circuits were having difficulty with their load. Just when James thought they may go out, they blazed to brighter than full strength before going back to normal.

"With all due respect," James said to Robbie. "It appears as if we may need your flashlight."

"Hotel has a backup generator for lighting and heat," he said. "You folks don't need to worry about that. Once they clear the roads, the owners will get a maintenance team up here. Lines are probably failing with all the heavy snow."

That's when the lights went out and plunged them into an almost complete darkness. He felt Vic grab his shoulder. As Robbie predicted, James heard a machine kick on. Within seconds, every third light turned back on at half strength. Heat continued to pour from the vents at their ankles. Vic released him.

Janey opened the door to the stairwell and descended into the darkness.

"Is that prudent?" Vic asked.

"No," James said. "Of course, it isn't. We should go after her."

"You mean drag her back up here, don't you?" Vic asked.

James thought about his answer. Janey mentioned she'd seen the ghost of the maintenance-man and the ghost wanted them all to go to the basement. No, probably not prudent, but the apparition may know something they didn't. And they couldn't let Janey go down there alone. He thought of the maintenance-man's melon squashed beneath the elevator carriage and winced.

"Vic," James said, "stay with the sheriff if you like, but I'm going to the basement with Janey. Let's just see if there's something to her story."

Robbie shuffled the papers around on Marion's desk. James supposed they didn't train officers how to react to a paranormal situation. Probably taught them to dig through all the hokey business and find the true root cause of the problem.

"But it's so dark," Vic whispered. "The lights are barely on."

"It'll be fine," James assured her.

Vic stared down the stairwell and let out a long breath. "Let's go and get this done with," Vic said. James noticed the set of her jaw.

James took her by the hand and walked toward the stairwell. "It'll be fine," he repeated. Then he glanced back at the sheriff. "You coming?"

The sheriff let out a sigh, a weak blast of air past his lips. He looked from the stairwell to the outside door and back to the stairwell, then nodded. "I'll be honest. I've got a kid out in the blizzard...and another kid wandering around following ghosts. I'm not sure which one to go after." He checked his cellphone then quickly stuffed it back into his pocket.

"You might find some answers downstairs," James said as he reached the green-carpeted stairwell. Janey had already rounded the corner to the next set of steps. He hurried as best he could while making sure Vic kept up.

Vic said in a determined voice, "I'm not a sissy. I just don't understand ghosts and such. Why are they after us?"

"I don't think the ghosts are, dear."

James heard Robbie's footfalls as the sheriff followed them down the stairwell.

"Something is," Vic said. "Something more than Marion."

"Yes, of course there is," James said. "Let's see if Janey can shed some light on the matter. Perhaps her extraordinary powers of perception can aid us. It can't hurt, at the very least."

"You forget we're walking into a creepy basement," Vic said. "That's where everyone gets killed in the horror movies. The characters always think it's this glorious idea to go down there and then they die gruesomely."

"We'll try and avoid that," James said.

"Best way is to go to your rooms," Robbie said from behind them. Then he flashed the round disc of light produced by his flashlight around like it was attached to a disco ball.

James followed the sounds of Janey's footfalls until he and Vic emptied out onto the cracked concrete floor. The basement smelled of damp things. About the same as when he explored earlier. *Nothing has changed.* This calmed him. All seemed normal and the lighting appeared even and as bright as one could reasonably expect under the low voltage of the generator. The walls wore a sheen of white over their cinderblocks. Moisture streaked down from cracks in the foundation in a couple spots. The fissures kept the drain in the far corner plenty busy, and James wondered if the hotel had invested in a sump-pump. These things raced through his head to avoid much more distressing thoughts.

Janey stood in front of the elevator shaft, which remained vacant as the car hung above them on the ground floor. The space lay bathed in inky darkness which undulated and stirred.

"Why do the shadows move so?" Vic asked.

Robbie swiveled his head and took in every dark corner. Still protecting, James thought, and this brought a measure of comfort.

"The maintenance guy wishes to show us something," Janey said. "Beyond this…but first, this."

Robbie walked up and looked over the top of the girl and down into the shaft. "I don't see anything except a dark elevator shaft. The movement could be a trick of our senses."

"You'll see," Janey said. "Look closer."

James watched as the shadows continued to stir. Then, he gasped. He watched the shadows coalesce into a shape which lay in the bottom of the shaft. James couldn't identify it at first.

Robbie stared hard, like a man who couldn't believe what he was seeing. Janey remained where she stood with a smile. Vic took a step back, hand over her mouth.

This all happened as James' felt a slight disconnect from the real world as the form took the shape of something he recognized. He fought to regulate his breathing and placed a hand on Vic's shoulder. On an intellectual level, he understood the rumor of this exact scenario, the image of a man squashed beneath the weight of the elevator carriage. It appeared as his mind had imagined the image when he first read about the phenomenon in the lobby.

Before him lay a man. His torso, arms, and legs lay outside the darkness of the shaft, contorted with pain. But the interior of the shaft held the remains of that which, at one juncture, must have resembled a human head.

Good Lord! It looks...busted open.

The bone shards splintered from the man's cranium stuck up through thinning gray hair in sharp slivers. A few of the larger chunks had become unattached and sat apart from the rest, but all lay within the puddle of red blood and curd-like brains. The right eyeball dangled from a thin red optic cord. The left must have disintegrated upon impact, because the socket remained empty except for an inky well of pure blackness. Cheekbones were splayed out like macabre butterfly wings. The chin no longer existed, powdered to nothingness beneath pulped skin. The nose was shoved well up inside the face and into the brainpan.

He resembles a dog, a pug maybe.

Vic pulled back, stumbled, then sat down on the concrete, tears in her eyes. "That poor man."

James placed his hands on her shoulders and rubbed gently, not wishing to continue his vigil but incapable of looking away. He finally helped her stand and they walked a few paces away.

Only Janey and Robbie retained front-row seats to the bloody manifestation.

James knew he should feel more fear than he did. If he'd seen this but hours ago, he would have grabbed Vic and headed for the room. But this ghost felt comparatively benign, a leftover tuft of energy from an event long past. Compared to the other events of the evening, this sight carried little to terrify. Just a decrepit bit of sadness depicting a tragic incident. James crossed himself, anyway, if not for his own well-being then for the benefit of the leftover bit of ectoplasm.

"Miles should have his camera here," Janey whispered. Then, as if it just occurred to her to worry about her brother, she repeated, "Miles."

The ghostly imprint before them began to blur, the details less defined. *Either that or I'm losing optic acuity.* It melted and blended, first at the edges, then the entire body sank into a morass of white light and concentric rings of stirred energy. The whole chaotic mess began to flicker like it never existed at all, until it disappeared into the bottom of the shaft. Nothing remained except dark shadows and years of debris.

"He's asking us to follow," Janey said. She pointed to an area to the left of the shaft. James noticed a small alcove.

"Where—where did it go?" Robbie asked.

"The revenant is before me," Janey said in a calm voice.

"I can't see it!" Robbie said. James could see the man's frustration and confusion as the sheriff looked more closely inside the elevator shaft.

James understood the sheriff looked for tangible facts, but also thought it obvious none of them could see the maintenance-man. If he'd ever watched a rudimentary ghost show, he would know ghosts came and went, even if you didn't believe in them.

"Cunt," Janey whispered. Just this once, James thought she was addressing the sheriff and not the psychic residue which littered her little-girl brain.

James shuffled to his left because he wanted to see the area Janey pointed out with her index finger. He noticed a rusty iron door, three-foot by three-foot in size, hinges at the top. It appeared old and decrepit, probably long forgotten.

"The ghost wishes us to go through there?" James asked the girl.

"Yes," she said.

"Through that little tiny door?" Vic asked. "Not a chance on God's green Earth. I'd rather die out here in the open, thank you, if that's what all this will come to."

Janey shrugged.

"What's he want with us?" Robbie asked. "What's through that door?"

"Hell," Janey announced, as if this detail should already be obvious to everyone. "A quiet hell, but hell all the same."

"Looks like an old coal chute," James said. He remembered such things from photos of the old hotel that was torn down near Hibbing, Minnesota. A student used them to enhance a particularly poor essay he'd written on the city's historic mining region. Nonetheless, James remembered the photos of the basement where the old boilers still existed and the chute for the coal lay in disrepair. "My guess is the doorway leads to a subbasement where the coal-boiler used to exist, before the hotel turned to water and steam."

"And why does this ghost want us there?" Robbie asked. "What will we find in this...hell?"

"Things you seek," Janey said, then shrugged.

"Manifestations, so I've heard, often possess intelligence we are not privy to," James said. "They tap into a stream of information of which only they have access." He'd heard this on a ghost show but decided to claim it as his own.

Janey looked over her shoulder at James and favored him with a small smile. "Still violet," she whispered.

James blushed. When he regained his composure, he asked, "So, what vested interest do we have in crawling around down there in the dirt and dark?"

"No interest at all," Vic said. "How dreadful, just the thought of it." She looked up and batted her eyes at James. "Let's take the sheriff's advice and go to our room." She said this in such a way that smacked of promises and interludes and much sex. "There's certain things you've always wanted to try."

"Violet and peach now," Janey said.

Good Lord! James shook his head as if he could lessen the peach-strain by this physical action alone. "As enticing as that sounds, my love, I think we should hear the child out." He turned to Janey. "What happens if we don't go down there?"

"Death," Janey said.

"Whose death?" Robbie asked. "Ours...or somebody else's?"

Janey shrugged. "The spirit didn't say."

"Can you ask it?"

"It's gone."

"Where?"

Janey shrugged. "Where they go."

Robbie exhaled a sigh of frustration. James noticed he fought to retain his composure.

"Cunt," Janey whispered, so low James barely heard.

"Screw it," Robbie said. "I'm going in there. It's either that or go after the boy. I need to do something, and in for a penny, in for a pound. If the girl knows what she's about, then I'm with her."

He released both flashlights from his belt, flipped the smaller one to James, and approached the top-hinged coal door. When the sheriff reached down to open the rusty door, James wondered what would become of them all. *Dead by dawn*, he supposed.

Chapter 19

The beast charged forward, feet pounding on the hardwood floor. It stopped faster than Angela thought possible and pondered Penny's corpse on the floor. A low rumble emanated from the thing and then the rumble grew to a scream of rage. It raised its ill-formed head toward the ceiling in anguish and the scream increased in volume until Angela needed to cover her ears.

Angela watched the beast stare at the body of the librarian. "Your minion failed," Angela said, unsure why this felt so good to say. Especially since she'd been the one to end the woman's life. A small ball of sadness sank like lead to the bottom of her stomach.

The beast looked up at her with those intense red eyes and the leaden ball in Angela's gut returned to liquidy terror.

"Truth," Miles added. "The librarian failed. She's dead, and you didn't even get to do the killing. I bet that's a pisser, ain't it?"

The beast's eyes grew brighter just before it let loose with a scream so vicious Angela thought she could feel the creature's hot breath on her flesh. "Don't antagonize it," she hissed. She realized her mistake. She'd allowed her defense mechanisms to take over, her sarcasm to blossom. And now she'd endangered them all. Instead of running, they were throwing useless epithets at something that could kill them like the swat of a bug.

"You did," Miles said.

"Touché," Em added.

Angela felt her face turn red. She needed to get them out of here. She looked back up at the creature just as it reached down and grabbed Penny's body like a child might a doll.

The beast held Penny up to where its face would exist if fully formed beyond the shadow state it favored. It brought the corpse closer until it merged with the beast. The coupling produced sucking sounds as the beast infused the human flesh with its own. Small pitter-pats of blood dropped to the floor like a gentle hot rain.

The smell of fresh blood rushed to Angela. And the use of her olfactory senses convinced her brain this was all real, not just an illusion. Her legs itched to bolt. She backpedaled with short measured steps. If she fell now…

"Holy crap!" Miles said. "It ate her."

"Not sure *ate* is the correct word," Angela whispered. "Let's get moving."

"Yeah, let's get out of here before it tries that little trick on us," Em said.

Angela stood taller and backpedaled toward the door, careful not to trip or become unbalanced in any way that may encourage the beast to attack.

The beast finished with the absorption of the body and a renewed odor of death filled the room as if an entire graveyard of freshly dead corpses stood before them. It took a gigantic step forward.

Angela heard when Em opened the door and then felt the snowy blast of cold on her back. *Good.* This meant she was nearing the exit. She turned to look and saw Miles and Em standing outside the threshold, waiting for her. They would all run, she knew, because no other plan existed. How could you combat this monstrosity with conventional weaponry? She'd cross that bridge when she got to it. First things first. They needed to put some distance between themselves and this thing. Then maybe she would have time to develop a strategy.

Miles beat her to it. "Get outside the door and stop," the kid said. "I have a plan."

With a last large backward step, Angela lifted her foot over the threshold and felt her boot sink into the newly fallen snow. "What plan?" she asked as she looked down at Miles.

"No time to explain," he said. He removed a pill-bottle sized vial from his coat pocket and approached the doorway. "But shoot at the thing when I tell you."

"Hey, now!" Angela said. She wouldn't put the burden of when to shoot on the kid. "Discharging my firearm is a serious choice."

"Please, ma'am," Miles said. He knelt by Angela's knees and took the cover from the bottle.

The shadow creature took another step forward, its eyes on Miles.

"What do I do?" Em asked. "Can I do something to help?"

"Bait," Miles said. His voice carried a grin. "Make sure that thing wants to come out here after you."

"Hold on!" Angela said. "What are you doing?" She glanced from Miles to the creature and back. "You better know what you're doing."

"Hey!" Em hollered. "Ya big buffoon! Come get me! Your miserable minions tried to sacrifice me. They failed. You come do it, if ya got the balls."

"Shit," Angela whispered, then knelt and aimed at the door. She held steady and felt the act a minor miracle. Somehow, the fear in her gut and brain didn't reach her arm as if her nerves realized she needed the separation.

"It's a little trick Janey and I have talked about," Miles said. He brushed the remaining snow away until the metal of the threshold shone like a new dime. Then he poured the contents of the bottle from jamb to jamb, creating a quarter inch line of white granules. He backed away, his eyes never leaving the beast.

The creature approached and Angela knew it was too late for any other plan but Miles'.

"Come finish what they couldn't," Em yelled. "You should have known they were too old and weak to handle the likes of me. I got more life in my pinky than you have in your whole ephemeral body."

"Don't overdo it," Angela said. "It's already stomping in this direction. You'll probably send it right through the roof in anger." She continued to stare down the sights of her Glock at the shadowy creature, careful not to aim anywhere near Miles. She took long calming breaths. Her heart pounded in her chest so hard Angela thought it would explode.

The beast raged with a mighty roar, each step sounding like a wood post pounded onto a concrete floor. Its stench preceded it, ripe and pungent. Red eyes lanced outward and into the snow, to the middle of Em's chest. It wanted her, bad—wanted the one chosen by its ineffectual cultists. Angela wouldn't allow this—would give herself up first. She hoped Miles knew his shit, because if he didn't, they may all end up dead long before dawn broke over the eastern horizon.

"Come get us," Miles shouted, then scurried behind Angela and her Glock.

Angela let out a breath of relief. She would never have dared shoot over the kid's head, but now the way was clear. She took several shuffling steps backward and then knelt.

The beast approached the doorway. If it wondered why they hadn't run away, the beast showed no indication. It continued toward them in a rage, hellbent on finishing whatever agenda it had.

"Just because your tribe was a bunch of douchebags," Em shouted, "doesn't mean you have to get after everyone else. I suppose you made a deal with the Devil, am I right? He helped you, you work for him, forever. That about size things up?"

A gigantic squall, louder than any of them had heard previous, erupted from the beast. It stormed toward them. The headdress and hatchet erupted from the black mass like symbols of the beast's rage.

"That did it," Miles said. "Must have hit a sore spot. Get ready, Angela!"

Angela stayed silent, sighted down the barrel to the creature's center-mass, waited for the kid to give her the word. Angela had little choice but to trust him. She continued to work on her breathing. If she thought about the shear odds of this stunt, she'd run screaming into the darkness. Angela concentrated on keeping her mind clear, a blank canvas. She would hold the line they drew with the salt.

Like an enraged gorilla, the beast hit the threshold, dark arms reaching, red eyes darting over Angela to Em. It bellowed and fell back a step when the arms reached the salt line and the thing appeared to reduce in size and take a more solid form. Angela thought she could make out a thin layer of fur and muscle beneath flesh. The tomahawk and headdress looked more solid than ghostly as the feathers fluttered in the vicious wind of the storm.

"Fire!" Miles shouted.

Angela squeezed the trigger, sights buried center-mass. When she went to deliver a follow-up round, the beast sank into the shadows and disappeared. Through the echo of her gun's report, Angela made out the sound of a huge body crashing through the patio door.

"Run for it!" Angela shouted. "To the jailhouse." Now or never, she knew. This opportunity may never come again. They needed to gain distance if they wished to survive. She'd picked the jailhouse because it represented law and order, safety, a place people went when they needed help. *Robbie!*

Trees whizzed by as Angela pumped her arms and legs. The snow had deepened even in the short time they'd been inside. She chugged along through knee-deep snow and when she heard Em and Miles next to her, Angela pushed forward with renewed energy. She would fight for them.

"What just happened?" Em asked. She sounded out of breath, air sucking in and out of her mouth like a car with a bad carburetor.

"We tricked it, and Angela wasted it!" Miles shouted. He whooped like a kid playing at the park. He ran next to Angela with little effort, not tired at all.

"I don't get it," Angela huffed. "Why'd you pour salt in the doorway?"

"Because it's pure and wonderful and really does a job on evil spirits, especially shifters."

"What's a shifter?" Em asked, falling a bit behind the others.

"Long story," Miles said. "I'll explain when we're safe. Let's just say Janey and I did some research before we came. All great investigators do. I just didn't think..."

"Didn't think it would come to all this?" Angela said. How could anybody have predicted this, even in their wildest of imaginations? She continued to run, her skier-knees giving her hell. White-hot bolts of pain, bone on bone, ripped through her.

"No way," Miles said. "Thought it was all made up. Just theories and stories for the tourists. Guess not."

Something clattered through the branches of a giant oak before them. Angela thought it sounded like a bear breaking branches up in the heights. This happened occasionally and Robbie would call in the game warden to trap the scared thing. She came to a sliding halt in the wet snow and glanced behind them to make sure nothing pursued. Nothing did. Then she looked up and noticed the flickering of shadows at the top of the oak, along with the cracking of large branches. Those shadows began to descend.

"Get out of here," she yelled. *It's like it can fly or jump from tree to tree!* Angela pumped her arms and legs, Glock waving like an L-shaped metal wand.

Angela could see the streetlights of the main street ahead. *Just two blocks to the jailhouse.* If they could just make it there, they could barricade the doors and fortify the windows and any other openings with the salt Harold kept in his desk. She felt in her heart if they could make it to sunrise, everything would turn out okay. They could then find a way off the side of this mountain.

Above them, branches cracked and, like a foghorn, the beast's rageful bellow called to them.

"I think you two just pissed it off, is all," Em said, huffing and puffing and stumbling through the drifts.

Something wet hit Angela's face—something much warmer than the snow. For a moment, she feared monster drool, infection, little squirmy pieces of the thing wiggling down her throat and into her insides. There, anything could happen. She imagined baby beasts bursting from her abdomen, grinning with bloody maws like in the movie Alien. But when she wiped her face, it came away red.

"I think it's bleeding," Angela said. "I might have winged it." A bloom of hope surged through her, bringing with it a shot of adrenaline. If it could be hurt, then it could be destroyed. She ran faster.

"Not enough to kill it, though," Em pointed out. "It seems to keep up fine and dandy."

"It's hurt, though," Miles said as he ran. "At least a little. My plan worked. Just wish we had a little more firepower. You got more guns at the jail?"

"Yeah," Angela said through clenched teeth. It hurt her lungs to speak. "Locked up, though. Only Robbie has the key. If we're lucky, we'll find it in his desk."

"Can't blame him hiding the key from Harold," Em said.

"Shut up and keep running," Angela said. God, her knees hurt. If she survived all this, she would stop smoking and get back to exercising. *That's for damn sure!*

Em screamed when more branches broke above. This time they sounded lower in the tree.

"It's wounded, not dead," Miles said.

"No shit," Em said, but kept running.

The lights of the main street grew closer and brighter. Only another hundred feet and they would make it.

Like a giant black panther, the beast leapt out in front of them and clung to a large oak branch about twenty feet off the ground. It swung like a giant ape but had transformed back into an amorphous black blob with red dots for eyes. In its free hand, it held Jeb's head aloft for them to see. It bellowed like an enraged bull and cocked its arm to throw the head.

Maybe that's where the blood came from. Maybe I didn't do shit for damage. Angela kept running, then veered left to avoid running beneath the thing. She didn't want to allow the demon to jump down or drop the head on top of them.

Em squawked as she tumbled through the snow like a shoulder-shot Mule deer. Jeb's head rolled off into the snow and came to a stop, eyes and mouth up, as if gasping for air. *The thing threw it!* Jeb's eyes bulged as if tiny beings inside her cranium were trying to shove them out.

"Em!" Angela raced over to her, coming to a sliding stop on her aching knees. She propped the woman up and held her close. Angela could feel Em's delightful breath against her neck.

"I'm fine," Em whispered. "I'll just have a helluva bruise. Maybe a headache." But she didn't try to get up. Angela thought she sounded woozy.

"Get back!" Miles shouted from somewhere behind them.

Angela turned to locate him and saw the boy waving the empty canister of salt like a weapon.

The beast dropped to the ground, halted, and stared at the kid.

"Get up," Angela told Em. "We can rest when we get to the jail."

"This seems like an okay spot," Em whispered, then nuzzled into Angela's neck. But when the beast let out with a roar which sounded like it wanted to rip out their spines, Em quit with the nuzzling and started to move. "Shit!"

Angela helped her up, and they both plodded through the snow. Angela yelled over her shoulder, "Come on, Miles!"

"Yeah!" he shouted and ran. He still held the salt in his right hand, his eyes wide and white, little legs pumping, feet scratching for every bit of purchase they could find in the twenty inches of powder.

Giant puffs of white snow and debris shot into the air with each step of the beast's monster feet. It pounded toward them and screamed the desire to rend and destroy. A giant blast of wind, as if it came directly from the creature's maw, whistled past them and brought the stench of decay and feces as if they were chased by a pitch-black outhouse.

The oak trees and their dead chattering leaves thinned out and the light from the main street grew brighter, pushing those horrible shadows back like a bulldozer moves dirt. Angela led them through a yard which bordered the street. There were lights on inside and movement behind the shades. And just as she noticed, the lights inside went out and the lights of the main street flickered, dimmed, burned brighter for a moment like supernovas, then went out altogether.

"What the actual fuck?" Em hissed. "This thing can control electricity, too?"

"Just the storm," Angela said. She hoped this was true. "Keep running for the jailhouse."

Miles pulled up next to the women, legs and arms pumping. "It's gaining," he said. "Better not to look."

The great thudding footfalls were all Angela needed to hear to tell how close the thing was to their ass-ends. It sounded like it could reach out with those long dark appendages and snare them up like rabbits. The stench encircled them like a physical presence.

Angela turned when she reached the main drag and raced down the middle of the street, holding hands with Em as she stumbled along, Miles racing next to them.

The beast bellowed and turned up the street behind them.

They raced down the abandoned street for a block. *Only one more to go.* Then Angela realized how quiet the night had become, enhanced by the buffering snow. She turned and realized the beast no longer followed. Angela didn't know where it had disappeared to. She wondered which was worse, the chase or the not knowing.

"Where is it?" Em asked as she came to a sliding stop.

Miles shrugged but looked around as if the beast might lie in wait behind any tree or any dark corner. He clutched the canister of salt like a lifeline.

"Let's go," Angela said. "We'll get to the jail, just another block, then worry about where it went. Don't let your guard down."

Em grabbed Angela's hand, turned, then led the group through the twenty inches of snow.

Angela couldn't help but wonder if the lights would ever come back on.

Chapter 20

"I don't understand why you're going down in that hole," Vic said. "Everything will be okay in the morning." She didn't sound as if she believed this.

"I trust the girl," James explained. "We've all seen enough to give her credit. If she says this is what we need do to stay alive, then I believe her. It's either that or go lock ourselves up in our room and hope nothing comes out of the mirror or smashes through the door or windows."

Vic peered down through the coal-door where Robbie's flashlight beam fluttered about like a lightsaber. Janey had already joined him and James could hear them whispering back and forth. Perhaps the sheriff would trust Janey enough to help find a solution.

"Stay here if you wish," James said, "but I'd only worry about you." He thought back to their wedding day, how beautiful she looked, and her bright smile. He rather missed it. The darkness of the basement sucked every ounce of joy from her. Even her strong libido had run off and abandoned her. He supposed fear could accomplish this and he felt bad he forced her to make this decision. But no other option seemed viable other than waiting alone in the dark for a sunrise which remained a long way off.

"Fine," Vic said, "I'm coming. But this will cost you some capital, Mr. Landes." She smiled at this.

Finally! "I understand, Mrs. Landes," James said, "and I fully intend to replenish the supply once we are off this mountain and out of danger—replenished to unprecedented levels."

Vic giggled despite her fear. James thought it a good sign. "Better get that tongue in shape and ready to go in that case."

"You wish me to read you stories then?"

Vic smacked him on the shoulder with the knuckles of her right hand. "You know damn well what I want that tongue doing." She grinned salaciously and without mercy.

"Yes, mum," he said and waggled the muscle inside his mouth to further help Vic forget her fear. "Strongest muscle in the human body, you know."

"Thank, God," she said. Her voice still shook, but she sounded better. "Now help me down before I change my mind."

"Look out below!" James announced, before hanging on to Vic's hand and lowering her down the chute and into the darkness of the subbasement. Sheriff Robbie grabbed her arm and set her upright, right before James sailed down the shoot and came up standing at the bottom. "Ta-dah!"

"Showoff," Vic said.

James bowed, then realized how much older this subbasement appeared than the rest of the hotel. "Must be original."

"Has to be," Robbie agreed and shone his light to reveal a corner filled with the remains of the final shipment of coal, just a few black chunks piled up as if someone might light up a barbeque. In another corner stood an ancient hunk of metal. Tubes ran from it and into the wood ceiling above like snakes from Medusa's head.

"The old coal burner, looks like," James announced and walked over. "Maybe there's something left inside it."

"Careful what you wish for," Janey mumbled from the dark.

James reached down to open the furnace door.

"Must you?" Vic asked. "No good can come of it, James. Mark my words."

"Where's your sense of adventure?" James clicked on the flashlight in his hand.

Robbie walked over just as James pulled the door open on reluctant hinges. They creaked and rust pattered to the floor in tiny chunks.

James jumped back. "Good Lord! There's bone in there." He worked up his nerve, made room for Robbie, and looked again.

"Sure enough," the sheriff said. "Looks like a human skull and a femur."

"They used to hold the ceremony here," Janey said. "Now they hold it down there." She pointed to the ground. "So says the conduit."

"How gruesome," James said, then turned to Janey. "Is that what Marion wanted, Janey, when she tried to murder Victoria? Would she have brought her body to the ceremony?"

"Of course," Janey said. "That's all they ever wanted. The spirits of their kills haunt this place. They're unhappy."

"I suppose," James said. "I would be." He glanced around to make sure the maintenance-man wasn't trying to manifest again. He felt sure this would push Vic back over the edge and ruin the little rally she now enjoyed.

Janey nodded and continued to point at the floor. "We need to go down below."

"We are below," Vic pointed out.

"Deeper," Janey explained. "To the place it will bring the cunt," she glanced at James with a clever grin, "*who* failed. And others."

James frowned.

Janey smiled but then walked toward a dark corner. She asked, "You sure?"

"Who are you speaking to?" Vic asked.

"The ghost," Janey mumbled. Then, "Okay." And she continued to walk into the darkness. Kneeling in the light produced by Robbie's flashlight, Janey tugged at something embedded in the floor and surrounded by a circle of round boulders. It looked to James like a chunk of rotten planking.

Robbie walked closer and shown his flashlight on the wood and stones. She continued to yank at the chunk of wood using a brass ring that was imbedded in the wood. She looked determined but James could see the frustration settle in as she tugged with no results.

"It feels like ghosts down here," Vic said. "Look at my arms. Just full of goosebumps. Must be those EMFs they always rave about on the network shows." She wrapped her arms around her torso. "It smells like it, too. Musty and just a hint of rot to go with. Yuck. I feel unclean and even an hour bath wouldn't wash me back to normal."

"I'll help you bathe later," James whispered, but then walked over to the girl. His dress-shoes clip-clopped off the ancient mud floor.

"Promises," Vic murmured.

When James approached Janey, the girl looked up with expectation. "Help me," she demanded. "The ghosts think we'll all join them soon if you don't."

"That's what they tell you?"

She nodded and her eyes pleaded with his. "I don't want to get trapped down here with them forever. They can't leave…and it uses them. And it wants to add more. Usually, just seven, but now as many as can be managed." She pointed at the floor.

"Because the ritual failed?"

She nodded once, then turned her attention back to the brass ring and tugged with renewed effort. James took this as a prompt for him to join in.

"Stand aside," the sheriff said. "Let me get some leverage on the thing. Then we'll see what is afoot and what we'll do about it." He looked behind him and handed the flashlight to James. "Hand that to Vic and give me a hand. We might as well see if Janey knows what she's talking about."

"Looks like an old chunk of wood in a firepit," James said and did as instructed.

Both men grabbed a side of the ring, and on the sheriff's count, they tugged and groaned and cursed like sailors.

"Cunt," Janey whispered, joining in.

"One more good tug!" James shouted. Both men pulled until their faces turned red and their cheeks puffed out with the breaths of their exertions.

With a tortured shriek, the chunk of wood splintered, then broke in half, outer edges still attached by metal hinges just inside the ring of rocks. James and Robbie flung their respective pieces upright and stared downward.

A foul breath of wind flowed up and out of the darkness below them. A stench of decay, feces and things long unwashed.

Vic stumbled backward. "My word, the smell. Enough to gag a maggot. No way I'm crawling down in there."

Even Janey stood and backed up, but only one step.

"A might putrid," James coughed, trying to breathe through his mouth so as not to plug his sinuses.

"Smells like it did upstairs, except a million times worse," Robbie said. He continued to stare into the hole despite the stench.

"They threw them down there," Janey whispered. "Then it came for them."

"This is where the cult threw the bodies, Janey?" James asked. "Is that what you mean?"

She nodded once, her ponytail bobbing then swaying. "After this place became tainted, its hunger outgrew their efforts. So, down they went. Deeper. Inside the mountain."

Robbie shone his flashlight down the hole. "Not much room to maneuver," he said. "Looks like some bones down there, too. Leg and arms, mostly, by the looks."

"Means they chopped them up," James said. Vic moaned at his words, and James wished he could take them back. He'd created an image for her she couldn't unsee.

Robbie grunted an affirmation.

"Don't be grotesque, James," Vic said. "And don't think for a moment I'm going to crawl down into that stinking hellhole. I'll take my chances upstairs with that thing. At least I can run away if necessary."

"Of course," James said. "I would never suggest…"

At that moment, the hinged coal-door clanged shut and extinguished what muted emergency light had come from above. Then the sound of a bolt sliding shut echoed in the chamber.

"They need us," Janey said. "They won't allow anyone to go back now. The only way is down."

Vic ran to the chute, placed her hands on the outside rails, then shimmied herself to the top. She rattled on the door until James imagined she would come tumbling back down even if she did manage to open the blasted thing. She grunted like a pig at the trough as she yanked and pulled. Desperate. After a few moments, she stopped and slid back down, defeated. She turned to them with wild eyes and a heaving chest. By way of the sheriff's flashlight, James noticed her shoes were ruined, black with coal dust.

"Sheriff," Vic said hotly, "shoot those hinges off that door, right this instant. I refuse to stay down here another moment."

"Those hinges are solid iron," Robbie explained. "Only thing that'll happen if I shoot them is us taking ricochets. Sorry, ma'am, but that's a big no-can-do."

Vic's shoulders dropped in disappointment, which James supposed would cost him even more in tongue-time. *It'll be cunnilingus city, cunnilingus Tourette's,* James mused. The Tourette's line made him think of the boy out in the blizzard. He wondered which would prove worse, to end up trapped down here or trapped out in the storm.

"Hey, where you going?" Robbie hollered, looking toward the ring of boulders.

James turned in time to watch Janey leap into the dark hole and disappear. *Good Lord!* He felt certain now which choice would prove worse. He and Robbie met at the hole and peered down to watch Janey drag her legs out of view and into a tunnel—a tunnel a gopher would feel claustrophobic in.

"Come back here!" Robbie said.

Nothing answered him except for the sounds of Janey crawling deeper into the darkness.

Chapter 21

Selected Scenes from a Terrorized Village

The old woman lay scared in her bed. *The ritual failed.* A ritual she no longer took part in because she couldn't use her damn legs, and she refused to sacrifice her family. She knew Marion, Harold, Penny, and Jeb had screwed up, failed. So, it would come for her, then her offspring. Maybe even the grandkids! She'd heard it bellow out there not but a few minutes ago, after the lights went out.

Marv—ol' not-a-lick-of-sense Marv—told her to keep quiet. "Just the wind howling," he had quipped. But he had known better, too, deep down. Harriot could sense it, like she could sense that thing out there stalking the night, making ready to kill them.

The last decade she'd tried to warn them, her family, to get them ready for this day. Tried to convince them they needed to join the good fight and keep this thing at bay. But she'd waited too long. By then she was old enough for them to imagine her falling into the first stages of senility, or maybe they accepted her wild claims as the first steps in going batshit crazy. The concept of sacrificing seven for the good of hundreds fell on, if not deaf then, disbelieving ears.

"Marv!" she heard Jackie yell. "Don't we have no more propane lanterns? The kids are cold." Her daughter-in-law must have been standing next to the thermostat, because then she said, "It's down to fifty-three in here. Thanks a lot for taking the chimney out last summer. Can't even have a fire."

Always the nag. If Harriot ever did possess the stomach to slaughter her own, Jackie would head the list. *No big loss.* But now they'd probably all die soon. Harriot wondered if the beast would not only rend her flesh but also steal her soul. Would she ride around for eternity inside its head as punishment for the failure?

Harriot felt a stab of indignation. How could blame be cast in her direction for a generation who didn't believe? Those who would rather spend time behind a video game system and play pretend than learn about the old ways—about what their elders did to keep them safe. Sure, she shared the stories, which they mocked with their silence, their rolled eyes, their smirks that told her they would only tolerate her, nothing more. Now, they'd pay.

Oh, yes.

A creaking board up on the roof caught her attention, then a steady tread which ended right above her. So it came to this, a measly few feet of sheetrock, rafters, plywood, and shingles between her and her ruin. It would come, and she wondered what route it would choose. It could shift between solid and spirit, she'd been told, even though the ritual always held in the past, so her only interaction with *it* involved the delivery of flesh. Harriot found herself woefully unprepared for what would come next. It never occurred to any of them what they would do if things went south. Thirty years had seemed like a damn eternity. Now, it felt like nothing at all.

"Mom, I'm cold!" a girl shouted. Macey, Harriot knew. Took after her ma, a whiney and fussy little one. Liked to complain and hear herself screech. *Number two on the list.*

Another tread from above, quieter this time, as if the thing was standing up there sniffing for her. Harriot glanced from the window next to her bed to the large antique mirror on the wall. She'd heard tell about the creature using old mirrors. Rumor carried it could come for her in that fashion. Harriot imagined it slipping out of the glass, not much more than a dark shadow, all arms and legs, and those retched red eyes. She held in a scream, because she would never wish herself part of the problem and not the solution. Harriot grabbed her Diamond Willow cane beside the bed and then pulled herself up.

Come on, if you're coming.

Her grandson, Billy, screamed from the next room. "I saw a face in the mirror. Its eyes were red! It's climbing out. It's coming."

"Knock it off," Jackie said, and Harriot heard the irritation in her voice. "You're gonna scare your sister with your foolishness."

Anything to protect her precious Macey. She never did care much for the boy.

"Marv? Where are you?" Jackie shouted, her voice shrill from being ignored. "Did you find more lanterns? Marv? What about blankets? We're gonna freeze to death before you find anything useful."

"It's coming," Billy yelled.

Harriot wondered how the thing could exist above her, up on the roof, and inside the mirror in the hallway at the same time. Perhaps the physical aspect of its existence stood on the roof while some spirit offshoot, like an old runner root, slithered out of the mirror—the matching mirror of the set to the one in her room.

"Stop with this foolishness," Jackie said. "When your father shows his face, I'll have him deal with you. It'll be spanking-city!"

Spanking Tourette's, Harriot thought but didn't understand why she would think this. It sounded stupid and made little sense, but it's what popped into her head. She found this a pitiful thing to think at a time like this.

The boy screamed.

"Mom!" Macey whined.

"That's it," Jackie said. Harriot heard her storm off down the hallway. "I'll spank you myself. You can't just scare your sister like that. The storm is bad enough." Then Jackie screamed, a high-pitched wail, ending with an even higher pitched shriek. The shriek ended with a wet gurgle. *Sounds like mud bubbling up out of an old well pipe.*

Footsteps thundered down the wing to Harriot's little mother-in-law suite, and both Macey and Billy tore into her room, wild-eyed and balling up a storm. Snot ran down from their noses to their quivering little lips and they stammered and screamed.

"Under the bed," Harriot ordered. She knew this maneuver wouldn't save them, but perhaps buy them an extra couple moments to say their little prayers, the ones Jackie taught them to say before bed. Perhaps their God would prove more merciful than her own.

Heavier footsteps pounded down the wing toward her room. Harriot listened, head cocked toward the roof, but she knew the physical manifestation had somehow maneuvered its way inside. The footsteps sounded like a four-hundred-pound pirate on a peg-leg, thundering down the hall. Harriot could make out a humongous black shadow—a shadow one shade darker than the darkness around it. Red eyes bloomed to life, bright enough for her to notice the heads it carried in each of its beefy paws.

That's where Marv got to. Now, Jackie's right there with him. Poetic.

Blood pattered from both necks and onto the hardwood floor, but it was the stench Harriot could have done without. That death-cabbage odor she hadn't noticed until those red eyes popped out of the darkness. She held her breath, then tightened her grip on the cane.

The kids screamed from beneath the bed.

"Come take me," Harriot said, cane raised above her head.

It did.

Mason paged through an old book by the light of a large lantern. He knew the refracted light formed dark shadows on his face, perfect for what he wanted to discuss with his parents.

"Says here the thing comes every thirty years and brings the big snow with it," Mason said. He enjoyed spooky things and now enjoyed scaring his family with these old stories he found in Grandpa Rick's attic. "I found an old journal up there in the attic, too. I think he killed some folks thirty years ago."

"Stop with the tall tales, Mason," Kelsey said. "You can go to Hell for lying, you know."

"Grandpa Rick didn't believe in Hell," Mason said and shook the book he held. "He believed in some other stuff. Weird stuff. Witchery, I think."

"Knock it off," his father, Luke, said. "Grandpa Rick's been dead three years, so I suppose he found out what's real and what's not. Let's not talk about him in a poor light, witch or not."

Mason smiled, because he knew his parents just didn't get it. He picked up his EMF detector. It was a Mel meter—one he found with Grandpa's boxes of stuff. It measured several ambient things at once: EMF in both K2 and Milligauss and air temp. It even utilized an EMF pump which created a magnetic resistance up in the antennae so any ghost who went by would set the alarm off. He turned the device on and a series of beeps and flashing lights erupted from the speaker as the sensors acclimated to their surroundings. Then it lay still.

"Grandpa Rick's books don't seem to give off any strange readings," Mason said, then dug in the box for the old journal that told about the slayings from years back. He held the book close to the device and the device whirred and blinked like when he'd turned it on. "But the journal does."

"How'd you make it do that?" Kelsey asked.

"I didn't," Mason said. "The journal did." He held the journal close and got the same response from the device. "Holy crap! Ambient EMF in this room is less than two Milligauss and Grandpa Rick's journal spikes it up to fifteen. Grandpa must've really been into some super-crazy stuff."

"Gotta be some trick," Luke said to Kelsey. "Just ignore him and he'll give up. No audience, no fibbing."

"I'm not fibbing," Mason said. He would remain patient with mom and dad because they were ignorant. He and Grandpa Rick knew the truth. Grandpa used to talk to him all the time. He told Mason to keep the things they discussed a secret, because his parents wouldn't understand. Boy, was he right.

Grandpa Rick always said the time would come. And here they were amid a snowstorm, just like the old man had explained. The thirty-year blizzard raged outside, electricity nothing but a memory, and now the beast Grandpa Rick talked to him about would come for them. Mason just knew it! He needed to get ready. Some of the stuff Grandpa Rick spoke of scared Mason, but like Grandpa always said, *if everyone does their jobs, there is nothing to be scared of.* Grandpa spoke often about the tasks: opening rituals, sacrifices, the delivery of the blessed flesh. Exciting stuff!

Mom would really flip out if I told her about that stuff. He decided if neither of them believed the books and journal, no way they would believe the stuff Grandpa told him. No, Mason would handle this himself. Using his equipment, he'd know what to do and when to do it. He poked a bit more at his EMF detector to make sure the sensitivity was adjusted to where he wanted it. He knew the K2 part could go off for several reasons, including when the water-heater turned on and when their cellphones updated. He hadn't had a signal in a while now, but better safe than sorry. He didn't want any false positives.

Mason's Mel meter whistled a signal for a huge EMF spike, immediately followed by a thud on the front door. The force of the heavy knock rattled the frame and most of the glass from the narrow window fell out and smashed on the floor.

"What the hell is that?" Kelsey asked, backing away from the door. "Luke, go check."

"Why me?" he asked.

Another thud and the jamb splintered, sending wood chunks onto the floor in a wild spray of debris. The remaining glass fell to the floor and smashed, cascading across the hardwood like little scrabbling insects. Snow whistled through the missing window and the widened crack between door and jamb.

"Whoa," Mason said, his detector still squawking like a scalded cat. "It's the beast, and it's mad. Stuff must have gone wrong."

"Get your shotgun," Kelsey said to Luke.

Mason smiled, then turned back to the door, hand with the Mel meter extended as if in offering.

Luke ran for the bedroom.

"What beast?" Kelsey asked, backing away. She grabbed at Mason, but the boy pulled away.

"The one from Grandpa's journal," Mason said, then turned and ran for his own room. "Be right back!"

Mason heard when the door flew inward and slammed off the doorstop. He listened as his mother screamed and something roared.

He heard his dad yell, "Get down so I can shoot." Then Mason grabbed the axe Grandpa gave him. Now he would fulfil his promise to Grandpa.

Mason raced down the hallway, then took in the scene before him. His mother's body lay on the floor, stump of her neck pumping crimson fluid all over the hardwood. The beast raised her head with a hairy hand, soulless eyes of Mason's mother staring off into the middle distance. *Whoa!* Mason's EMF detector continued to screech.

With a vengeful scream, mouth wide, Luke raised the shotgun and fired. The shot and wad sailed right through the beast and blew out the picture window behind it. Glass exploded out into the falling snow.

Grandpa had been right, Mason figured. Nothing could kill this beast. He admired how the thing fluctuated from pure shadow with red eyes and a hairy beast of a creature which looked as solid as he did. *Cool!* Only one thing to do, Mason knew, as he raised the axe and approached his father from behind. He needed to save all the folks in this village, even if it meant the death of a few. Just like Grandpa always said.

The beast's eyes pulsed an even deeper shade of red as Mason hefted the axe way over his head and drove it down into his father's skull. Luke dropped to the floor, right next to Kelsey, twitched for a moment, then lay still as he bled out a sticky morass of plasma and brain-matter.

The beast roared in triumph, then turned and carried Kelsey's head out into the swirling snow.

Conrad sat in his armchair, inside the glow of the fireplace. He loved the fireplace, having built the house around the big stone walk-in hearth. He took a sip of bourbon from the glass in his right hand, considered things, then took a much longer swig. The booze stung the back of his throat like only a fine bourbon could. He figured he might as well get smashed. He wouldn't feel the sting so bad when the end came.

No, unlike the others, Conrad never felt the answer to their dilemma ever rested on the sacrifices. If they all dug a bit deeper into the folklore and facts from the past, they would have found an alternative. But Conrad never had, even though it'd been a good thirty-year try. Thirty years of booze, divorce, his kids moving on to bigger and better, taking the grandkids with them. Not to mention his declining health. Now he sat here with a stiff drink in hand, waiting for the end.

A bout of guilt hit him hard. Perhaps if he'd sucked it up and helped the others, things could have turned out different. *Kill a few to save the rest,* as they always said. Conrad liked to think he never helped with the sacrifices out of some concern for the welfare of others. That sentiment did exist to some degree, but mostly he could chalk it up to his own fear. How could he look someone in the eye as he drained the life from their bodies?

He took another swill of bourbon, felt the burn, and then the spin of his lightheaded cranium as the booze kicked in. *Good, finally.* Now he could face whatever came for him. His other hand trembled like a fish out of water on his left knee. Conrad took a deep breath and tried to enjoy the glow of the booze in his system. In the back of his mind, the plan would always be—always had been—to drink to oblivion. If he woke the next morning, great. If he didn't, well, he wouldn't know it. One couldn't wake up dead, after all.

But what if I did? As a ghost…a revenant…a disciple of that—that thing. It took a huge portion of what remained in his glass to calm him. Conrad reached down for the bottle and tipped it to fill his glass, stopped, then mumbled, "Fuck it." He raised the whole bottle to his lips and poured a generous measure down his throat.

The bottle shook in Conrad's hand, both from old age and fear. He knew it would come—come for him and punish him for his cowardice. If only the booze acted faster. Sure, Conrad felt the twinges of drunkenness, but none of the glorious blackout darkness of complete annihilation.

The fire in the hearth flickered and licked at the wood Conrad had heaped in there. The warmth helped with his arthritis but did little for his high blood pressure and cholesterol. If the booze wouldn't take him down in time, he hoped for a massive stroke or heart attack. Not the little kind that only left you paralyzed yet aware. No, he wanted the massive kind that stole consciousness and life all in one fell swoop. Then the beast would come and find him already deceased.

Conrad laughed. The very thought of the beast finding him already dead gave him pleasure. It would be glorious if things worked out that way. He imagined the big stinking thing standing over him, puzzled, trying to piece the whole thing together. Conrad fought through another round of giggles, then raised the bottle to his lips and drank a few shots' worth of liquid. He began to feel numb, but definitely not near inebriated enough.

Conrad drank again, trying for that glorious blackout darkness—cursed that he'd become so tolerant of drink it took so much damn bourbon—and noticed motion outside his picture window. And there it stood, great big and stupid, swinging someone's head around like a bowling ball, huge body black against the falling snow. Conrad couldn't swill enough liquor to deal with this image. He panicked as the beast wound up and threw the bloody sphere through the glass.

Glass, melting snow, teeth, and a few tufts of bloody hair remained stuck in Kelsey's—the next-door neighbor's—head as it careened off his better knee, sailed past the flickering light of the fireplace, and came to rest eyes down in a dark corner. A splatter of blood marked the head's path.

The beast, fully formed and not only the shadow with red eyes, stood in the window and gloated. The thing stank, and Conrad really would have liked to have passed on long before exposure to such eye-watering putridness. But here things were, as a good old-fashioned pessimist would have expected.

The beast heaved one hairy leg over the threshold, and Conrad took a last swill of bourbon—the last he'd ever take. He savored the burn in his throat, then hefted the bottle as one big hairy foot hit the hardwood beneath the window and the stinking hulk dragged the other inside. Conrad shrugged. Worse ways existed. He tipped the bottle over his head until the second half of the bourbon saturated his upper body. Quickly, Conrad lit a cigar, careful not to set himself ablaze quite yet, and took a quick drag.

After what seemed an exorbitant amount of time the creature stood between him and the window. All shadow now, the beast's eyes glowed red like the coals in the bottom of Conrad's fireplace.

That gave Conrad an idea. He'd planned on burning himself up in the chair, but that plan seemed doomed. The thing would get to him before he burned enough to finish himself off. He wanted to achieve complete unconsciousness before this thing decided to brutalize him. He couldn't face that.

Braced by the consumption of a half bottle of mighty fine bourbon, Conrad ignored his fussy joints and ran like a much younger man for the fireplace. Conrad leapt inside as he screamed, "Fuck you!" Those were the last words he'd ever say. Conrad erupted into flame and screamed until reaching his wished-for oblivion. His last conscious thought flickered to regret—regret he hadn't slammed the whole damn bottle.

Renee applied one more smear of yellow to her sunset and then smiled, her teeth as bright as the panorama before her on the canvas. A chunk of wood in the fireplace next to her popped, and she felt the heat renew and warm the bones which lay beneath her thin nude frame.

Adam already lay in bed, exhausted by their activities an hour earlier. As for her, the physical activity, and a good healthy orgasm or two or three, always invigorated her. Not only physically but creatively. So, here she sat, alone with her work. She ran a hand through her short blonde hair, then applied more pigment to the sunset. She nodded. Now it didn't appear so blood-red. Before the application of yellow, the sun looked like a doomsday sun and that wouldn't do. Suns were meant to look cheery and inviting, not bloody and depressing.

Renee smiled again, then stretched her arms over her head. She enjoyed the way her body felt after expressing herself creatively and after good sex. Even better when the two were combined. A combination of a sated mind and body.

Something moved above the flaming hearth and when Renee glanced in that direction, she couldn't tell if the movement belonged to the portrait of Adam's mother or the antique mirror next to it. Now that she looked closer, it did appear as though the mirror sat askew.

Nothing worse than a crooked wall-hanging. She stood and her legs quivered because of the past physical effort. She could still feel Adam's hands on her and him in her, and the postcoital memory warmed her. She thought she would join him in bed after she straightened this damn mirror. And after she cleaned her brushes, of course. Her responsible nature bade her not neglect them any more than she would neglect her own hygiene.

A glance out the window confirmed the blizzard still raged outside. This suited Renee just fine. No need to leave the house in the morning for work, the candy shop for her and Adam down in the valley at the copper refinery. No, they could stay in bed all day tomorrow if they wished. And Renee thought she just might, especially since Adam's wife wasn't due back for a couple more days. For sure she'd sleep nude tonight, because the thought of waking up to Adam touching her made for an exciting prospect.

Something banged off the window where she had just checked the weather and the sudden noise made her jump. She felt compelled to cover herself, an arm across up top and a hand down below, in case someone out there was peeping. What if Adam's wife returned early? Renee enjoyed working nude, but the thought of a spy made her feel awkward. Vulnerable. She backed up toward the bedroom for a robe.

It angered her she need cover up when she'd begun to enjoy the warmth of the fire on her bare skin.

Before she reached the bedroom, breaking glass erupted, forcing Renee to rethink her plan. *What's going on?* First the mirror, then the bang on the window, now this. It sounded like a window shattering. She heard Adam get up and stomp about and wanted to shout out to him but decided to wait. Then she heard a strangled cry and a gurgle from back there in the darkness. Perhaps his wife was home...and angry.

"Adam?" she finally managed.

Then she heard faltering footsteps from the bedroom, bare feet on hardwood.

"Babe?"

Back in the darkness, Adam fell face first like a dead fish. His body twitched a couple times, then lay still. Blood pumped from the stump where his head should be and spread across the hardwood.

Renee backed up, her mind still not registering the need to flee out into the night, nude or not. Her eyes darted from the corpse of her lover back into the bedroom where shadows moved in the darkness. She attempted to calm herself despite her lover's body lying before her. Perhaps he tripped and fell through the window, did this to himself somehow, her mind too numb to think much beyond this simple reasoning.

She stood next to the fire, her skin beginning to sting a bit with the heat in such proximity. Then she heard the mirror above her shift again. She pried her eyes from Adam to glance upward. From the mirror, two long dark appendages reached for her.

Too much for her mind, Renee didn't feel much when the claw-tipped appendages grabbed her shoulders, claws slicing through skin, and lifted her lithe frame hard and fast toward the glass. She felt the rupturing of her cheeks and brow until one last bolt of pain took her to darkness.

Chapter 22

Angela fumbled with her keys, her fingers ice cold, only to discover the door to the jailhouse already ajar. She wondered if Robbie had returned to check on Harold and left the door open. It wouldn't surprise her.

She bumped the door open with her hip, then waved Miles and Em inside. The escape from the wind and snow felt incredible. Angela savored it for a moment, eyes closed, before shutting the door. When she opened her eyes, she knew things weren't right. Angela scanned the darkness.

By the light of the battery-operated exit signs, Angela noticed the puddles of thick liquid which had pooled in front of both holding cells. The odor of iron hit her and something round lay wedged between two of the bars fronting Harold's cell.

"Harold?" Angela asked, the whisper sounding loud in the dead silence.

No answer.

Miles walked over by the cell. He studied the round thing, scrunched his nose, then took a step back. "Don't think he's gonna answer you, Angela."

"Gross," Em said. "Please tell me that's not Harold's head."

Why would it be Harold's head? Angela thought. Her mind refused to go here. But it would. If she allowed herself to drown in the whys of the day, she would miss something vitally important in the here and now.

"I could tell ya that," Miles said, "but I hate to lie to ya. Looks like blood all over the floor, too." He walked over to Jeb's cell, careful to stay out of the red puddles. "If the head belongs to Harold, then that Jeb you told me about is gone, if this is where he was locked up. Looks like that thing squeezed 'em out right between the bars, except Harold's head must've been too fat and got stuck."

"Get away from there," Angela said. "That's evidence." She didn't know if she said that because of any procedural concerns or if she just didn't care for the idea of a kid being so comfortable with gore. Probably the latter, she figured. But why should the kid change now? She sighed and wasn't surprised Jeb's body was gone. If the beast had his head, his body couldn't be far away out in the snow where his head was by now buried.

"How can we stop this thing?" Em asked, voice soft, almost a whisper. "I mean, if it can get to folks through solid-steel bars, we're so screwed."

"We have any more salt?" Miles asked. "Seemed to work the first time, least for a little while. Your shot looked like it hit, even if it didn't hurt it bad."

"Harold's desk," Angela said. "He uses a huge container, the kind with the little metal pour spout, for his hard-boiled eggs. Eats them—ate them," she corrected, "like the world might run out. Every day he'd bring a few in. Must have kept the local chicken farmers in business."

Em walked over, grabbed the cylindrical container from next to Harold's pen and pencil holder, then threw it over to Miles. "Knock yourself out. You know more than we do." She returned to Angela as if her physical presence alone could make everything okay.

Angela felt Em shiver as the girl nestled into her, then watched closely as Miles poured a robust line of salt across the threshold of the door and each window casing. Angela shifted so she could stroke Em's cheek and better watch Miles, then ran a hand through Em's auburn wisps. Strange how she never enjoyed cuddling before. Angela sighed. It felt so good to relax for a moment. She could smell the peach of Em's shampoo. If they got through this, she would take Em somewhere nice, a long way from here. Somewhere hot and tropical. Angela figured every town needed cops. They could live in a lot of places—anywhere but here.

"We gonna be okay?" Em asked. "I mean, not to sound whiney or anything, but just hearing we would be okay even if you don't mean it would go a long way. You know?"

"We're gonna be fine," Angela said. When Em opened her mouth to argue, Angela kissed the girl so deep she thought they would touch tonsils. Em tasted like a combination of beer, corn nuts, and the peppermint Lifesaver she just sucked on. Not bad for a first kiss, Angela reckoned.

When they parted, Em said, "Yep; I feel better now, thanks." The girl beamed from ear to ear and ran a hand through her hair flirtatiously.

With men from her past, Angela found picking up on social cues wasn't her thing. But with Em, that all seemed to change. Not only could she pick up cues but seemed to understand what Em thought and how she felt without burning out her brain trying to figure things out. Men left her confused, while Em left her wanting more—so much more.

"If that's my last kiss ever," Em said, "I can live with that fact, because it was the best ever." She stared at Angela and Angela could see the blue depths inside Em, the layers of intelligence, caring, and, yes, longing. Em's breathing became ragged. A tear slipped from her left eye. "I want to live...to be with you. I don't want to die."

"I got you, babe," Angela said. "I got your back and every other part of you. We'll get through this."

Miles coughed. "If you two are done fussing over each other, maybe we should come up with a plan. That thing doesn't give two shits if you guys love each other or not."

"Yessir," Em said with a salute. "Right away, sir."

Angela laughed because it felt good to hear Em joke around. She hugged her, then separated herself. The absence of Em pressed against her felt cold and lonely. What she wouldn't give to cuddle in under covers and fall asleep with Em in her arms. After this situation ran its course, they could sleep for hours, days, and hold each other. Angela walked over to the cells and confirmed the blood and Harold's head. It did appear too big for even the creature to squeeze it through the bars. Harold's eyes appeared forlorn, mourning the loss of his body.

Jeb's head must have managed the journey okay, because nothing but blood and chunky residue remained of it. Angela wondered how the beast got in. Perhaps it happened after Robbie left the door open. Both mirrors were broken, so even if it could travel via that route as Harold had insisted, it couldn't now. Perhaps as a spirit it could travel wherever it wished. This gave Angela a surge of goosebumps. This thing, other than a spot of trouble with the salt, seemed unstoppable.

"Who are you here with?" Em asked.

Miles finished with the salt and Angela watched him walk toward Em. "My aunt Kayla. She's attending that writing convention…or was. I guess it's probably cancelled."

"And your sister is still up at the hotel, too?" Em asked. "With your aunt?"

Miles nodded.

"Tell me about your sister." Angela knew Em was trying to distract Miles from the blood, although she didn't think it bothered the kid much.

"She's possessed by some spirit from a Ouija board. It makes her use the word cunt a lot."

"That's not a very nice word," Em said, but grinned.

"Janey's not a nice girl," Miles retorted. "But she's clairvoyant, and can talk with spirits, and can scry through mirrors, and kinda knows shit others don't."

Em nodded. "Like you heard us talk about at the library, we read a book that said this thing might be the spirit of a Native American who killed his tribe and himself, way back in the old days. Did Janey say anything like that?"

Miles thought about it. "No, but she's never that clear. She mumbled a bunch of stuff about how mad it is, rage and stuff, and how only its own rage can stop it. You know, useless crap like that."

"Might not be," Em suggested. "It does seem grouchy. Maybe there's a way to use that against it."

Miles nodded. "Yeah, the salt worked. It chased us and couldn't push past it. The monster seemed to firm up and then Angela winged it. Maybe we can try that trick again, except be smarter about what we do. Doubt it would fall for the same thing twice, but ya never know."

"Your sister was possessed?" Angela asked, walking over. The only thing she knew about possession she either learned from *The Exorcist* movie she watched with her parents when she was twelve or from the subsequent internet searches. Those offerings were always light on detail yet heavy on supposition and superstitious bullshit. They never offered anything useful.

"Ouija board," he answered with a nod.

Angela thought she recalled reading Ouija boards could be dangerous if you believed in all that. She never had believed, but now she felt the macabre things she'd read about as a kid might hold some truth.

"And you mentioned your mother was murdered," Em said. Angela thought she sounded motherly herself, sweet and soft. "That's horrible. And now you're mixed up in all this."

"Well," Miles said, "it hasn't been a cakewalk, but we still have dad and Tracey. And supernatural goings-on are just par for the course with us. Maybe not this extreme all the time, but we've seen bad stuff before."

Em shook her head and looked like she wanted to hug the kid.

Angela doubted Miles was much of a hugger. Kinda like she used to feel about cuddly stuff. Until now.

Miles looked at Angela and sighed, hands on hips. "Look, I don't want to upset you again, but you should probably get ready to shoot. If that thing tries to get us, you gotta shoot it. A lot. Wait until it touches the salt. Hopefully it'll get mad enough to fall for it twice, but even if not, we oughta give it something to think about."

"No worries," Angela said. She patted the butt of her Glock. "I got it."

"Where's those other guns?" Miles said. "Maybe we could all have one, and you could upgrade to something with more firepower, like a grenade launcher or a flamethrower."

"We're in a small-town sheriff's office, not the National Guard," Angela said. "I think there's another Glock and a shotgun...and maybe Robbie's deer rifle back in the safe." She walked to Robbie's desk and found the key lying inside his pencil drawer. Robbie didn't know it, but sometimes he was easy to keep in the dark. He was too trusting.

With long strides, Angela reached the safe and inserted the key. The safe opened on well-oiled hinges. She took out the Glock and a pistol-grip shotgun and made sure they were both loaded. The shotgun made her feel better. She left the deer rifle because it had a scope which would be a hindrance at close range.

"Thought Robbie didn't give out the key," Em said.

"He doesn't," Angela answered.

Em and Miles giggled.

"Here," Angela said, handing the extra Glock to Em. "You always wanted to be a cop, and you've been to the range with me enough, so here you go. I just deputized you." She winked. "Careful where you point it." She reloaded her own Glock and then shucked a round into the breach of the shotgun. It felt really good to have the extra firepower whether it would do any damage to the beast or not. "Okay, best we can do."

"Don't I get one?" Miles asked.

Both women shouted, "No," at the same instance and then turned to each other with smiles.

"Aw, geez," Miles said. "I been through more than both of you, but ya treat me like a kid."

"About time someone did," Angela said. She felt bad for him. He could probably handle a firearm, but he needed to stay a kid for as long as possible. His life seemed to have fallen off the rails after his mom died and someone needed to reign him in. His sister, too, by the sounds of things. The caretaker in her wanted to protect his innocence. She was a peace-officer, after all. "If that thing shows up, I want you out of the way. And I know you understand a lot, but you can share that information without endangering yourself. I don't want you hurt. Not on my watch."

Miles huffed but stayed silent. A small smile played at his lips, like he might feel good about someone caring.

And Angela did. She wondered if it had anything to do with the kid she never got the chance to meet, an overcompensation for the miscarriage. Perhaps her psyche wanted her to pay penance even though her heart told her she did no wrong. But Angela could still see the hurt in her ex's eyes, the betrayal, the anger. Like his love for her had only been tied to that small bundle of cells growing in her belly and nothing else. Angela took a deep breath before a tear could leak out. She didn't need to explain these particular tears to Em right now.

"Let's try to hold out until morning," Angela said. "Then we'll go up to the hotel and see if we can find your sister, Miles. Maybe we can all come up with a plan to get off this mountainside."

"Morning's a long way off," Miles mumbled.

"And it's already cold in here," Em said. "And if you think I'm going to spend the night with you for the first time on one of those cots where Harold and Jeb died, you better wake up now, because…because, not gonna happen."

"What do you two suggest, then?" Angela asked, arms over chest.

Miles kicked the salt container around like a soccer ball but stayed silent, a scowl on his face. "I don't know."

"I'm sorry if I sounded mad," Em said, then rubbed her hand over Angela's shoulder. "I'm just cold and scared and hungry. Well, I'm always hungry…but cold and scared, for sure."

Angela nodded. She didn't want to sleep in those cells either, not with the stench of blood. Not that it smelled much better here in the office, but at least it wasn't so potent. "Look, I'll round up some clean blankets, and we'll sleep on the floor here in the office. We'll all huddle together for warmth."

"You two gonna smooch some more?" Miles asked. He scrunched up his nose and eyes. "If you are, I'd rather sleep out by the blood and guts, thanks."

Angela and Em both laughed but promised to refrain. Angela couldn't help but feel Miles' fussing about affection was a smokescreen. Something about the set of his knowing eyes, the uptick of the right side of his mouth as if stifling a grin. He knew things. Probably a lot of things, but something about the boy's reluctance to slide away from innocence felt refreshing and right to Angela. Even amidst all these things that very much weren't.

Angela knows she must have fallen asleep and is now experiencing a dreamscape based on the previous day's experiences. The world lays enveloped in white snow, and white fog, until all that white seems to have seeped inside her—into her mind. She feels cold and prickly, her skin clammy with the cold moisture. Her joints ache and she wonders how this sensation is possible inside a dream.

The answers don't matter, Angela understands, except for the one answer she must derive from the images her mind provides. Somewhere in this swirling white mist lays an answer for which she's always sought. And one that may prove useful in the hours to come. Somehow, she knows this.

Somewhere out in the white stillness, Angela hears the swish of skiers, metal edges on snow. She will never forget the scraping and carving sounds, never forget the feel of her own feet in ski-boots as they maneuver her skis like an extension of her own body. She feels like she is close to seeing the other skiers, so very close, if only she could open her eyes and clear the blinding white fog. Angela can almost see the others as they flit through the powder on their way to a warm chalet for suds or hot chocolate, depending on their mood.

Then she sees the red swatch of bright blood on the new snow, like a red sun glinting off a sheet of glass. How anything can remain so clear and distinct in this swirl of white eludes her. She only knows she's meant to see this. Like the flip of a switch, Angela stands directly above the swath and understands she should recognize this scene. And she does, and she cries, white tears rolling down frost-white cheeks.

The blood sings to her. "Not your fault, mommy. Not your fault." And at first, she thinks the voice must belong to Miles who sleeps next to her back in the waking world. But why would Miles call her mommy or, for that matter, reside in her dreams? He's just some kid she has met. But she knows, deep down, knows to whom the voice must surely belong. She often wonders what that voice would sound like had things turned out favorably. Like an angel, she thinks. More tears spill onto the white vastness of snow.

"Mommy, I died before you fell. Days before. Live your life. Survive. Fight."

But I have so little to fight for, she thinks. The knowledge of her own innocence in the matter brings no solace as she feels it should have. Her body betrayed her. Perhaps she ate too much, not enough, didn't take the proper vitamins, possessed the wrong cells and genes and flesh and DNA or whatever other host of possible maladies. Surely, she was to blame in some fashion, in some way. After all, he had blamed her.

"He no longer holds sway," the child says. "You have always wanted softer, something more tender. She has now fallen into your arms and you should fight."

"But—but, then you will never see the world."

"I've seen."

Angela wonders about this, wishes to ask if the child liked what it saw, or if the child understood the world as a place it never wished to travel and chose, instead, to remain in the other place. The place with no pain or intolerance. No sharp edges or harsh angles. No confusion. No spirit form beasts intent on death and torture. No daddy's who blame and belittle and leave mommy's alone in their moment of greatest grief.

"Fight," the child whispers, and it sounds a lot like snow and wind and ice.

Angela stirred awake, back stiff, brain a muddled mess of nightmares and dreams. She remembered her conversation with her unborn child and wept in the dark. Her heart raced inside her chest.

In her sleep, as if she knew what roamed in Angela's mind, Em had placed a soft gentle arm around Angela and held her close. The warmth felt divine yet innocent, sensual yet not provocative.

How a touch should feel. Her ex's touches always contained a hardness Angela could never enjoy, an ulterior motive, punchy, scratchy, abrasive, rough. So many horrible things in which Em proved the polar opposite. Her warmth nurtured and healed. Even Em's imperfections complimented Angela's own instead of making them worse. They were strong, whole onto themselves as individuals, but even stronger when caught in the same orbit of energy.

Angela concentrated on her breathing, matched it with Em's, then focused on Miles who slept beside them. His blond locks lay skewed with sleep, and his eyelids fluttered with some movement of his eyes. Perhaps he also dreamt.

Fight. The word echoed in Angela's mind. Her eyes widened.

No warning! With a blast of wind, snow, and a big hairy foot, the door to the jail flew open with such force the doorstop broke off and rattled away. A roar reverberated through the jailhouse and seemed to come from everywhere at once. The thing's stench, much worse than the irony bisque of the blood, plugged Angela's sinuses.

Em and Miles stirred, confused, pulled harshly from their slumbers.

At the threshold between outside and in, the creature bellowed as it attempted to cross the salt defenses. White and red sparks flew like fireworks in a night sky as the beast struggled to gain entrance. In its rage and bloodlust, the creature remained rooted in the doorway a moment too long.

"The salt is working...see the colors," Miles said sleepily.

Angela, with a maneuver born of instinct, snapped the Glock to position and fired center mass. *Fight!*

The creature screamed with fury but backed away. In the sheen of the emergency lighting, the mist of red hovered then caught the wind and dissipated. Angela hoped the blood loss was enough. Perhaps the creature lay just beyond the door, in the snow, dead or dying.

"Did you get it?" Miles asked.

"Angela?" Em asked. She sounded confused, like a little girl, like she couldn't quite remember why she was here. Then she said a peculiar thing. "I saved you from the fog and snow. After he spoke to you." She blinked her eyes rapidly as if to dispel a dream.

Angela kissed her cheek. "I know, babe. We'll talk later." Her heart thumped harder, and another tear streaked her cheek. She wanted nothing more than to hold Em in her arms. But there was too much else to do, like stay alive until morning.

Miles ran to the door. "I don't see it out here," he said. "A few drops of blood, but not enough. Takes a lot of blood loss to drain a big son of a bitch like that. But you hurt it, made it think twice. Maybe it'll move on."

The wind answered from outside with a hefty gust which brought more snow and cold. A drift had already snaked inside the door and seemed sentient in the manner of a large white serpent. If the drift formed red beady eyes, Angela would unload her Glock until the drift lay spread around the jailhouse.

It didn't.

"Oh, God," Em whispered. "There in the dark." Angela felt Em's body tense, and the girl's hand gripped Angela's bicep like a vice with jagged metal teeth.

Miles also noticed and began to back away from the hallway which led to the holding cells. "It found a way around the salt. Is there another mirror in this place?"

Angela knew there was one in the women's restroom, but didn't answer Miles. She should have thought of it.

A set of red eyes bobbed like fireflies in the darkness, disembodied, hovering right above the two pools of coagulated blood outside the cells. Angela could feel the beast's malice and rage sifting into her psyche like an infection. For a moment, she felt what it felt. Yes, rage and bloodlust, the need for retribution, but also a modicum of confusion. Angela wondered if it no longer understood the world in which it found itself. The lack of faith—the lack of belief in deities and spirits and gods.

"It's become obsolete," Em whispered. "Just like Harold and Jeb."

Angela appreciated she and Em being on the same wavelength, but felt compelled to mention, "But not yet ineffectual."

Em nodded.

Miles said, "Back off!" Angela noticed the boy still held his original vial of salt, what remained of it. Or maybe he had filled it from another of Harold's stash while she was preoccupied.

The red eyes considered him, then floated, midair, toward the office. The stench grew worse and a dark body began to manifest around the red orbs like fog around a lighthouse. The headdress and tomahawk returned, peeking from within the black mass only to be reabsorbed as the thing traveled.

"Leave us alone," Angela said. Then she thought of an angle. "You can abandon your rage. The ritual is over."

"Yeah," Miles said. "The gig's up."

The beast screamed as if it understood but would not relinquish its claim on the flesh due it. It stomped forward on ephemeral legs that made a lot of noise despite their lack of flesh and bone. All this as if the beast held sway over the very essence of reality or wished the three bags of flesh before it to believe this.

Em trembled behind Angela, arm still wrapped around her. The woman's breaths whispered off the skin of Angela's neck and beneath a different set of circumstances she may have found the blow of air lovely and tantalizing.

Angela stood frozen in front of Em as the boy darted between the beast and them. Miles held the vial before him to ward off the menace which approached with purpose. Miles reached back, then hurled the salt from out of the vial like a baseball pitcher off a dirt mound. The small cloud of white granules floated and spread. Angela timed her draw to the exact moment salt met beast—for that magic time when the beast would become solid. This didn't happen.

It's learned, Angela thought as she watched the thing take evasive maneuvers.

The beast twisted around the salt like a demonic kite, the beast more agile than Angela would have thought.

We're truly fucked.

Miles hurled the salt container itself at the beast as it reformed to its former glory, red eyes and all. The container sparked white as it passed through but offered no more resistance than a pop-can thrown at a dust storm.

It threw Miles against the wall as it passed him. The boy slumped to the baseboards, his eyes closed. Then it approached Angela, and she rose to her full height. She would *fight*.

Angela trembled, her body attempting to betray her. She could also feel Em shudder behind her. She wished she could blend inside Em, form a kind of superwoman with which to fight this evil. Even as she thought this, the opposite happened.

Angela felt her body drift away from Em and she couldn't stop it. Then she was flying, arms grasping for purchase, legs striving for the floor. She landed on her side next to Miles. Her body ached and complained with the force. How she had gotten from there to here so fast eluded her. Angela shook her head. The beast's touch had made her thoughts sluggish. Events played out before her in bits and pieces, as if she floated in and out of consciousness. Em's screams brought Angela back to the here and now.

Angela blinked.

The creature surrounded Em in a kerfuffle of tornadic motion until it seemed Angela watched Em scream on the screen of an old-time black and white feature film.

"Leave her alone!" Angela shouted. She felt impotent and useless.

The black tornado rose from the floor, Em within its influence. She didn't spin, but appeared to float within the creature's center, inside the eye of the storm. It approached the door.

Angela stood, her head spinning, then rushed the black mass. She pumped her arms and legs, determined to save Em. She flung herself at the mass, shoulder first, as it hovered before the whiteness outside. Angela found herself spun around and flung across the room, coming to rest just short of the pool of Harold's blood. Unable to move, Angela refused to remove her eyes from Em.

Harold's face appeared to laugh at her as it sat perched between the metal bars.

"Angela," Em pleaded. The look of hopelessness and despair on Em's face, the wide eyes, mouth stretched in fear, the wrinkled forehead, broke her heart.

"I'm coming, Em!" Angela screamed. Tears streamed down her cheeks. She couldn't yet stand, so she dug her elbows into the hardwood of the floor and crawled, pulling her body along. The skin on her elbows scraped against the rough surface, but she ignored the pain and dug forward. She wanted Em's last image on this earth to consist of someone caring for her, loving her, wanting her.

And then Em and the black mass were gone, out the door and into the swirling white storm. Her soft, beautiful Em. She'd allowed her to be taken. The loss burned inside, mixed there with the never-sated grief of her miscarriage. Could she save anyone? Angela shrieked into the night like a wolf into the face of the moon.

Chapter 23

James lowered Vic down into the pit where Robbie stood, arms up, ready to catch her. She reminded him of a cat who didn't wish to be handled. He would pay for talking her into this madness, but he hoped that day came. That would mean they'd lived, that they'd made it through this darkness to tomorrow. Once they were on their way off this cliff, Vic could yell at him until she turned blue in the face, and he would have no choice but to take it with a smile.

She yelled, "I don't understand why we are going to crawl like gophers down that filthy rat-hole. It stinks to high Heaven down there. And it looks muddy."

James couldn't help but feel she'd asked the wrong question. The question that floated through his mind had more to do with how powerful a ghost must be to lock them in like that. The ghost of the maintenance man must have really wanted them down here. He hadn't even believed in ghosts as little as forty-five minutes ago, and now they were following the girl.

"We can't leave Janey to fend for herself," he said.

"Let the sheriff go retrieve her," Vic said as the sheriff grabbed a hold of her and set her down on the dirt floor.

James jumped down, the impact hurting his knees. Then he stood with the others, a hand on Vic's shoulder.

"Janey seems more capable than any of us," Vic said. Are you sure she needs all of us?"

"I think we should," James said and removed his hand from her shoulder. "I think we can all agree something beyond comprehension is occurring and we're all a part of it. We should stick together."

"Yes," the Sheriff said, "Down here, together is the safest. I'll be the first to admit I don't know if I can keep everyone from harm, but I'm going to try. And that means we follow the girl."

They all stared at the hole. Good Lord, James thought. They were all going to actually crawl down in there. He wondered where it led.

A horrid stench came from the crawlspace and James envisioned a tomb. The girl had been adamant cultists had used this tunnel to transport bodies to the creature. Maybe this would end up a disastrous idea, but there was nowhere else to go. They burnt that bridge when they jumped down here with no way back up. The walls of the pit were smooth as a baby's ass.

"I'll go first," Robbie said, but James thought he sounded reluctant. "James, you bring up the rear." He threw James his smaller flashlight, then Robbie assumed a crawling position and stuck his head inside. He paused, swore about the stink, and then continued into the dark.

James watched Robbie crawl and disappear into the hole. He could hear the man grunt with exertion as he pulled his way along. There was barely room for his beefy shoulders to fit.

"It stinks, and it's dark in there," Vic said, as if they all didn't know that already.

"You're up," James said. He didn't want to rush Vic, but he also didn't want to fall behind the sheriff.

Vic turned to him. "I came here to write, hang out with writers, and fuck you silly. What happened?" She sounded disappointed.

James shrugged. "A blizzard, ghosts, a clairvoyant child, some creature… I don't know."

"Wouldn't you rather be up in our room, betwixt my legs?"

"Of course, darling," he said, knowing she was stalling. "But such is not our plight." He nodded at the hole in the dirt.

"We could wait here, in the pit," she said. "We could make this place work for us." By the light of the flashlight he held, James watched Vic wink at him. "I'm sure they'll send someone to fetch us after they get out."

James shook his head and thought back to their honeymoon. They'd made love in a cave in Missouri on a bed of moldering leaves. So, her suggestions weren't without precedent, but he found it difficult to imagine any form of arousal in this filthy, stinking place. Besides, he knew she wasn't serious about the sex, only the staying behind.

James heard a scratching noise come from the wall of the pit. It sounded like an animal pawing at the dirt. But he knew no animal could live down in these dank depths. That left ghosts or bugs, neither of which he cared to encounter. Especially, he wished to never again look upon the apparition of the maintenance guy. The splattered image was one thing up in the light, but down here it would break his psyche.

"I think we better get going," he said.

Vic glanced around the pit, then at James. "Fine." She put a tentative knee down then picked it up. "Oh, God, its damp and horrible."

"Like every option available to us," James said. "Hurry now, before we're left behind."

Vic grumbled, put one knee back down, grimaced at James, then placed the other next to the first. She lifted the palm of each hand in turn to look at the dirt which clung to them. "Gross." Then she began to crawl. "I can't see a damn thing!" She sounded muffled. As she entered, the darkness of the pit seemed to swallow her alive.

The scratching came again, and James wanted to exit the pit and get in the hole, sure that's what the spirit wanted. He felt another minute spent in this pit would introduce him to things he would rather not meet. The moment Vic's shoes disappeared, James held his breath and started into the darkness. The dirt did feel damp and infectious, but it beat the hell out of seeing the insides of the maintenance man again.

James couldn't see a damn thing, so he shone the flashlight Robbie gave him into the hole in time to watch Vic pull her feet further in. The sides and ceiling of the tight hole were nothing but dirt, as if a giant earthworm had bored through this spot and moved on. He hoped the walls wouldn't cave in.

He could hear Vic shuffle and make noises of discontent out in front of him. The air in the narrow tunnel felt dead and too warm. Within moments, his pits and crotch were bathed in sweat.

The sound he heard next, from right behind him, stole what little confidence in safety he had retained. The scratching sound from the pit now followed him inside the confines of this claustrophobic hellhole. The ghost must be traveling behind him to make sure James didn't change his mind and go back. James wanted to move faster, but when he did, Vic's right Louis Viton kicked him in the nose. He let out a gasp of air and brought his hand up. It felt like someone set the bridge of his nose aflame. The flashlight flickered around wildly.

James saw stars in the darkness and tried to speak but the blood traveling down his throat turned it into a scratchy rasp. Instead, he squeezed her foot to tell her she should keep on.

"Please tell me that was you," Vic said, voice shaky. "If it was a rat or worse, I'll scream."

"Yeah," James said, but that's all he could get out. His voice sounded like his nose was plugged with cotton. "Me."

"By the sound of you, I suppose your nose is broke," Vic said. Her voice sounded muffled and far away. "I felt it in my foot and ankle when it struck you. Can you keep going? I'll check you out when we get somewhere less enclosed."

"Yeah," James said. He wished to tell her about the ghost but couldn't speak well enough to do so, blood dripping down his throat and out his nostrils. *I'll sure look a fright.*

Vic stopped trying to turn around and finally started to move again.

"Something grabbed my ankle," the sheriff shouted from further in the tunnel.

To hear better, James tilted his head. In the process, he smashed it into the top of the tunnel and dirt cascaded down. James had already found it necessary to breathe from his mouth due to his damaged nose. Now, as he breathed, dust from the falling dirt pushed its way inside and caused him to choke and spit. He imagined it tasted like ash from a crematorium. *What else?*

Vic must have heard his struggles. "What are you up to, James?"

He couldn't answer. Then the scratching sound came from right next to him, as if the ghost noticed the opportunity to kill him and decided to take it. James reacted and rammed his right shoulder into the side of the tunnel. He grunted but adrenaline kept his momentum traveling forward. Dirt continued to fall until James felt certain he would soon find himself buried and they would need to dig his broken corpse out of here or just leave this God-forsaken place as his tomb. He panicked, which caused more dirt to dump down onto his head and shoulders. He spit and grunted and bled.

"It empties out into a cavern," Robbie shouted. "Keep crawling. You're almost out."

This provided James with hope and he scurried forward, his right hand accidently groping Vic's ass and down a little further past the taint to her private area.

Vic huffed and kept crawling. "Oh, no you don't. The pit back there wasn't good enough to fuck me in. Don't think you'll get any action in here."

He knew she wasn't serious, that she knew it was an accident, but his nose, throat and mouth were too filled with blood and dirt to acknowledge her attempt at humor.

The scratching noise sounded off again, mocking him, propelling him forward like a herded steer.

James grunted and crawled as close to Vic as he dared. They finally spilled out onto the floor of a cavern. Robbie stared at them, blinking, as if they'd just shot out the ass-end of an elephant.

"You're a damn bloody mess," the sheriff said.

Vic squatted next to him and looked at his nose, and then touched it with a gentle finger. "Darling, that looks horrible."

James nodded wearily and then noticed the girl peering at some drawings on the cavern wall. *Let her have them.* He turned off his flashlight and flopped to his back and groaned.

"Are you okay?" Vic whispered. She attempted to wipe some of the incrusted blood away from his nostrils but only succeeded in making him wince. "You'll need the doctor when we crawl our asses out of here."

James nodded, closed his eyes, and tried to breathe normally.

"What's this ya got here?" James heard Robbie ask the girl.

James cracked one eye and noticed Janey was standing in front of the drawings, her dress filthy and neck smeared with mud. She stared up at some goofy looking stick figures drawn with what looked like white chalk. Hieroglyphs, he thought. Or something like that. James wondered how ancient peoples got down here and why.

"They wanted it dead even then," Janey said.

James, who had closed his eyes again, opened them and noticed the cave-painting in its entirety. Several smaller stick figures, holding spears, surrounded a bigger stick figure with teeth as big as its head. A story about fighting a monster, it appeared.

"Anasazi…early Apache?" Robbie asked.

The girl shrugged. "They failed…cunt."

"Where do we go now?" Vic asked. "We followed the girl, but I don't intend to crawl back through that hell."

Janey turned and looked at her, eyes hooded, whites tinged with red. "It'll find a new hell for you."

"Wonderful," Vic whispered, shaking her head, and wiped a smear of mud from James' temple. The dirt cascaded down, tumbled, and then James was sure he felt it enter his ear canal.

James turned his head and felt the detritus dislodge and fall out. He spit more blood. While turning to spit, he noticed an ancient firepit, complete with a circle of rocks, a few bits of bone, and the charred remains of branches.

Janey glanced at the firepit, then at James. "Violet, not yet dead," she said. She turned and walked toward a tunnel that would only require walking carefully and not, *thank goodness*, crawling.

"Where are you going?" the sheriff asked.

Janey didn't answer and walked into the darkness.

Girl has balls the size of King Kong's. James admired the girl's courage.

"Come on," Vic said and reached down to help him up. "I know you are hurting, but we might as well not get left behind now that we're down here." Vic ran her other hand through her hair. "I must look irresistible."

James heard the sarcasm and made an effort to smile at her. He nodded. She normally was, just not right at this moment. He winced at the bit of mud which lay smeared from her upper lip to her left cheekbone. It looked like dogshit.

With Vic's assistance, he stood. James closed his eyes to quell the spinning in his head and then followed her toward the next tunnel. He turned the flashlight back on and scanned the floor before them. It lay littered with debris of rock and bone and some dried wood pieces. When he heard scratching from behind them in the previous tunnel, James hurried forward.

Robbie's flashlight shone off the cavern walls ahead. The walls looked like polished stone, so much different than the muddy hell through which they just traveled. He wondered if the shiny walls were caused by traffic, more of a beaten path than the other passages. In the brightened space, James noticed more cave drawings, these in color, yet faded with age. He could make out figures with bows, spears, and knives.

In one section, several warriors bickered and fought with men dressed in red robes and chainmail. In another portion, warriors battled what appeared to James as the same creature in the primitive drawings, only more fully fleshed out. It possessed a full body of hair, long arms and legs, and a puffy chest. Its head sat atop a stocky neck, mouth filled with red-tinted fangs. Each hand featured claw-tipped fingers. The beast carried a human head around like a bowling ball.

James shuddered. *Must have been tough back in those days.* Then he considered their current situation and wondered how different things were after all.

"It was just a stupid creature back in those days," Janey said from somewhere up front. "Simple. They came here to fight it. Later, they came to feed it. After."

"After what?" Robbie asked.

When Janey didn't answer Robbie said, "We must be in the old copper-mine shafts by now, or close. It's like walking through a huge time capsule in here. Lots of history. Must date back centuries." He glanced at Janey. "Can you tell? Are these from two different tribes, older and more recent?"

Janey didn't answer. But then she continued down the passageway, her little feet making small sounds on the hard-packed surface. James couldn't help admire the confidence of the kid, like she understood fully what she had gotten them all into. And herself.

As if she read his mind, Janey turned to him and smiled. She whispered something, one word, but James couldn't hear. But he knew. It rhymed with runt.

Janey led them all off into the gloom.

James sent off a little prayer that all would end well, with no further fatalities and nobody injured. He didn't feel an abundance of hope toward this end. James shone the flashlight around, took in the images of Native Americans fighting a monster. He wondered how all this hidden history came to be. How two different tribes, from separate eras, traveled to the same place to create murals and fight monsters. And why.

Then he heard the scratching noise, back behind them in the dark, and he hurried along to rejoin the others. James, as before, felt herded by some unseen watchdog and didn't care for the sensation.

Chapter 24

Angela shook her cobwebs away with an oscillation of her head and then helped Miles off the floor. The boy staggered for a moment, then looked around the room. She'd allowed it to take Em. If anything happened to the woman, she'd never forgive herself.

"She's gone," Miles said solemnly. He though a moment then shook his head. "What would Tracey do?" He rubbed his fingers over the pubescent dusting of fuzz on his chin.

"That your stepmom?"

Miles nodded. "Dad's girlfriend, if we're splitting hairs. Anyway, I think she would go after the thing, track it down. She enjoys diving headfirst into stuff without a plan, kinda reactive versus proactive. But it usually works out for her. It's her deal."

Kinda sounds like me. "Grab your coat," she said. "I'm gonna try to track this thing. Hopefully, it left footprints like before." She considered Miles for a moment. "You can stay here where it's a little warmer and safer. I need to find Em; I promised her."

"I'm with you," Miles said. "If I know Janey, she's hot on the trail of the ghosts of the Jerome Grand. I'll bet she's recording." He looked thoughtful for a moment. Then he walked over and grabbed his jacket and fished a video-camera out of the pocket. "Kind of a shame I haven't gotten anything on the SD card except a little at the library. Tracey will skin me when she hears what I saw but didn't get on film."

"We were running for our lives!"

"Still." He fiddled with the device and it turned on. He opened and stared at the viewing panel. "Looks no worse for wear. I'll get some footage yet." He slipped on his jacket. "Let's go find your girlfriend."

Angela opened her mouth, about to tell the kid he couldn't go, but decided not to. If she was being honest, Miles knew more than she did about this thing. And Em needed him. She loved Em.

"All right," Angela said. "You'll be safer with me, anyway."

"And you'll be safer with me." Miles smiled big and continued to point the roving eye of the camera at her. "Can I have a gun now?"

"No." Then Angela checked her ammo and picked up the shotgun. "Let's go. Bring your salt." She walked out the door. The snow still fell in white sheets and plumes. If there were tracks, they wouldn't be there for long. She searched the ground and her heart leapt when she noticed the large tracks filling with snow.

Miles spoke to her from the threshold of the door. "Hang on, I'm out." He began to scoop salt from where he'd laid it across the metal.

Angela thought about this. When the creature found them it couldn't pass through the salt, it used the mirror in the bathroom. She glanced at Miles who was screwing the top back on his canister. She took a deep breath and decided to trust his judgment. "How do...things like this work, Miles? What has Tracey taught you? What are we dealing with?"

"Tracey says, these kinds of things build power over time, merge with other energies. That goes double if folks worship them like these people have over the years. It thinks itself invincible...and that gives us an advantage."

Angela nodded and then looked back at the disappearing tracks. She needed to get to Em. The woman had already suffered enough over the years at the hands of the men from this town. She didn't need this on top of it. Angela revisited the haunted look in Em's eyes as the creature took her, the desperation, the hopelessness. With a flurry of rage, Angela plowed through the knee-deep snow and followed the tracks. When she turned the corner of the building and entered an even deeper darkness, Angela unclipped her flashlight and shone it into the gloom. The tracks were easier to see between buildings where the wind didn't whip the snow.

The tracks led out back. Angela stopped where they plunged down the cliff face into a field of rubble and broken cement. As she shone her light, Angela could make out the ruins of the old jailhouse below where it had slid down the mountainside due to the collapse of some of the mine shafts. *Shit.* She put her hands on her hips and thought for a moment, and then turned and ran back the way she had come.

Just as Angela hit her stride, churning through the snow, she almost ran over Miles.

"Where you going?" he asked.

"Wait here," she answered. "I'll be right back." She ran as fast as she could, arms and legs pumping. Angela reached the jailhouse and slammed through the broken door, jumped over the patches of dried blood, past Harold's lonesome head, and raced for the storage room. Once inside the storage room, she used her flashlight to look for what she wanted. They were in here somewhere, buried beneath both piles of junk and horrible memories. Old desk chairs flew, careening off walls and other junk. An old lamp soared and smashed off the cement floor. She shoved an old wooden file cabinet out of the way and there they were. Right where she'd left them.

Angela took a deep breath and unzipped the long vinyl ski-tote. The set of K2 skis fell out of the bag into her practiced hand. Beneath the skis, she found her competition ski-boots and slid them on. They fit like a glove, felt like her own feet. Satisfied with the fit, Angela threw the skis and poles over her right shoulder and used the flashlight with her left.

The going was slower with the heavier ski-boots, but she made good time. She burst out the door, not bothering to secure it, and raced into the space between buildings.

Miles looked up at her with bewilderment. "Holy shit! You gonna ski down that cliff?"

"Goddamn right! It's the only thing I'm really good at!" Angela didn't care if the beast heard her. "You're gonna get on my back and hang on. If you fall, you'll spill all the way to the bottom."

"Awesome," the boy exclaimed and ran behind her to the edge of the precipice.

Angela shook her head. *Awesome?* She guessed she would never understand, so she let it go.

Angela flopped the skis onto the ground, careful not to bury the bindings in the ever-increasing powder. After she stepped into the bindings, Angela lifted each ski to make sure the fit was snug and secure, and then continued to step until the snow beneath became packed and manageable.

Ready to rock and roll. She knelt low and turned to Miles. "Okay, get on my back. You're going to hang on around my neck, but low, so you don't cut off my breathing. Wrap your legs around my waist. You're also gonna shine the flashlight out in front of us. Can you do that?"

"Hells to the yes!" Miles said and approached and took the large flashlight. "This is gonna rock so hard!"

After Miles latched on, Angela stood, pole in each hand, and stared down the mountain. Her hair flapped in the brutal wind. The terrain would prove steep and rough, she knew, but nothing she couldn't handle if everything went okay. The powder would help with speed and help her to turn without using the steel edges of the skis much.

The tracks of the beast barreled straight down the steep slope and disappeared out beyond the reach of the flashlight Miles held.

"Here I come, babe," Angela whispered. The wind caught her words and whisked them away. She slid the skis back and forth to warm the wax on the bottoms with friction, and then released off into the abyss.

They free fell for a moment, weightless, and then right before impact with the powdery slope, Angela angled her skis in a slight turn to the right. Then they hit. Angela did not properly gauge the effect Miles' weight would have, and when she tried to brace against the powder for a left slalom turn, her knee buckled. They plowed straight forward into an unplanned course.

"Holy shit!" Miles screamed yet managed to keep the light of the flashlight out in front of them.

They began to pick up unwanted speed, and Angela knew she needed to reduce it by making a turn. Then they could get back on the tracks of the beast. It wouldn't take much out here on this slope, in this blizzard, to get to a point of no return. They could end up at the bottom of the mountain if she wasn't careful.

Millions of individual snowflakes whizzed by the light in streaks of white. Angela fought to see through them, to keep them from hypnotizing her. Then she spotted a lump in the snow. Just what she needed. As they approached, Angela lowered her center of gravity and began to dig her skis in to the left. When they reached the bump, the skis struck, and she used the momentum to turn left further in the direction Angela wanted to go. They whizzed left and Angela immediately scanned for another obstruction from which to help her turn right and reduce speed.

With a shake of her head, Angela cursed herself for not digging deeper into the pile of crap for her ski-goggles. The snow filled her eyes and collected on her lashes. From experience, she understood her eyelashes and eyebrows and bangs would soon freeze into a slurry of frost which would impede her vision further.

"Miles!" she yelled. "Wipe off my hair and my face. The snow and frost. Can you get it out of my eyes?" She searched in a mad frenzy for her next turn. Beneath, the tracks of the beast whizzed by. They would have to turn soon to stay on course.

Miles swiped with his hand that held the flashlight. The hard metal casing of the light banged off her head.

"Ouch! Take it easy, Miles."

"Sorry," he said. "I need my other hand to hold on." He tried again, more gently, and this time the action only stung her windburned skin. She felt cold moisture fall inside her jacket and cool her sweaty cleavage and pits. She fought to look around his hands. Even though Miles tried his best to do both things at once, the light of the flashlight danced around and made things difficult to see in the near whiteout.

In fact, Angela didn't see the next bump until her skis nearly crashed into it. The tips began to lift into nothing but air when she repositioned her hips and initiated the right-hand turn of her skis. Angela prayed the momentum shift would be enough to get the skis turned in time. She felt her edges grab and they darted right as she hoped to, but they were traveling too fast. Snow whizzed by her head and stung her eyes. The tracks appeared then disappeared again beneath her skis.

Against her training, Angela initiated a small snowplow maneuver, in order to cut speed. She knew she couldn't sustain this maneuver for long, because her edges would catch debris beneath the snow and flip them. Then they would tumble out into the abyss and the patrols wouldn't find their corpses until the spring thaw. That's if they were lucky. Many a cadaver got picked clean by Golden Eagles before any rescuers could find them.

To her right, Angela noticed a slight ridge, an old foundation poking through where the wind eroded away a portion of the accumulated snow.

"Hang on!" she said.

Miles tightened his grip yet managed to keep the light out front.

As they approached the old foundation, Angela lowered her center of gravity, and then leaned back. Her core muscles screamed, and a bolt of raucous heat ripped across her belly and ribcage. She knew she would be lucky to avoid a hernia or torn musculature. She held the weight distribution despite the discomfort and dug in her edges to glance off the cement foundation of the old jailhouse and careen back to the left. She straightened, and the immediate relief on her core felt glorious as blood rushed back to the spots it had vacated. She made a couple of small turns down the ledge and then began to search for her next major turning point.

They built speed, and the footprints, fresher now, whizzed by beneath them. *We're getting closer.*

Miles reestablished his grip and, like an old pro, wiped some of the hoarfrost from her face and hair. Again, it traveled inside her clothing and cooled her.

Then she noticed it, a large section of foundation looming before them. She turned in an evasive maneuver, forcing the skis and her body weight to the right. The tips just missed the concrete, edges scraping along, her left shoulder bouncing off the five-foot section.

"Whoa!" Miles screamed. "That was too close!"

But then they were turned and heading straight downhill, foundation on their left. No way she could cut further right without reducing speed. She clattered her left pole along the concrete, trying to find a hole to lodge it in, anything to slow their speed. Angela dug the other pole into the snow on her right, desperate now, knowing that any faster and they would plunge off the end of the world and carom to the bottom of the mountain.

"Look out!" Miles yelled and shone the flashlight on the white ramp before them.

Angela recognized it as a huge slab of wall that had, at some point in its fall from grace, tipped forward but not fallen all the way to earth. *No avoiding it.* She kept her weight back when she felt them hit the incline. Instinct told Angela the abyss lay just on the other side of this anomaly, certain death. *They'll pick our remains out of a quarter mile stretch of rubble down below!*

Miles shrieked.

Then her tips were heading up the giant mound and she knew only one way to slow their momentum. As they approached the lip, Angela swung her right arm and pole counterclockwise, whipping it past her face and around to the left. She allowed her head to follow. This forced her body to rotate, and as they reached the apex of the mound, the skis were already twisting around and catching snow.

They exploded through the powder at the top in mid-turn. Angela felt solid ground slide away and her skis rotated the rest of the way after launch. A full three-sixty later, she noticed the gut-wrenching sights of the lights at the bottom of the mountain. Briefly, she felt jealous they retained their power down at the base. The lights from the huge copper refinery loomed savage and bold, ready to eat them if they fell that far. She lost balance.

"Motherfucker!" Miles said and Angela felt him squeeze harder just below her throat.

Please let us have slowed enough! She closed her eyes and fell backward and sideways, trying to keep her weight off Miles at impact.

Terror flooded Angela. She understood the impact could very well happen thousands of feet below them. She screamed.

Chapter 25

Will this cavern never end? James thought. The packed dirt floors and copper-veined walls were all they had seen for what felt like miles. The infernal scratching noises persisted whenever they lagged on a timeline James wasn't privy to. This never failed to give him the heebie-jeebies. The tunnel walls, in strategic places only the artists understood, were adorned in that same symbolism of warriors and the occasional monster with red eyes.

The girl stayed up front, wandering, ponytail swinging from side to side. She took in all the artwork as if their stroll took place in a lovely art gallery. James didn't understand her calm demeanor when he felt so panicked. He knew Janey understood things they didn't. Occasionally, she would glance back and grin.

"Keep that light coming," Vic said, turning to him. "You keep getting distracted and then I can't see where I'm stepping."

"Yes, dear," he said, then added, "but you do realize the going is obstacle free. You can see sheriff Robbie's light well enough. And this tunnel almost glows. I want to get a look at the walls. They may hold clues."

"Clues?" she asked. "And what will you do with a clue even if you recognize one as such? Maybe it would be better to stay close to the sheriff."

"You never know," James said. Vic's comment stung a little, but he knew she meant well. "I might stumble onto something."

"You might stumble, yes," Vic said, and James heard the humor in her voice. "That, I believe."

"Ha ha," James whispered to her.

Vic smiled at him through the grime on her face.

James trudged along. The only thing he wished to hear less than his wife's teasing, despite her light tone, were the little scratch-scratch noises out in the dark behind him. For that reason alone, James pushed forward and ignored the cave drawings.

Robbie yelled back, "Tunnel widens into a cavern up here. Looks pretty big."

James watched Janey disappear into the gloom ahead, little legs pushing her forward, as if she didn't require illumination. He wondered if she could see in the dark like an animal. But as James approached the cavern, he noticed a little refracted light went a long way. Several shiny chunks of metal, not quite mirrors but close in their luster, stuck out of the dirt and stone. James supposed they were made of copper and the plates of polished metal allowed the weak flashlights to cast a wider arc.

The scratching intensified behind James as he hesitated at the cavern's entrance, impatient noises, never giving him a spare moment. He glanced back with reluctance, in time to watch an off-white slender chunk of something come scrabbling down the corridor. His eyes grew wide when he noticed it could only be a long chunk of bone. It clattered to his feet, and James danced away to avoid its touch.

"What is wrong with you?" Vic asked when he bumped into her. "I've never seen you so squirrely."

He pointed at the bone. "It came at me," he explained.

"That old bone?"

"Yes, what else?"

Vic shook her head. "Your imagination is running full force, love." She smiled at him then as if he were a child and didn't believe him.

This upset James, but he held his tongue.

"It means for you to understand," Janey said. How she had walked up to him without making a sound, James had no clue.

"Understand what?" he asked after he collected his wits. He felt led by his nose like a bull and this made him uncomfortable.

Vic ignored them both and walked toward the light.

"Everything," Janey said, and then turned to follow Vic toward Robbie and the alcove.

Robbie had stuck his entire head inside the hole in the wall and was reaching for something deep inside.

"Good Lord," James muttered, and then followed along before he could hear the scratching again or have another bone flung at him from down the passage. The closer he got to Robbie, the better he could see the man struggle, trying to pull something out of the grotto. *Some things should remain left alone.* Yes, he'd agreed to follow Janey, but he considered anything inside a dark grotto within a tunnel system as something to avoid.

"Earth to James," Vic said as she approached him.

"What?"

"You were just standing there muttering to yourself like a proper ass-hat," she explained to him. "What's the matter with you?"

"Just convincing myself we'll be okay," he said.

She stared at him a moment, a scowl on her luscious lips. "Knock it off," she said finally. "Don't pick a tunnel system I didn't want any part of, in the dark, to fall apart on me. You can have a breakdown later, once we get back to our room and are packing our bags to leave this nightmare."

"I'm not losing my…" Something hit him in the back of the head, hard enough to smart. Whatever hit him, it fell to the ground and clattered away into a dark corner. He could see, even from here, the bone from before had followed him down the tunnel.

"Even the spirits wish to tell you a thing or two," Janey said. "They mean for you to be a part of something."

"A part of what?"

Janey shrugged.

"We can't argue with ghosts," Vic said to James. "It's probably that poor maintenance man."

"Since when have you embraced ghosts?" He disliked the way she pretended the whole situation didn't freak her out. Just moments ago, back in the dark, she'd been the one to whimper and grouse. But he supposed this was better. He didn't want her to feel scared.

"I've written paranormal romance," she said, as if this should explain her change of demeanor, but James thought it had more to do with the well-lit environment they now found themselves in.

James smiled softly. "Pretty sure that doesn't qualify you as an expert, dear." When Vic frowned, he quickly added, "But you are an expert at romance."

"Well, I..." Vic started but didn't finish. She smiled instead when the last compliment sunk in. Vic nodded and said, "Let's just give the ghost what it wants and get out of here."

"It wants you to shut up and pay attention," Janey said.

James' eyes snapped from Vic's to Janey, and then to the grotto in the wall where Robbie still dug around. He knew exploring the grotto was the only way to stave off another assault from the spirit in the tunnel behind them. They needed to proceed. As he walked toward it, Vic slipped a hand in the crook of his arm. James took this as a good sign.

Robbie hauled something wrapped in a white cloth out into the light.

"A burial shroud," he said, "with something inside it. This must be hundreds of years old."

"There are more," Vic said and pointed down the cavern wall. "Several of them. This must be a burial ground."

"A sacrifice room," Janey said. "With seven grottos, seven bodies, seven spirits. Even long ago, they realized the benefit of killing a few to save many."

Hieroglyphs of live people carrying dead people stood out between the grottos dug into the cavern walls. Some of the figures carried knives, tips tainted red. One picture depicted a great beast sitting upon a throne fashioned from stick figures. Goosebumps formed on James' arms. The implications frightened him, and he hoped the sheriff and Janey could help them stay safe. The girl sounded like a human encyclopedia of fucked up shit, but the spirit inside her seemed to understand what was happening.

"Gross," James mumbled and realized this ritual had gone on for an eternity. He understood what Marion tried to do up in that room to Vic, before she failed and the beast came for her. *The cunt who failed*. And now he truly understood the whole ritual had failed. The one accomplished several times before but not this time, the killing of seven to save the rest.

"That's why we're here," Janey whispered as she stared, as if she peered directly into his soul. "It needs to end. So says the conduit."

Doesn't the girl ever blink?

Then she did and James blinked several times himself, and he knew she could read his thoughts. He took a step backward.

"Cunt," Janey mouthed, but no sound came out. "Violet turning black," she said out loud. When James could only shake his head, Janey turned. "We need to keep going. There is more we are intended to see. Before."

"Before what?" Robbie asked, hand on his Glock.

"Before the end," she whispered and walked on toward another tunnel entrance. Her ponytail swayed as she walked, and her tennis-shoes made soft little padding noises off the packed dirt. James tried to imagine her carrying a Hello Kitty lunchbox and couldn't quite envision it.

James' skin crawled. He didn't want to be a hero. He didn't want to save the world. Nor did he want to be sacrificed for the common good. He only wanted to go home with Vic, back to his residence where nothing exciting happened except the occasional sexcapade in the backyard. Vic especially enjoyed nudity within the confines of the backyard bushes. Then James heard the bone rattle again, back in the dark corner, and decided to get on his way before it hit him once more. The ghost didn't have to tell him twice.

"By the end, do you figure she means death? Are we going to die?" Vic rubbed her hands together. "If so, I want time to prepare. I mean, do I pray or what?"

"Of course, we won't die," James said, trying to sound reassuring. "But praying can't hurt." He couldn't remember the last time they'd attended services or prayed before they ate. Even when they had, earlier on, Vic never really participated. And, although they never discussed the matter, he would have guessed Vic an atheist. Religion just never came up.

"Do you believe in a higher power?" James asked, trying the theory on for size.

"I didn't. No. But, then again, I didn't believe in ghosts and cultists until recently. With all that's happened, well…I don't know. Ghosts speak to an afterlife. Maybe I shouldn't error on the side of being left outside the pearly gates." Vic looked around the large cavern before ducking inside the tunnel. "I'm frightened, James. And I'm woefully unprepared for my demise. What if I end up in the wrong place? What if we never have sex again?"

"Good Lord, Vic," James said as he entered the tunnel. "Why would you worry about that of all things?" Only Vic could worry about not making it into Heaven and never fucking again in the same thought.

"Because it's the only advantage we have over the spirits," she whispered. "We get to have an orgasm and they can't. Otherwise, they get to fly and float and stay invisible and mess with us. Fun things. So, I hate to take for granted the only thing we can hold over them."

James laughed and shook his head. Her logic didn't always hold, but he wouldn't point this out. No sense in it. She would only argue and keep them both from watching their backs. "Not to worry, Vic. We haven't screwed our last; I'm sure of it."

They trudged on down the shaft. Nothing rattled or scratched behind him or nailed him in the head. *Small blessings.* Then he heard Robbie yell something unintelligible from further up the tunnel.

"Do you think something is wrong up there?" Vic asked, stopping now.

James stopped behind her, feeling uncomfortable. He'd been punished a couple times already for not hurrying quickly enough. "Only one way to find out."

"Who wants to?"

"It's either that or go back the way we came, which leads nowhere but a pit we can't get out of." He paused. "I'm sure if it were too much to worry about, you know, the creature or worse, Robbie would have fired shots by now."

"One would think," Vic said. "What if he has lost his head, so to speak?" She laughed at this as she did sometimes, at her own jokes.

James didn't find this one very funny at all. Quite the contrary. The vision of Robbie beheaded, gun on the floor, blood flowing, rattled him to his core. That would mean the thing which caused said beheading would soon come for them. He imagined the thing turning from the sheriff and stomping toward them in the darkness. James took a deep breath. "I can do without the gallows humor."

Vic rolled her eyes. "Sometimes you're no fun at all." She swatted his ass, which echoed all around them and down the tunnel.

James winced, but knew she was wound up and on edge. Sex and bad jokes were her way of decompressing and making light of the situation.

"Violet and peach," Janey said.

Janey? His eyes snapped up to the child who was standing in front of them as if she had only materialized there in that moment.

"Move," she said. "There are things to see ahead."

"Easy," Vic said, her brow scrunched, lips twisted in a thoughtful pout. "We'll get there."

Janey turned and walked, and they followed.

James wondered how she managed that trick. She moved like a ghost herself and this scared him almost as much as real ghosts, cultists, and the creature itself. *Good Lord, she moves as quiet as a cat.* He continued behind her, obedient. *Like a sheep.*

After walking several paces, James could see the tunnel emptied into yet another cavern, this one better lit than the previous. As they drew closer, he noticed more of the shiny rocks wedged into the walls, and then he noticed Robbie walking around lighting torches that hung on the walls. He used a cigarette lighter.

With the good lighting, James could see what Robbie had raised his voice about. Piles of bone lay every so many yards, a human skull atop each. These bones looked newer, fresher, definitely in better condition than the ones back in the grottos. *More than the usual seven sets of piles. There must be a hundred.* James wondered if a rebellion amongst the people had occurred. *Or perhaps a failure.* And this was the price. The death of many because the death of the few failed. *Oh, no.*

"Who..." Janey whispered from right next to James. She stared at him, a serious look on her face, and then she grinned. The grin didn't reach her eyes. Her little-kid teeth looked dingy in the refracted light.

"Yes, no need to keep saying it," James whispered. He felt a tightening in his chest. The girl's eyes shone as if with their own light.

She grinned a moment longer and then walked through the field of bone piles like a macabre queen in her kingdom of horror. Then it hit him. This wasn't her kingdom, as appropriate as that seemed. No, this kingdom belonged to the thing that ripped off Marion's head and Jack Dowling's face. The thing that tried to come through the mirror. He looked up at Janey with respect. They needed her—he needed her. Only she could protect them; he knew this.

"Oh, James," Vic moaned. "This is too much. These poor people. What does it all mean?"

"Don't you see, Vic? It's like Janey's been telling us. They failed. They failed the creature, so it punished them by killing everyone. Or, at least, as many as it could get its hands on. It brought them here and then played with the bones." He imagined bits of gristle and red muscle and guts strewn about until time rendered them to nothing.

Vic's lips quivered as if she would refute his ideas but couldn't find the proper words. She looked around at all the piles and then at Robbie, who walked about looking at the piles as if he may recognize someone he knew.

Vic shook her head, and a tear swept down her cheek. James wasn't sure what the tear meant but supposed either fear or sorrow for the dead. He felt a twinge of guilt for convincing her to crawl down into the caverns. She was his wife, and he didn't want her frightened.

Janey stood in front of the next tunnel. "There is so much more," she said, just loud enough to hear.

The others remained frozen, as if waiting for something they couldn't see to tell them otherwise. It felt like the quiet before a storm—bigger than the storm outside.

And then it hit. The bones in each pile shook and rattled, the skull atop each dancing like a little person jumped up and down inside them.

"Good Lord!" Vic shrieked and grabbed her hair and whirled around to look everywhere at once.

Robbie spun around with his Glock, looking for a flesh and blood target.

"The spirits demand a recompense," Janey shouted over the din.

"The ones from the hotel or the ones from…here?" James asked. And he felt pleased with himself that he could articulate such a question given the unfortunate set of circumstances. While everyone else fell apart around him, he could still ask a pertinent question. Despite his forced bravery, James felt himself quake with fear.

"All of them," she said. "Isn't that the point?"

James wasn't sure that was the point at all.

Unhearing, uncaring about anything save striking out, Vic took a swing at the nearest pile of bones and sent them scattering to the floor like large white beetles. The skull from the top hit the ground, bounced once, and then landed in Vic's waiting arms. She screamed and flung the skull at another pile as if it were nothing but a carnival game. This started a domino effect which toppled several of the closer stacks of bones. James watched as they washed over and around Robbie's feet.

The piles kept falling. The cavern rang with the skittering of bones of various sizes and shapes, a deafening roar which forced James to cover his ears. He watched Robbie walk carefully through the bones, trying to reach Janey.

Janey stood staring into the darkness ahead like she didn't notice the bones rattling around her little feet. Her ponytail swung in lazy arcs, blowing in her personal existential winds.

"Take that!" Vic screamed. Her eyes were wide and white, hands on hips, chest heaving. "You don't scare me." A lie, James knew. She stumbled through the tide of bones and buried her head in James' shoulder and sobbed. "I can't take this."

With Vic's head in the crook of his arm, James stroked her hair and whispered into her ear, "It's going to be okay. You'll see."

James knew they were in trouble when he looked up from attending to Vic and all the piles were back in place, as if Vic never toppled them, the skulls on top like a cherry on a sundae. Robbie looked perplexed, ready to kill. Janey had already disappeared into the darkness.

Good Lord! What next?

Chapter 26

Snow exploded into a powdery deluge and obscured Angela's vision. The mound before them disappeared and then they were in midair amid snow and ice.

Angela couldn't see land, although, admittedly, she could see very little at all, some twinkling lights from the valley below and that was it. Miles' wielded the flashlight in wild strobes as he fought to hold on and this added to Angela's disorientation. As they completed their revolution, Angela wondered if they would continue to fall out into that dark void until they joined the lights of the copper refinery and homes way down below.

As this thought took root and panic filled her belly, a ridge of rocky earth sprang out of the blizzard before them. Angela's ski tips hit first, and one, the right, snapped off and disappeared out into the darkness. The remainder of the right ski dug in as the left slid its way up the escarpment, turning Angela upside down, right knee wrenching beneath her with a stab of pain while her torso twisted, and she landed on her stomach.

A softball sized rock down beneath the snow rammed into her ribcage and knocked the wind from her, but at least they seemed to have stopped. Although the world continued to spin. She could still feel Miles' arms around her neck and heard him moan. Angela fought her PTSD down, her brain reminding her of the last wipeout—the one that wiped out her little bundle of cells. *No, it wasn't the wipeout! Your doctor told you that!* Still, she would always blame herself, just in case. She took deep breaths and tried not to shed tears, for Miles' sake. Slowly, her limbs began to stop shaking.

"Oh, shit," Miles said. He let out a little sigh of pain, but Angela could tell he was trying not to show his discomfort to her. "That was close. Nice skiing, Angela. Another foot and it would have been meat-explosion city way down below."

Angela groaned and tried to decide if she dare move. She opened her eyes and noticed the three-foot ridge of rock before them, a lifesaver, the only thing between them and five-thousand feet of air. When she tried to imagine what a fall like that would feel like, Angela felt a twinge of nausea and her head spun more. "Ugh," she groaned, air finally entering her lungs again. "You okay, Miles?"

"I'll live," he said. "Just a little tender on my left hip. You okay?" Miles shone the flashlight right in her face.

"Yeah," she said, "now get that thing out of my eyes, please. Damn." Angela rubbed her belly, then her sore knee. The blow to the gut would cause some rib pain, and the knee may prove twisted but no worse. She would live, albeit in pain for a time. Angela lifted herself and came to rest on her good knee. She let out a breath. "Shit, that hurts."

"Hey, look!" Miles shouted. "Footprints!"

Everything rushed back to her then. *Em!* Indeed, a set of giant footprints led into the gloom behind them. And as Miles played the flashlight beam across the mountainside, she noticed the tracks disappeared into the jagged opening to a cave or mineshaft. The weak light did little except get eaten by the gloom of the cavern before them, but Angela could see the huge tracks went inside.

"Let's go," she said. Angela used her poles to release both bindings, then used them as an aid to bring herself to a standing position. Once up, grimacing with the effort, she immediately regretted not throwing her service-boots in a backpack. Now she would need to walk into the cave in the heavy ski boots. They would prove slippery and cumbersome, Angela knew, but no other choices existed unless she wanted to continue in stocking feet. *Not an option.* She took the flashlight from Miles and hobbled forward.

At the entrance, Angela could see an old set of mining-cart tracks headed inward. Before the landscape had eroded into a ledge and carried tons of earth away and into the valley, this opening had been a staging area for copper, and she knew carts upon carts came through this opening every day. Now the tracks lay tarnished and unused. Only, something else used the shaft now.

The smell from within raged against her sinuses, a combination of wet animal, feces, and rotted meat. Like the smell of the beast but somehow worse in this confined space. Angela wished she had a respirator for herself and Miles. Hell, she didn't even know if the air in the shaft was breathable. Didn't carbon monoxide sometimes push out all the air and create toxic environments? Then she thought of Em and drew her Glock. Thank God she hadn't lost it in the crash. Angela couldn't remember where the shotgun ended up and regretted not paying more attention. She'd been in too much of a hurry to save Em.

"Smells like Bigfoot shit on a rotten cucumber in here," Miles said.

Angela nodded, tried not to laugh at the kid because it hurt, and hobbled forward. Warmer in here, drops of fetid moisture fell from the ceiling and more moisture ran in dark streaks down the shaft walls. The timbers used to hold tons of rock in place lay covered in black slimy mold and looked close to disintegrating.

In for a penny, in for a pound, Angela thought and moved along. The shaft angled downward in a slight grade as they moved further inside the earth. Her heavy ski boots clacked off railroad beams and echoed out before them. In a puddle of moist dirt, a distinctive footprint lay right in the middle. The footprint looked gigantic, at least eighteen inches long, eight inches wide, and the huge toes were tipped with the imprints of rather intimidating claws.

"How can a spirit make a footprint?" Angela asked. She knew Miles understood this world better than she did in this regard. "I mean, you mentioned a spirit form. What's that mean, exactly?" She kept the Glock and flashlight pointed forward.

Miles held his salt canister like a weapon. "Well," he started, "some Squatchers think Bigfoot, you know, Sasquatch, the Yeti, cryptids like that, are spirit form creatures. That means they can take the form of a flesh and blood creature or of a spirit. So, theory holds. Anyway, that's why we don't find dead Bigfoots lying around, or their shit-piles, or much of anything else, except for a few tufts of hair and some footprints."

"But Bigfoot doesn't usually run around ripping heads off people," Angela said. "And don't, to the best of my knowledge, have a cult-following."

Miles shrugged. "Yeah, seems effed up, I know. There must be some explanation. Janey would know more, would feel it, sense it." He looked up at Angela with sad eyes. "I hope she's okay."

Angela nodded. "Soon as we find Em, we'll go find Janey. I promise."

Miles nodded back. "You must really love Em like crazy to follow her down there." He pointed forward into the darkness beyond the flashlight beam.

"I think so," Angela said. "I mean, we just kinda started this thing, where we're more than acquaintances, but, yeah, it feels strong like love."

"Then let's save her," Miles said. "I mean, seems as though adults were meant to couple up and you two aren't getting any younger. Just saying." He grinned.

"Whatever!" Angela admonished, but with a smile. She liked this kid and a small part of her wished she could have a kid like this. *Not in the cards*. She continued marching forward through the muck so as not to tear up in front of the kid. "I'm not that old. Anyway, what about you? Any friends that are girls at school or anywhere?"

By the light of the flashlight, Miles blushed. "Nah," he said. "Janey and I are half-assed home-schooled. So, we don't play with other kids much. Besides, girls are mostly gross. I mean, not you and Em, or even Janey and Tracy, but ones who, you know, wanna kiss and get mushy with me and crap." He shook his head.

"Your attitude will change," Angela said.

"Hope not," Miles said, but Angela didn't hear much conviction in the answer. She figured he liked girls fine and had probably already entertained the idea of girls as more than friends.

"So, what else do you know about these spirit form creatures?" Angela asked, changing the subject to something more useful. "There some secret trick to get rid of them?"

Miles shrugged. "Just like all ghosts and the paranormal and stuff like that, nobody ever knows for sure. Not like they ever carry on a full conversation with anyone." He paused. "Except Janey, sometimes...and other mediums. I mean, they say the spirits talk to them, but nobody ever believes because they can only hear one side of the whole thing, so they think Janey makes shit up and is a little bit crazy. I mean, she is, because she's possessed, but not because of her abilities. She's sharp as a tack there and is almost never wrong."

"Wish she was here," Angela said.

"Yeah," Miles agreed, "me, too. I guess."

"You guess?"

"You know?" He smiled. "Little sisters...pains in the ass. Sometimes she smells because she refuses to shower or take her bath, and she gets God-awful mad for no reason and sometimes she won't even talk at all. But I think that's when spirits are talking to her. Anyway, a lot of times she's sarcastic, and she cusses a lot. Stuff like that."

"Yeah, I get it," Angela said. "I have a little brother. But, for the record, you cuss like a sailor, too."

"Yeah, but I'm fourteen," Miles announced.

Angela smiled, then allowed a small puff of air to pass her lips which could have accounted for a laugh. They continued forward down the iron rails. The further down they went, the warmer and wetter it got. Her ski boots trudged through three inches of muck. She disliked this, but when she attempted to use the rails or the timbers, her feet would slip, so better the muck and hope for the best. The only good thing was the footprints trailed off out in front of them on a regular basis.

As she followed the behemoth tracks, Angela couldn't help but think about her own bundle of cells—the only ones she would ever likely carry—and wondered if her child would have ended up like either Janey or Miles. Part of her hoped so, but part hoped not, in equal measure. Although she dug Miles, he spouted off a lot, seemed to have no fear whatsoever, and pretty much did what he pleased. Could she have handled a child who didn't depend on her, who, at fourteen, would light off after a cryptid in the darkness instead of hiding and trembling in fear? Angela didn't know the answer to that. Although, strange as he often seemed, she liked Miles and imagined she would enjoy Janey as much. A tear slipped from her eye and she angrily wiped it away before Miles got snoopy.

Through the film of moisture, Angela could make out something on the tunnel wall ahead. A symbol. More specifically, a star with a circle drawn around it.

"A pentagram!" Miles said.

"Is that bad?" Angela asked, Glock still raised.

"Depends," Miles said. "Right side up, well, then that's okay. See, lots of well-meaning religions use a right-side-up pentagram. But—but, not this one. You see, it's upside down and that's never good. Only bad witches casting dark magic, conjuring dark spirits, would use that. Tracy says demons use them as their calling cards."

"Great," Angela said. Part of her hoped someone had used the pentagram to try to rid the place of this spirit form beast. But, according to Miles, the opposite may prove true. Perhaps someone used it to conjure the thing or to enhance or harness its powers.

The cavern, with its dark and wet walls, seemed to shrink around her, encapsulate her and Miles until it felt like a tomb. Angela forced herself to trudge on before panic set in.

A little further up, on the left-hand side of the tunnel, a small rockslide had formed a pile of rubble on the ground and uncovered a tunnel, at least that's what the dark maw looked like to Angela. And, as luck would have it, the tracks led right into the darkness of the newer side-tunnel.

"Holy shit, look!" Miles said and rushed forward. He knelt by the pile of rubble.

When Angela arrived, she also noticed the pile of bones, a human skull, and a pickaxe buried, in part, beneath.

Miles wrestled the axe-handle away from the skeleton and hefted the pickaxe. The thing looked old, handle splintered, the iron pick-head tarnished with orange oxidation. He swung it a couple times. "Kick ass!" he said. "Now, I can fight."

Angela, against her better judgment, decided to let him keep the thing, then turned her attention to the slide. The dirt and rock looked newer, fresher, meaning it hadn't been exposed as long. So, a newer development than the mining efforts, Angela reckoned. How new, she possessed no idea, but by the looks of the skeleton, quite a bit of time had elapsed since.

"The stink is coming from that way," Miles said, pointing into the darkness of the newer tunnel. He looked at the pile and the remains. "Looks like the miners might have discovered more than they bargained for."

"Looks that way," Angela agreed. She imagined the miner, whose remains lay beneath the rubble, chopping at a copper vein, doing his job, when the mine collapsed inward. The man probably got crushed and then suffocated. *And they left him here. Why?* She didn't think she wanted to know the answer, but part of her already did.

As if he read her mind, Miles said, "They dug into its lair by accident. Bet they regretted that."

Angela thought about the landslide which brought the old jailhouse down. She remembered how Harold wouldn't let any of them go down and retrieve stuff. *He knew*, Angela thought. *He knew and covered it up. Probably thought he was saving lives.*

"Bet this thing lived back in here forever, way before the mining started," Miles said. "Cryptids like dark out-of-the-way places."

"Sure," Angela said. She shivered despite the temperature and imagined eyes on her back, scanning, waiting for the perfect moment to strike. "But that doesn't explain the cult and the pentagram and all the other stuff."

Miles shrugged and nodded. "Guess we better go up in there." He peered into the black tunnel.

Angela nodded. Is this what she really wanted to do, drag this kid up into the beast's lair? As a deputy, she thought maybe the kid's safety should come first. But then what of Em? Angela set her jaw and decided, then stepped past Miles and into the gloom. They would go save Em and Angela would keep the kid as safe as reasonably possible. She found she needed to plug her nose cavity with her tongue pressed to the roof of her mouth, so the stink didn't pollute her. The flashlight bounced off rock walls which looked as if they were fashioned from a different material altogether. Once inside the opening, Angela noticed the breach had erupted when the mining tunnel got too close to this tunnel. The slide had occurred where the two tunnels shared a wall that got too thin. The older tunnel went off in two directions, just as the newer one had.

"Which way?" Miles asked.

Angela turned toward the mountain, the direction which would take them beneath the city of Jerome, way deeper than any storm drains or utility tunnels. The bottom of this tunnel appeared packed hard, and no footprints showed the way, but Angela felt sure they should travel toward the heart of the mountain. The terrain in this direction appeared to run uphill, the other down, the opposite of the mine shaft. *What a stroke of misfortune that these two shafts bisected at all.*

"This way," Angela answered and began to creep upward, flashlight and Glock pointed ahead, ski boots thumping on the packed dirt. She seemed to feel a presence, a coldness. She never believed in evil, but now knew this is what it felt like. If Em lay in this direction, then this direction she would go.

"High EMF," Miles said. "I can feel it. Some people need a device to tell them, but I've been doing this so long I would know that feeling anywhere. You know, goosebumps on the neck, skin crawling on my scalp."

"That mean we're heading in the correct direction?"

"Depends on your definition of correct," Miles said, a grin on his face. He swung his axe for good measure.

"The direction it took Em," Angela clarified.

"If I was a betting man, yep. Which I totally would be if dad let me go to the casinos, but he won't on account of he thinks I would blow all my money and such."

"Well, you would," Angela said.

Miles sighed. "You're as bad as him."

They continued, the grade still uphill but not so uphill one needed to lean forward or dig their toes into the mud. Just enough to tax Angela's sore knee, especially while walking in the stiff ski boot. She rubbed at it, careful to keep her eyes and flashlight forward.

Miles practiced swinging the pickaxe again, as if he could defeat this creature on his own. If bullets couldn't stop it, even when in solid form, then how would a hand tool fare? Angela felt skeptical but figured the actions made the kid feel better, more in control of his situation. Kids needed that control, she knew.

As they trudged on, Angela's head felt more and more buzzy, as if more of what Miles called EMF floated in the air. Goosebumps formed on her arms and her heart pounded harder than when they had almost spilled out over the ledge. Angela wanted to burst from her skin, wanted to shoot her Glock into the darkness until no bullets remained. Even a small part of her thought suicide would prove a far better option than continuing into the den of this beast. The air became thicker, both with energy and stench, and Angela found it hard to breath. If not for Em, she would have turned back. Just the thought of the woman in the possession of this monster gave energy to her tired limbs.

Fight!

"Is that light up there?" Miles asked, finger pointing up into the darkness.

Angela turned off the flashlight, and when she did, her imagination nagged at her, whispered that the beast now stood right behind her, ready to pounce and decapitate her. She took deep breaths and forced herself to remain calm. After a moment, when her eyes adjusted enough, Angela noticed a weak light from somewhere off in the distance.

"I think so," Angela whispered. "Let's go."

Then Angela heard a gunshot. Shortly after, a woman screamed. That woman sounded like Em! Angela ran as best she could in the cumbersome boots, legs and arms pumping, flashlight wavering around like a disco-ball, breaths coming out fast and short. She needed to get to the woman she loved.

Chapter 27

"Now, Vic..." James started. He knew this may be too much for her. His broken nose throbbed from just saying the words.

Vic scanned the room and looked as though she was about to scream, eyes teary and bright, mouth open. "How? Who picked all the bones back up? Why?" She looked James in the eye. "Did you see? How did the piles get back to their original place?"

"I didn't see," James said. "But does anything surprise you? Perhaps it was all a hallucination meant to frighten us." *Or warn us.* He touched his nose with an index finger.

Vic looked at him and, despite the scare from the bones, looked like she might say something kind about his nose situation.

Someone screamed from down the next tunnel. A female, James thought. The tone of the voice sounded frightened or lost and made the hairs on his neck raise.

"This way!" Robbie said, walking off into the dark tunnel. "That didn't sound like Janey. And I don't know what just happened here, but I don't think it's safe to stay put."

"Who screamed?" Vic asked.

"Well, I'm not sure," James said. "I think we're about to find out, if we follow the sheriff."

"She sounded terrified," Vic said. "I seriously hope there's not more trouble ahead. Who else would have crawled down in these tunnels?"

James thought about that and didn't have a good answer. It could be anybody. Maybe the kids' aunt came looking for them. But that made little sense, because how could she know where they were? "Let's just follow the sheriff. It seems the safest, and most prudent, course of action for now." He tried to breathe through his nose and found it impossible.

The skulls began to bounce atop their piles, making a clackity rhythm which sounded a lot like coarse laughter. He stared at them, hoping not to see red eyes staring back at him. He imagined all the bones shifting and forming into one large monster, a Transformer from the bowels of Hell.

Vic stood where she was and stared, mouth still open.

"Let's go," James said, voice as firm as he dared use with Vic and with the pain in his nose. He felt the need to take control before the bones decided on something insidious. "I think we need to follow the man with the gun, and I have no idea where Janey got to."

"Rattling bones or a screaming woman," Vic said. "Some choice."

Vic stumbled forward toward the tunnel. James shown the light at her feet so she didn't trip over any of the stray bones that didn't belong to the still-rattling piles. A moan arose from her throat as if she were a flesh-eater from a Romero movie. Then Vic seemed to catch herself and stopped.

James gave one last look behind them to make sure nothing had snuck up from behind. *Thank, God.*

"Don't leave me in the dark," Vic said.

"I'm coming," James said. "I needed to check our rears. We can't be too careful."

"I don't see why," Vic said. "There is no safe place down here." After a huff of breath, she moved forward.

Somewhere up in front of them, James could make out a faint light. It seemed more subdued than a flashlight. *Perhaps a door to the outside*. He could see neither Robbie nor the girl. He hoped nothing untoward came at them, out of the darkness. Without Robbie's gun or the girl's arcane knowledge, such as the spirit inside her allowed, they were doomed. The stench down here alone could make a maggot vomit.

After he and Vic walked a couple tentative steps, James heard Robbie shout from up ahead. It sounded like a loud conversation or someone pleading their case. *Maybe there's a maniac up there, or a ghost, or, worse yet, the thing who decapitated Marion and skinned Dowling and tried to come through the mirror and grab Janey.* James considered going back. Maybe they could boost each other out of the pit and he and Vic could then find a way to get the locked coal-door open.

"Are you coming?" Vic asked when she noticed he had dropped behind. "Because we need that flashlight." She seemed to think a moment. "I see. You're frightened. I can see it in your eyes, James. Well, you should have thought it through more thoroughly before you jumped into that pit after the girl. I tried to tell you, but now we're locked into this course of action. Ghosts or no ghosts, we need to move forward. The sheriff and the girl are up there."

James found himself in the peculiar situation where he could still hear the bones of the dead rattling around back there in the dark and the heated conversation up ahead. He didn't understand any of this, except this must be the beast's hideout, and here they were, moving right into the belly of the thing. His imagination told him that in the past, the thing had fed upon the flesh which once populated those bones. It likely popped out their eyeballs and gorged its maw, strands of flesh removed and thrust down the thing's ephemeral throat, brains turned into dessert. James closed his eyes and took a deep breath. He knew he had absolutely zero proof any of that happened. He prided himself in always making the prudent choice, so how could he have failed with such great success this time? How could any of this exist in the reality which he'd so finely crafted for himself? He taught school kids how to enjoy great American literature, for God's sake. Things like this didn't happen to prudent men like him.

"James!" Vic snapped. "Give me the flashlight. I see your life flashing before your eyes, so if you're going to pick this moment to break down, let me have our only saving grace, please. I know your nose hurts, but I need you with me." She placed one hand on her left hip while the other extended toward him.

Shit! He needed to snap out of his doldrums and act. Instead of handing her the flashlight, James grabbed Vic's hand and said, "Let's go." They moved together toward what looked like another well-lit cavern.

James thought perhaps—as Vic wasn't one who exercised to any great degree—she would tire, or become winded, but the closer they got to the light, the faster she pushed herself forward. Whether motivated by the bones behind them or the fact her psyche couldn't handle the possibility of a situation where they were left alone for dead, James didn't know. But he figured some internal motivation must be at the root of this energetic fast-paced walk.

Sometimes she got like this in bed, as if making love to him would save her life, sweat dripping, impaled upon him, hips striving back and forth, and then up and down. Finally, she would drop to his chest in exhaustion. Yes, her burst of energy would cost her, and they would see just how expensive the bill was in the end. In their bedroom, she could fall asleep. Here, deep within the earth, the dip in energy level may keep them from running if needed.

They finally staggered into the light of the next cavern and looked around. Vic's skin looked pale and thin, a sheen of sweat built up from the scurry through the dark, and the woman's dishwater blonde locks appeared sweat-laden and untidy. *But she'll push through,* he thought.

Vic, as James suspected she might, collapsed against him, head on his chest. He could feel her heart pounding, and her breaths came hard and heavy. He figured this exhaustion was from a combination of physical exertion and fear. "Oh, God," Vic whispered and brought her hand to her mouth.

"Easy now," he whispered even as he glanced up. More of the shiny glass rocks enhanced the light of four flickering torches. *Good Lord!* This was a lot to take in. James understood where the scream and loud conversation originated. Robbie was speaking with a pretty gal standing inside a wooden cage above his head. Then James took in the whole cavern and took a step backward.

On top of seven more alcoves in the walls, a wooden stick-built chair sat in a corner. Inset within the folds of wood, white bones stuck out like large macabre porcupine quills which forced James to recall the art on the cavern wall. The complete skeleton of a Native American chief, decorated with headdress and bejeweled hatchet on a belt at his side, sat upon the chair like it was his throne to rule this underworld. In front of the throne, sitting in a circle on the cavern floor for the chief's inspection, were four headless corpses. They were fully clothed and possessed all their flesh as if they'd just died and appeared here.

James found this too much to process all at once. The smell in here alone made him want to vomit, and the sight of so much death made him think he may be the next to start his long dirt-nap in this underground chamber. Whatever killed all these people would most certainly come for the rest of them.

"My God," Vic whispered as she pressed against him so hard James got the impression she wanted to hide inside of him.

James noticed Janey walking over by the chief, hands behind her back as if she were out on a family picnic. Then he remembered her family and thought a family picnic may consist of such things, old hat for the girl, as boring as walking to the Department of Natural Resources outhouse for a potty break at the local beach area. Her lips moved in a continuous quivering thrum as if she carried on with a never-ending conversation only she and the chief could hear. Then James watched as Janey picked up an old clay container and looked inside it. Her button-nose scrunched.

The container looked ancient with designs carved into the top, which matched some that also decorated the walls in the cavern.

Robbie asked a question of the girl up in the cage. "Who put you way up there, Em? Who killed these people?" Robbie walked over to the circle of fresh kills and pointed at one dressed in a deputy's uniform. "Who killed Harold?" His voice sounded high-pitched with disbelief. "And here's Jeb and Marion and Penny! Even headless, I can tell that much."

"I told you," Em said. She hung on to the bars as the cage rocked back and forth with a slight motion. Her eyes were wide with fear. "This huge monster grabbed me from the jailhouse and brought me here. It must have brought all them here. Angela and I tried to stop it, but it's too strong."

"Where's Angela?" Robbie asked.

"Looking for me, I hope," Em said. "Her and Miles, although I kinda hope she left the boy behind. This is no place for a kid." She glanced at the girl. "That's got to be Janey."

Janey looked up at Em. "Miles," she whispered.

Em nodded and smiled. "He's okay," she said. "Last I saw. He's a brave kid. Kinda wild."

Janey smirked and turned back to the container as if it held the answers to all the mysteries of this place.

Em turned her attention back to Robbie. "You gotta get me down from here before it gets back." Tears formed at the bottoms of her eyes and slid down her cheeks. "It showed me," Em tapped at her skull, "in here, what it would do to me. Please, get me down." She wrapped both arms around herself and held her legs close together. Suddenly, James understood what the beast must have shown her. It didn't just plan to decapitate her, but violate her first.

"My God," Vic repeated. Then she walked slowly toward the cage. "Let's get her down. Can't you see she's frightened? No offense, but who gives a rat's ass-end about a deputy who's already deceased? I mean, look at him, all of them. They're dead, and she's alive. Your answers can come later." She stood with hands on her hips and James noticed the color returning to her face. Vic could go from zero to sixty and back down just as quickly when properly motivated. Or when it suited her.

James wondered when Vic had grown a pair. But it fit right into her erratic behavior as of late, terrified one moment, defiant and haughty the next. Her response to stress, James assumed. He rather enjoyed it.

"Well, easier said than done," Robbie said, looking up. "That cage is fifteen feet off the ground and tied to something on the ceiling. I don't see a ladder. And I can't shoot the rope up there because I have no way to catch the cage when it falls. Besides, the bullets could hit one of you...or myself."

"Wait," Janey said. Then she turned to a passageway which exited the cavern. "Miles."

"What?" James asked. "What about your brother?"

A chorus of shouts drifted from the darkness. James heard shuffling feet, and for a moment, he feared the beast was upon them, ready to take their heads. He braced himself for action, but then Miles and a female deputy ran into the cavern, breathing hard and looking everywhere at once. The woman wore heavy ski boots and Miles carried a dangerous looking pickaxe.

Good Lord! James thought. *He'll kill himself or someone else with that rusty old thing.*

"Em!" the female deputy shouted. She glanced from Em to all the dark corners of the cavern as if the creature may lay in wait for her. She ran on the clunky ski boots until she stood beneath the girl in the cage. "Where is it?"

"I knew you'd come!" Em said, a huge smile on her face, eyes love-crazed and shiny. James remembered that look coming from Vic in years gone by. "Oh, my God, I love you." She must have realized what the deputy asked her, because she shook her head. "It's not here. It locked me up in this shithole and then split."

"Angela?" Robbie asked, confused. "Where did you come from?"

Janey approached Miles, a stern look about her, hands behind her back, lips in a straight line, eyes glaring. "Cunt," she whispered, then she smiled in a way that smacked to James of collusion in crime.

"Missed you, too," Miles said to Janey and punched her in the shoulder. "What you got figured out?" Both kids were huddled together, whispering to each other. Miles nodded a lot and then spoke a little. Janey whisper-hissed, her rasping voice making her sound like a fiend.

Angela looked to Robbie. "I followed the creature's tracks down the old cliff on skis, then I followed them into an old mine shaft. The shaft bisects this place." Angela spread her arms to represent the cavern. Then she looked back up at Em. "How we gonna get her down?"

James thought the deputy appeared more desperate to free Em than she was to save the rest of them. He wondered how this may play out if the situation called for quick action or a prudent exit strategy.

One never knew about new love and the actions of the infected, how these plans often excluded all others.

"We were just discussing that," Robbie said. He squinted at her. "Are you serious? There really is a creature. I've seen some things I can't explain tonight, a lot, and I may need to reconsider my beliefs about ghosts. But a creature, an actual monster, is hard to swallow."

"You've seen the cave drawings," James said.

Robbie nodded.

"You best wrap your mind around it, Mister," Miles said. "We've fought that thing off all night."

"Fought it?" James asked.

"Yep," Miles said as he swung his pickaxe, "with salt and bullets. And it still got Em." He pointed at Em up in the cage, his eyes sad. "We gotta get her down."

Robbie nodded and looked around the cavern and then up at Em.

"You are a brave young man," James said. Most of the kids he taught would be hiding somewhere. It did bother him a kid found the need to fight this thing when there were adults around who should have stepped in, but he supposed Miles and Janey were different than most kids he'd ever met. "Can you help us adults formulate a plan?"

"James," Vic said. "Really? You want to be part of the planning now? What would your plan be, per se?" She smiled at him in a way which told him she was kidding but not kidding.

"Violet turning black," Janey said, and she sounded displeased, arms crossed over her chest, eyes stormy and wicked. "The one older than time shall return. So says the conduit."

"I don't really understand a thing these kids are talking about, and I'd feel more comfortable if I were the one doing the questioning and getting the answers to those questions." When everyone turned to Robbie like maybe he was missing the point, he added, "Yes, of course, the kids know things, and I'll take those things into account."

Everyone began to speak at once about what they knew and what they thought they knew. Miles talked about the creature, Vic about wanting out of here, the sheriff trying to ask questions, and Em screaming she wanted the fuck down from her high-rise apartment because the slumlord who owned the wooden piece of shit wanted to brutalize her.

That's when Angela broke proper police protocol and shot her Glock at the ceiling.

Chapter 28

The Demon and its Beast

Dark energy from the demon teamed inside the simple beast. The beast had proven to be the perfect vessel, made of both spirit and flesh, and the only creature large and powerful enough to carry such a substantial spiritual load. It provided other advantages, as well. The seven sacrifices had failed for the first time in centuries. Now, instead of only seven sacks of flesh and blood, it could feast upon the souls and flesh of whomever it pleased. Its lair would be full of flesh once more.

The demon forced the simple beast forward toward a house with a running generator. It contemplated how to enter. As a spirit or flesh-and-blood? Both provided certain advantages but nothing could beat the pleasures felt when it allowed the simple beast to roam in flesh-and-blood mode. It could feel every nerve fire, every synapse, every tasty emotion. *Orgasms!* Especially, it enjoyed drinking the fear of its victims. The only drawback: this state left the simple beast vulnerable to physical harm, but nobody remained to harm it.

Lights blossomed from within and the beast trudged on stump-like legs through thirty inches of snow, the white precipitation still falling and collecting on the simple beast's dark fur. The moisture caused the simple beast to stink, foul and pungent, and this increased the humans' fear. And the more fear they felt, the more energy the demon received.

The demon wondered how these humans would react. Would they put up any form of resistance? It doubted this and finally settled on a plan, a level of depravity it hadn't yet achieved. It felt emboldened without the constraints of the ritual. It would begin with a good scalping and the wearing of said scalp. Yes, that should sufficiently cow the rest of the household while the simple beast ran around with mommy's bloody scalp on its huge head.

Such a sordid act would break the man-of-the-house's mind and reduce the offspring to blathering idiots. Then the real fun could begin. Not just heads ripped off this time. *Full tilt boogie!*

Thoughtfully, the demon considered entering through the basement windows. A basement was a luxury in these parts, but the windows made the demon feel uneasy. It would avoid them.

The simple beast loped up the front walk, moved across the front porch, and then the demon made it smash in the front door. Sure, it could have slithered in through the antique mirror it sensed hung on the bathroom wall, but the demon was tired of subtlety.

On screeching hinges bent past their usefulness, the door tore away, the lock mechanism bursting from the doorjamb in a spray of wooden splinters. The door crashed to the floor, toppled once, and then came to rest against a couch.

The demon wished the simple beast's talents extended to speech, because it wanted so badly to scream, "Here's Johnny!" He wished for an axe with such an intensity the simple beast drooled long strings of saliva. The demon waited with expectation, but no humans screamed or ran around pissing themselves. In fact, not a single soul took notice. This didn't feel right, nor did it feel satisfying in the visceral way it had come to expect.

It forced the simple beast to bellow and stomp its huge feet, just in case the humans in this household were late to the party or disabled in a way which prevented their display of terror.

Nothing.

Perhaps the human flesh had exited out the back, but the demon didn't think so. It would have sensed this. Or the simple beast, whose hearing proved impeccable, would have heard their flight. No, this house felt pre-naturally quiet. The quiet of spells and dark magic.

The demon forced the simple creature to creep along as slow as possible for its large frame. The only sound came from the generator which hummed from somewhere in the back of the house.

Then it remembered the basement, and the windows for which it had not cared. In the heat of the moment, during the climax of entry, the demon had given the basement little thought. It paused to contemplate the implications. Perhaps these humans knew a little something about protections and wards and spells, even a ritual or two or three. No matter, their skill could not equal his, but a thrum of excitement for a good chase coursed through the demon's dark energy.

Let's dance, it thought. *And when I'm done dancing with you, I will enjoy dancing on your desiccated bodies and within the pool of human blood spilled from them.* For effect, it made the beast chortle, the sound like dead cornstalks in a stiff wind.

The demon watched through the beast's eyes as the hairy thing moved through the quiet home. The walls were covered with dreamcatchers. *A house of some pretense then.* The dreamcatchers amused the demon as firecrackers may amuse a soldier or, in some cases, annoy them or cause flashbacks. But the demon held no such inconvenience. It had never been bested and didn't intend to be this time.

It walked down a hallway and into a well-lit kitchen. The kitchen sparkled with cleanliness and smelled faintly of cleaning products. The demon wished to defile the place, litter it with human remains, drive the stench of clean and innocent from the home and replace it with the odor of flayed human, of bowels, and excrement and blood.

Dark energy seethed and roiled within the simple beast's infested mind, the desire to rend growing. It would turn these humans to red pulp and mist, but not before much agony. It would begin at their feet and work its way up, leaving no pain-center unexplored. It would rend their outsides and their insides, and they would live long enough to feel every exploration.

Then it noticed the basement door. Just a basic wooden door with eight raised panels, easily destroyed and dispatched. But upon the wood rectangle, carved right through the ridges that bisected each panel of wood, a pentagram stared at the demon like an unblinking eye. Whoever crafted this could revel in the fact they did the job correctly, the pentagonal point thrust upward like a middle finger.

This gave the demon pause. This pentagram would not prove to be the work of a minion or one of the cultists or any other type of familiar. No, the human responsible for this would lay on the other side of the door, with the righteous—with those who the demon abhorred and enjoyed defiling. *The innocent.*

A growl ripped from deep inside the simple creature. The pentagram reminded it too much of the boy and the girl and their magic and their salt.

The simple creature, upon the demon's command, reached out and touched the pentagram. The demon felt the small—*miniscule*—vibration and tingle of electricity. *Laughable.* It forced the beast to push through the slight discomfort and smash the wooden door.

Upon impact, the door folded inward, and then the half not attached to the hinges teetered and finally bounced down the basement stairs with a loud clatter.

The demon listened for screams—the screaming induced by the failure of the humans' meager and ineffectual protections.

Silence.

They can't be so gifted as this. The demon imagined how amusing the situation would be if nobody hid down in the basement at all, if he forced the beast downstairs only to find a basement devoid of flesh.

No, the demon was sure they were down there. *Waiting.*

Patience gone, the demon turned the beast's body and pounded down the basement steps. One board broke and the beast's foot fell through, but the demon's rage was enough to force the appendage back out and it continued down the steps.

To the right lay a laundry room, dark and devoid of human flesh—at least flesh the demon could sense. It decided to trust its abilities which had never failed it, and it continued down a poorly lit hallway. This lack of illumination puzzled the demon. Never had it encountered humans who didn't enjoy the comfort of every bit of light they could get, especially when frightened.

The demon wanted the humans to whimper and screech but when this didn't happen, it pounded down the hallway and spilled out into a large living area. In the far-right corner of the room sat an old skeleton in a white rocking chair. Gray hair stood out from the back of the skeleton's cranium and dusty clothing covered some but not all the remains. The skull grinned at the demon.

What is this devilry? It didn't recognize the deceased woman in the chair, nor did it care to, but where had it come from? Had the humans who lived here kept this stinking corpse in the rocking chair all this time? If so, they were like no humans the demon had ever encountered. *They must be deranged.* Not even the cultists kept corpses lying about in their homes. Sure, they gave them willingly to the demon every thirty years but didn't save any for themselves so they could peer at them from time to time. Then the demon began to wonder. *Are they worshipping another of my kind?*

A human voice reached out to it from behind. "Got you right where we want you," the voice said. "Grandma told us you'd show up sooner or later."

Bless the dark lord. The demon forced the simple beast to turn and explore the darkness behind it. It noticed the writing, written in a cuneiform spell-script, on the walls and wondered how it hadn't noticed this detail before. It heard a noise behind it and turned to find the rocking chair rocking back and forth. *A ghost then?* Well, it could swallow ghost energy just as well as a living soul. Then it noticed for the first time the simple beast stood within another pentagram. *Oh, shit.*

"Grandma says you're fucked," the voice said. A teenage girl stepped out of the gloom of the hallway, black hair pulled up behind her, exposing a thin neck adorned with a plethora of vine and flora tattoos. Her dark eyes watched the beast with a mix of fascination and disdain. She wore black formfitting flower-print leggings, the kind that made the demon wonder what lay beneath. It would like to find out but somehow doubted it would get the opportunity. Thinking this made the beast drool, large globs of spittle falling to the floor.

"You're gross," the girl said, and then began to speak in the old language, the language of the dark ones, the old gods. "Grandma taught me about scum like you and it's time to return you back to your master." She continued whispering in the old language.

The demon took a step toward the girl, making ready to rip her pretty head from her willowy body. Then he'd use her upturned head to drink the last vestiges of plasma pumping from her neck like a human stein. When the demon forced a second step, it found something held the beast's foot stationary.

Looking back, the demon noticed the pentagram had turned into a gateway of darkness and a tentacle had encircled the simple beast's ankle. A crude and simple trick at best. It didn't sense the pentagram, nor the minor demon, possessed enough energy to hold the simple beast for long—not coupled with the demon's own powers.

The rocking chair continued to rock, and the demon wished the revenant would cease with its little parlor trick, because it felt like a distraction. The beast bellowed with rage.

The girl walked toward it, chanting some arcane words the demon had never heard before, and it could feel her meager—*very meager*—power encircle the beast's shoulders. With the tentacle and the meager energy, the demon felt the slightest bit off-balance but managed to hold its ground.

Shaking it side to side, the dark-haired girl held a canister of salt in her right hand. The demon wondered how so many people had learned the properties of salt as related to the demonic. Did some new grimoire exist which spelled out the use of salt so exactly? It didn't matter. The demon planned to end this game right now.

The demon forced the simple beast into its spirit form and then slipped from the tentacled grasp like black vapor. It hovered in the air a moment, enraged by the smug girl, but flew upward before she could hurl a wave of salt at it. It thought about going right back down and showing the black-haired girl what it did to its victims but then thought better. It would come back after it fueled up, when nothing could stop it. Not a girl with salt, or a deceased grandmother, or even a stupid tentacled minor demon.

Enraged, it flew out and into the blizzard. Someone would pay, and the demon knew who. The girl inside the wooden cage would feel its wrath and sate its need for retribution. It would split her in two using the simple beast's assets. Yes, that would do the trick. This would fuel the demon's depleted energy levels. And after it accomplished this, it would come back for the black-haired girl and her ghostly grandmother. And the stupid minor demon would become the simple beast's calamari.

Chapter 29

"Do I have your attention now?" Angela shouted.

"Holy shit!" Miles exclaimed. "How could you not? 'Cept now my ears are ringing."

Janey didn't seem to notice and continued to study the corpse of the old chief sitting on the throne.

"Em needs our undivided attention," Angela said, Glock still pointed at the ceiling.

"Take it easy," Robbie said. "No need to discharge your piece. I'm still the sheriff and..."

"I don't give two fucks about the authority structure," Angela said. "It means nothing here and now. And when this is all done," she turned her head upward to Em, "you can't fire me because I quit."

"That's right," Em said. "We'll move to a warm place and start our new life. We'll find a nice rent-friendly bungalow within walking distance of the beach and shack up and cuddle and watch movies and—and other stuff."

"Stuff like kissing," Miles said, grinning. He bounced his canister of salt in his right hand, the pickaxe gripped in his left. Angela thought he looked ready for battle.

"I've been through this with the others," Robbie said. "There's no ladder. And I don't dare shoot the cage down. The fall might kill her."

Janey continued to examine the skeleton of the chief, hands behind her back like the grim curator of a macabre museum display.

Angela thought about what Robbie said, her mind trying to find another solution. They'd need to go for a ladder. She noticed the man Robbie called James and the woman who must be his wife speak quietly to each other. James looked like he wanted to come talk with her, but his wife kept holding his chin and demanding his attention.

Robbie walked over to her. "What do you propose then? Even if we get her down, can we get out the way you came in? Because there's no going back the way we came." He looked sincere and just as confused as everyone else. Angela wondered what horrors he had already encountered.

"Listen to Miles for one," Angela said. "He seems to know about the kind of things we're dealing with here." Robbie seemed to contemplate this as he looked to the schoolteacher for support. But James was looking down and shuffling his feet beneath the gaze of his wife. Robbie let out a breath and shook his head.

"I've spent time with both children, and they do seem knowledgeable about the things that plague us," James said. His wife kept glancing from him to the dark tunnel behind them as if she expected something to lurch out of it. "As adults, we may need to take a backseat and listen."

"By all means," Robbie finally said, and then glanced up at Em, frowned as if disappointed in something, and finally turned to Janey. "She has been communicating with the spirits down here."

Janey ignored Robbie and stared at the dark opening in the cavern where Angela and Miles had come from. "It comes," she whispered.

"What comes?" Robbie asked. "More ghosts? The monster?"

Miles hefted his pickaxe, and Angela involuntarily placed her hand on the butt of her Glock which she had finally just holstered. Ice spiders raced up her spine. Adrenaline flowed and buzzed through her like a swarm of tingly bees. She knew what was coming.

"Yes," Janey said. "The thing made from ghosts, a simple beast and that which is older than time. So says the conduit." Her ponytail swung as if in a breeze or as if a ghostly hand tussled it in a friendly gesture.

"This creature," Robbie said and then paused. Angela saw doubt wash over his features. Finally, "how do we stop it?"

"It's real," Angela said to Robbie. She nodded her head and gritted her teeth. "I've seen it and it's real…really mad, and really dangerous." Angela needed Robbie one-hundred percent on board and ready to fight. She glanced back up at Em and decided the only thing she could do was protect the woman.

"Okay," Robbie said with a sigh built into the words. "It's real. What do we do?"

Janey took a step toward the entrance and stared. Miles crept behind her with his axe, ready to defend her.

"Janey?" Robbie asked. "What do I do?"

"Finish what they couldn't," Janey said and pointed at the circle of four headless corpses. She seemed to think a moment. She whispered in a much deeper tone, "That's not correct. Not what they started. We need to kill it, not fuel it." She paused. "Yes," she agreed with nobody anyone could see. Then Janey walked up to the circle of four bodies.

"Don't touch those," James said. "They're unsanitary. Can't you smell them?"

His wife elbowed him in the ribs. "Is that really important right now? I don't think Janey needs an ear full of your mansplaining to keep herself...sanitary. Now shush and let the girl and the authorities arrive at a solution."

James nodded and Angela was only moderately surprised when the man gave his wife a hug.

Janey, with a sudden burst of activity, kicked and spit on one of the corpses. "The cunt *who* failed," Janey said. "But I won't." She spat again, and the glob landed on the poor woman's neck stump and mingled with the dried blood.

"She's possessed for sure," Miles said. "Dad's gonna be pissed."

"Who are you?" Angela asked, because it felt right, even though she couldn't explain her feelings. "You're not just a girl."

Janey glanced at Angela with pitch-black eyes and smirked. "Cunt," she whispered. "I'm Janey...and the spirit from the board. The spirit from the board...and Janey." Angela felt a bolt of shock at this. Even the girl's voice sounded different from what she'd heard previous. She thought back to what Miles had explained about the incident with the Ouija board and now believed every word.

"Tracy is gonna be pissed too," Miles said. He swung his pickaxe.

Robbie looked to Miles as if he might say something about pickaxes and safety, but Angela noticed when he changed his mind and turned his attention back to Janey.

"I will help Tracy in ways she has not yet anticipated," either Janey or the spirit said. "She'll learn to accept." Janey picked up something which resembled a vase from where it had sat in a small alcove in the cavern wall. "We must return the demon to its *Vessel of the Diablo Si.*"

Janey carried the vessel up to the wooden throne where the corpse of the Native American chief sat in regal authority. She glanced at Miles. "Come, brother," she said. "Bring your canister of salt. It's almost time."

The others looked on in fascination. Even Robbie, usually ready to jump in and keep folks safe, watched the kids. A sense of calm and awe enveloped the group like a shroud. Janey ran her hand along the shoulder bones of the great chief. Dust and ancient skin fell off in clumps to land on the mud floor as Janey mumbled and whispered words Angela couldn't hear.

Miles approached Janey. "So, the story is true." He pointed at the chief and then at the seven sets of bones in the wall. "An old chief offed his clan and then himself and conjured a demon."

"Yes," Janey agreed. "So says the conduit. But he got more. The demon wished for help and got it."

"The Bigfoot, Yeti, Sasquatch, Mogollon Monster, pick your poison," Miles said. He seemed to be speaking to everyone now, not only Janey. "It's a spirit form, just like I figured."

Janey grinned, small teeth gleaming in the muted light. Angela noticed the look of admiration for her brother in her eyes, a slight softening around the edges. They made a great team.

Angela glanced up at Em and smiled. *We'll make a great team, too.* Em smiled back and then cast a nervous glance into the darkness of the cavern mouth.

"Good Lord," James said. "The thing that ripped the face from Jack Dowling and the head from receptionist Marion is a Bigfoot?"

"The cunt who failed," Janey corrected.

"Yes, yes," James said.

"How do I kill it?" Robbie asked, grim-faced and sullen.

"Magic," Janey said.

Robbie shook his head and stared at his feet. Not the answer he wanted, but Angela knew enough to realize it was the only one that made sense. They needed to rely on Janey.

The sounds of heavy plodding footsteps raced toward them. They sounded like they were created by something heavy and fast.

"Good Lord," James said. "It sounds like a pair of trees are stomping their way up a hill." He shifted to a position in front of his wife.

Angela glanced at the couple, and then up at Em. The woman she loved stared at the tunnel-mouth in horror and despair. Angela felt overwhelmed with emotion. They had no time now to go get a ladder to get Em down. She moved until she stood beneath the cage. The beast would have to get through her to get at Em. She would fire every round from her Glock and then fight hand, nail, and tooth afterward, if she had to.

"Quickly," Janey said to Miles. She pointed at the wooden throne.

"Got it," Miles said, and ran to the throne and poured salt from the canister around the wood legs until he almost completed a full circle.

"Not all the way," Janey said. "Not yet."

Miles nodded and left the front of the throne unadorned with the salt.

Robbie drew his Glock and took a step toward the opening. "Sounds like an elephant coming," he whispered. "This can't be happening." Louder, he said, "Everyone, stay back. Let me handle this." The sheriff pointed his pistol at the entrance, but Angela could see how much it was shaking. This surprised her, because Robbie was not a coward, but she also understood his fear of the unknown.

Angela, already blessed with knowledge, would hold no such fear and would remain rock-solid for her love. A lie, she knew. Her heart beat faster, and she hoped it matched Em's in perfect harmony. She glanced up to find Em peering down at her.

The girl mouthed, "I love you, babe." Angela could see the fear in her eyes.

Angela nodded, winked a reassuring wink at Em, and then returned her attention back to the darkness. The footfalls grew louder and closer. This was it.

A wave of dark energy pushed out ahead of the beast as it blasted forward. Angela could feel it building against her like a physical wall.

"Good Lord," James said. "It's coming. It'll have our heads." Keeping his wife behind him, arms outstretched as if to shelter her from viewing whatever approached, he moved backward a few steps, Vic stumbling with him. Angela knew the man hoped she would save him with her gun.

Angela felt the couple should run instead of fight. Take the kids with them and let the trained cops take on this monstrosity. But deep down she knew their survival really depended on Janey and Miles.

Pounding footsteps slowed as the creature approached. A deafening bellow roared into the cavern from the darkness and shook the bones in their alcoves. Angela knew the bellow of rage was intended to frighten and intimidate. She could feel it in her mind and her rankled nerves.

Fear and oppression increased inside Angela, and she knew the feelings would slow her actions if she allowed them to. The energy would force her from her skin and onto the floor where she would writhe about as nothing but a chunk of red grisly muscle and bone. Her eyes would pop under the strain for sure and this would save her the need to see what killed her—to see what violated and then killed Em. Blindness would prove best, yes. And then she remembered her dream and her unborn child. She couldn't give up now.

Fight!

Angela took deep breaths and drew her Glock, focused her attention to a pinprick of consciousness, until no room existed for fear or any other emotional clutter. Angela could hear Em breathing deeply above her, and this added to her courage and convictions.

The creature howled with rage and then, like a phantom, stomped into the entrance. Angela froze as she tried to understand what she looked at. It looked so much bigger and angrier than it had at the library or the jail. More real. A giant creature, at least twelve feet tall, which morphed in and out of spirit form without a discernible rhyme or reason, perhaps at the whim of the evil inside it. The spirit form creature wore a coat of dark fur, and its massive head held eyes that were much too big. It opened its mouth to roar and exposed two rows of razor-sharp teeth.

Robbie took three quick shots, center mass, which caused no physical harm. The report echoed off the walls of the cavern and masked some of the beast's howls.

The creature seemed to understand perfectly well when it needed to revert to spirit form to avoid harm, like the flip of a switch. Angela had no idea how to kill this thing, but she hoped the spirit inside Janey did.

On huge feet, the creature took a step toward Angela and glanced upward. It woofed a greeting to Em, and Angela almost vomited when the creature licked its giant lips as it stared at the woman above. It seemed transfixed on Em, as if it had dreamt of this moment. It licked its lips again and took another gigantic step.

"You are so gross," Angela hissed. She took a quick shot, hoping to catch the beast in a moment of transition. Her shot passed right through the giant to no effect. "Shit!"

"Oh, God!" Em screamed. "Please, no." Em pushed back to the rear of the cage, causing the large entrapment to swing backward.

Angela stepped forward to intercept the thing before it could get to Em.

"Over here!" Janey screamed, even louder than Em. "You better kill me first. I'm the only one who knows your filthy secrets."

The beast glanced one more time, longingly, Angela thought, up at Em. Then it turned its attention to Janey.

Janey ran inside the circle of salt and appeared to hide behind the throne, as if frightened. A nice ruse, Angela thought, because she had never seen the girl even approach an emotion which resembled fear or anxiety.

"Cunt," Janey said, as the beast pounded toward her.

Robbie fired again, this time at the beast's head. When it didn't even slow the thing down, he rushed forward, screaming, "Leave the girl alone!"

Robbie leapt at the creature as if he intended to grapple with it. The creature turned to face him. As the two bodies collided, Robbie's seemed to absorb into the creature's, as if the beast had wrapped Robbie in a shroud of darkness. Angela could hear Robbie scream, but it sounded like the screams originated from outside a closed window or door.

After one last strangled screech from Robbie, a blast of red moisture and body parts exploded out of the creature like a crimson curtain of filth. Angela felt Robbie's blood and viscera strike her face and one particularly slimy chunk squirted past her pressed lips and into her mouth. She couldn't spit the salty bisque out fast enough. Then she opened her eyes and blinked rapidly. She stumbled back a step.

"Oh my God...Robbie!" Em said. Angela heard the cage rock back and forth as Em moved. "Angela, run!"

She wouldn't run. Angela would save Em or die trying.

Vic screamed from behind Angela, and she heard both she and James shuffling away from the creature. James spoke to her quietly, but she could still hear his fear and panic. She hoped they would run down the other tunnel and give Angela two less people to worry about saving.

Angela stole a glance up at Em, took deep breaths, and then tried to think about what she needed to do. Someday she would process this, but she couldn't let Robbie's death paralyze her. Too many lives were at stake. Em's life.

The beast, Robbie already forgotten, turned toward the chair where both kids hid behind the throne which dripped with a rope of intestine and blood. What looked like Robbie's colon slid down the side of the chief's skull and plopped onto his collarbone and stuck there.

"Good Lord," James said from further away, and Angela could hear his wife gagging behind her.

Em grabbed the bars of her cage and yanked on them like a gorilla in its enclosure, trying to pry one loose. She yelled obscenities as she yanked, trying to wrestle the beast's attention away from the kids. But Angela understood the kids had worked out a plan between each other and Janey's current spirit guide.

The possessed cryptid stalked toward the wooden throne, and then stood before it and roared.

In response, Janey screamed. She looked terrified, her face a mask of fear.

A ruse, Angela thought.

Miles, salt canister in hand, crawled on his belly beneath and to the front of the large wooden chair. The skeletal feet of the chief moved as Miles wormed his arm between them.

The beast didn't notice Miles because of Janey's hollering, and Angela knew the kid would try to complete the circle of salt once the creature was inside. Could it be trapped? Angela wavered somewhere between action and inaction. The realist in her knew this was the Miles and Janey show now. But the adult and cop in her wanted to save them and spare the kids any pain.

Janey, done with her act, taunted the creature. "Come for me, you stupid cunt!"

The beast did, aggravated and aggressive. Angela could tell it harbored zero fear, probably thought itself invincible. It approached the throne.

"Get away from them!" Em screamed. "Bring that bloated carcass over here and fight me!"

The demon ignored her, saving its attentions for later, for when they were alone and would have no interruptions. Angela knew this.

But first it would have to escape the kids' trap and get through her. She would fight to the death for Em.

"Good Lord, stop shouting," James said. Angela thought he had moved even further back. She could tell he was torn between keeping he and his wife from harm and helping the others.

With a roar that sounded like the thirty-year blizzard and death, the beast stepped inside the unfinished circle of salt and reached around the throne, trying for Janey. It missed.

"Now!" Janey yelled as she ran around the throne.

"I say," James said. "This isn't a game. Run, you two. Run now!"

Before the large beast could get turned around and pursue Janey, Miles reached out and finished the circle of salt, connecting both ends and creating an infinite line of white. When the creature reached for him, Miles rolled out of the way, stood, and then joined his sister at a safe distance.

When the demon made the creature step forward, and its foot went to move over the line of salt, sparks flew into the air and the smell of burnt sulfur filled Angela's nostrils.

"You stink!" Em yelled. "That a demon fart or what?"

"It worked!" Miles whooped.

"Is it trapped?" Vic asked. Angela heard the hope in her voice and mirrored her own.

Angela couldn't bring herself to feel safe yet, to declare victory. The thing was still very much alive and pissed off. Trapped, yes, but that could change in a heartbeat. If it escaped, it would kill them all. Its red eyes flashed about like twin lasers.

Janey swayed before the demon like a willow in a stiff breeze. She appeared to contemplate her next move. Then she spoke, voice soft yet stern. "No need for you to stay any longer," she said. "I'm speaking to the flesh vessel, not the demon who dwells inside. So says the conduit."

The beast roared and switched between its spirit and solid forms. Angela thought the beast sounded confused, as if it hadn't understood it could free itself from the demon.

"That's right," Janey said. "You're free to go—free to roam the forest and the swamps and the mountains. Free to do as you desire. Free of the evil inside you."

More of the sulfur stench filled the air. Angela recognized this as the demon's stench, separate from the cryptid's fetid odor.

The cryptid shuffled a tentative hairy foot toward the salt, and when the fur grazed the white granules, sparks flew, and the creature bellowed in discomfort. Doggedly, the cryptid continued, despite the pain, until the appendage moved past the field. Its eyes went wide and lit up with a childlike glee. A smile erupted on its simple face. It continued to pull itself outside the salt like a paperclip traveling to the bottom of a cup of glue.

As the hairy beast moved outside the ring of salt, a growing shadow danced in its wake, inside the ring, agitated and in a fury. The demon was losing its toy and didn't care for the fact. The flesh of the cryptid, while it remained in solid form, could slip outside the salt while the demon remained behind, trapped. Angela now saw the wisdom in Janey's plan.

"Pull!" Janey encouraged. "You are so close to freedom. Taste it, hairy one. Your unshackling is at hand."

"It's escaping," James said. "Janey, get away from that thing."

Angela turned to the couple. "I think she knows what she's doing." She smiled to tell them it would all be okay.

With one last behemoth roar and a giant tug, the cryptid tore itself free of the salt and the demon and stumbled out into the cavern. It turned its gigantic head and peered at the demon inside the salt. For just a moment, Angela thought the cryptid would give up its newly earned freedom and return to the demon, but then it sprinted toward the exit. Right as it reached the mouth of the exit tunnel, it morphed into spirit form, hovered a moment, and then disappeared into the darkness.

"That was cool," Em said. Then she shouted at the demon. "Whose body you gonna use to do your dirty work now, asshole?"

"You're funny," Miles said to Em. He looked at the demon. "See, now you're all alone. The cryptid never cared for you. You made it stay with ya. You're a pathetic piece of shit of a demon."

"Miles," James said. "Please don't antagonize the thing. It still looks dangerous."

"It can't do shit anymore," Miles said.

Janey turned to the demon which floated inside the ring of salt. Angela thought it looked diminished, nothing but a demonic black kite with red eyes. It moved with quick flashing movements, looking for an escape from the ring of salt. The sulfur smell lay thick in the cavern and created a haze of eye-stinging smoke that made Angela's eyes water.

"You may all leave," Janey said. She spread her arms wide in a gesture of freedom.

Angela watched as spirits began to wriggle free of the demon like maggots wiggling out of roadkill. The demon appeared to go into convulsions. First, Harold's spirit sprung out, looked around, and then floated toward the ceiling of the cavern. Jeb followed, then Marion and Penny. Several more followed who Angela didn't recognize. All the souls it had stolen over the centuries, Angela figured. The last were Native American wearing buckskin and shawls fashioned from beautifully woven fabric. They all traveled the same route, up and out, to whatever Heaven awaited them.

"My God," Vic said.

Janey walked to the very edge of the salt. "I know you feel shame, but it's time for you to depart. You are also free." She seemed to speak to one final soul.

The demon fought hard to hold this one in, contorting its shadow-body around and around, trying to prevent the final soul's escape. Then, one arm popped out of the darkness, then two, and finally a head with a large headdress. *The chief.* He struggled upward as the demon fought to hold him. After a few moments, the chief tore free and floated above the demon. It glanced longingly at its own remains sitting on the throne and then turned to the bones of the ancestors which he had slain. Angela watched a tear streak down his ephemeral face.

"You will pay your penance," Janey assured him. "But you will know peace again. One day."

The chief looked at Janey, nodded, and then streaked out through the cavern's roof in a line of orange, red, and white contrails.

"Show off," Janey whispered. Then she turned to the demon who floated within the circle of salt. "Cunt. You're all alone now. Nobody left to do your bidding." She picked up the clay jar and its lid off the floor, then held it toward the demon. "Inside," she said.

Like a dark-winged bullet, the demon slammed into the invisible force which held it, attempting to get at the girl.

Janey didn't flinch.

More sulfur filled the air as the demon growled a far different rumble than the beefy screech of the cryptid. The demon's red eyes burned with an intense gaze which flickered over Janey. Angela knew if the thing escaped, the girl wouldn't stand a chance against the angry apparition.

"The chief who summoned you and began the curse has returned home and so shall you." Janey held out the vessel.

This time the demon streaked toward the cavern roof.

"It's trying to get away!" James said.

Oh, no. Angela knew it would try to escape straight up. If it did, it may figure a way outside the salt ring. How far vertically did the salt's influence extend? It no longer possessed the cryptid's body, but it could go find the poor creature or, worse, possess one of them.

Janey put her hands behind her back as she watched.

Easy for her. She's already possessed.

Angela watched the demon approach the cavern's ceiling and build speed. It wasn't much more than a rapidly moving shadow when it struck the rocky surface. With a blinding flash of light, the demon fell back to the floor like a moth from a light.

"Holy shit!" Miles said.

"You got that right," Em said. "I can't believe it."

Angela heard the couple behind her gasp and then whisper to each other. She could also hear Em's heavy breaths from above.

"The curse still holds you," Janey said. She held the vessel up again. "If you're ready, I will set it inside the ring."

When the demon seemed reluctant to comply, Janey said, "Miles."

"You got it," Miles said and walked the cannister of salt over. "Either you go in that *Vessel of the Diablo Si* or I'll burn you into extinction. You pick. Either way works for me."

The demon studied Miles, its red eyes glowing. When Miles prepared to launch the salt, it looked upward as if to prepare for death.

Miles must have sensed its true intention. "Don't even try it. I have a strong enough arm to reach the ceiling."

The demon withered, then stole one more longing glance up at Em.

"You can't have her," Angela said. She wondered how it felt to go from something so powerful to the nothingness the thing now faced. It had to be a shock, something to process. It would have plenty of time to think inside the clay jar.

"What's it gonna be?" Miles asked, voice stern.

Janey sat the vessel inside the salt ring. Angela breathed a sigh of relief when the demon didn't attack her. Either it couldn't or it was afraid of getting dowsed with salt.

"Let's go," Miles said. He shook the cannister. A skiff of salt fell to the cavern floor.

The demon tracked the salt with its red eyes before finally growling one last time. Then it turned to a black vapor and entered the *Vessel of the Diablo Si* like a genie into a bottle.

"Is it...is it gone?" James asked.

"Not gone," Janey said as she entered the salt ring and picked up the vessel.

Miles stepped forward, ready with the salt should the demon launch out and attack her.

Janey placed the lid on the vessel. "Not gone but trapped."

"What are you going to do with that?" Angela asked.

"Only I will know," she said.

Angela nodded, trusting the kid to do the right thing. Part of her didn't want to—wanted to take that thing herself and bury it away in the middle of the desert where nobody would ever find it. But they might. She imagined some archeologist in the future digging up the vessel and opening it. Angela shook her head. No, she'd rather not know where it ended up.

"Wanna get me down?" Em asked.

"I wanna do more than that," Angela answered.

Em giggled. "Love you, babe."

Miles said, "Gross."

James embraced his wife as she sobbed tears of relief.

For once, Janey didn't say *cunt*. She walked into the darkness of the passage with the *Vessel of the Diablo Si*.

Chapter 30

James white-knuckled the steering wheel. The switchbacks down the mountain still contained ice, but the plow had at least voided them of the snow that lay almost forty inches everywhere else.

James had to admit, the snow looked beautiful out in the trees, how it covered the pine branches and held them low. The unbroken expanse of white and green seemed endless.

To the left lay the abyss, five thousand feet straight down. Even with a short metal fence, designed to slow a car but probably not stop it. James felt safer looking up and into the woods. A few birds flitted about. They passed a Mule deer doe who had dug down to munch some greenery beneath the layers of snow as she watched them pass.

The sun peeked through the branches and reflected off the white brilliance of winter's wonder. They had stayed one more night to get some rest, but sleep proved difficult with all that had happened. James imagined sleep may prove difficult for some nights to come. This time, when he heard the gurney out in the hall, James had just turned over and tried to sleep. No more ghosts for him. He'd seen enough of the paranormal for a lifetime. It had been a relief to give the kids back to their aunt. They found her passed out, an empty bottle of Glenfiddich and a prescription bottle of sleeping pills on the nightstand. Even now, more law-enforcement than he'd ever seen accumulated in one place, were scurrying around the hotel like ants. They'd questioned him and Vic, not liking the answers they received, but allowed them to leave after collecting their contact information.

"I can't believe any of this," Vic said, looking out her window. "Jack Dowling. Dead. Face torn off by a possessed cryptid of all things. Ghosts." Vic sighed. "Before this weekend, I would never have believed any of it. Still wouldn't if I didn't live through it."

"Well, we did, my love," James said.

"Yes, we did," Vic said, then she leaned over to kiss his cheek.

The roads were still slick even as they approached the valley floor, despite how hard the plows had worked to free them from snow and ice. The sand they had spread helped, but he could still feel the tires slide around the switchbacks. James figured they were three-quarters to the bottom and drawing nearer every moment. He could see the tops of the pines below, a great sign they were nearing the bottom.

"Almost there," Vic said. She maneuvered lower, blowing on his right nipple through his shirt, and then even lower as she kissed a small patch of exposed stomach skin right above James' belt. "You wore a belt why? You have no desire to feel good?"

"Good Lord," James said. "I didn't think, with all that just transpired, you'd be in any mood to give a blow."

"It'll take my mind off things," she said, continuing to kiss his skin. Then she fiddled with his belt. "By the time you finish, hopefully we'll be at the bottom of this infernal mountain. Besides, what better way to end a romance writer's convention. Even a horrid one."

"If you insist," James said. "Who am I to argue?" He smiled at her.

"You're a lucky man, James Landes."

"I've known that for years." *Climax city, climax Tourette's.*

Vic lowered her head to begin.

That's when he noticed it, the streak of brown hairy fur rocketing toward them out of the woods on two legs. James swerved toward the ledge, hoping the bipedal monster would miss them.

Vic pulled her head away from his lap. "What in the hell is going on? Had I known you'd go off the road, I would have never gone down on you in the first place."

The creature rammed into Vic's side of the car. James could have sworn the creature screamed the words, "Violet and peach!" as it collided with them. The jolt sent them careening toward the guardrail. Sparks flew as metal tasted metal. It took everything James had to get the car back to the middle of the road.

"What the hell?" Vic said and grabbed onto James' shoulder and neck.

James didn't respond, only watched the creature disappear as he maneuvered the car around a sharp corner, heart beating rapidly in his chest. *We could have died. The irony.* He wondered if their lives would ever return to normal.

The creature watched from the middle of the road as the car disappeared around the corner. The spirit who had once inhabited Janey slipped out of the creature and the cryptid turned and ran off, back into the forest to live out its life in peace.

Angela felt the burn of the hot sand on her back even through the plush beach-towel. Em lay next to her, breaths steady and light as she napped. Angela squinted to avoid the unforgiving sunlight and could barely make out the ocean of blue as it met the even bluer sky on the horizon. She took a deep breath and let it go, trying to finally relax.

Aruba felt like paradise after the cold and snow. And demons and cryptids and occultists. True to their word, Angela and Em left Jerome the next day and headed for warmer climates. A great decision as they'd known it would be. The first night with Em in the bungalow on the beach had felt like Heaven. Angela reached over and placed her fingertips in the palm of Em's left hand. Em squeezed them in her sleep and the gesture made Angela smile. She loved this woman so much.

A shout from the boardwalk behind them roused Angela from her warm thoughts. The shouting grated on her nerves. Angela only wanted to relax and unwind. The frightened tones became more urgent. Finally, disgusted with the noise, Angela looked over her shoulder to where the vendors set up their food carts and crafts.

A black-haired man with several bleeding wounds was chattering to a security guard who shook his head and rolled his eyes at the story.

The man said, "A large creature chased us and took Charles…my brother-in-law. It just ran off with him into the jungle."

"I suppose you're going to tell me it was an Orang Pendek," the guard said. He sounded like he didn't believe the man.

"It did have an orange hue to the fur," the man said.

The guard laughed.

This behavior made Angela angry. He was a man of rules and regulations and should take this citizen or guest seriously. She was no longer a cop, at least for now, and all she wanted was a break. But the man needed help, whether or not a creature existed. His words resonated with Angela and she thought of what she and Em just went through. She flipped over to her stomach, and the action disturbed Em who then opened her eyes and also flipped over to her front.

"What's happening?" Em asked.

Angela nodded toward the dark-haired man still speaking with the disbelieving guard.

Em listened and then glanced at Angela quizzically. She smiled. "What are the odds?"

Angela looked her in the eye and saw the emotion and energy there. Finally, she asked, "You up for an Orang Pendek hunt?"

Em nodded, and both women got up, kissed, and then made their way toward the boardwalk, hand in hand, to offer their assistance. They were experts, after all.

Acknowledgements

No book is produced in a silo, and this one is no exception. A big thank you to the staff at Silver Shamrock with an extra big shout-out to editor extraordinaire, Kenneth W. Cain, who helped shape this book into something special. Big thanks to Jeremy Hepler, Brendan Deneen, and Jonathan Janz, who either read this up front or offered much-needed encouragement, or both. A special shout-out to Brian Keene: I would never have started writing if not for you…thank you for all you do. Last but certainly not least, thanks to my wife, Ali, who puts up with me when I have too much to write, and also when I don't have enough.

Justin Holley is the author of the three-novel Bruised series, as well as, several short stories published in magazines and anthologies around the world. He also investigates the paranormal with a TAPS-family group and plays volleyball twice a week. Correspondence from his fans is encouraged, and the best way to contact him is through his website: www.justinholley.com

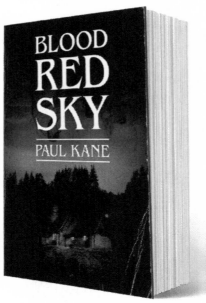

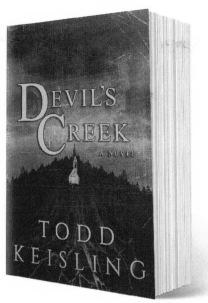

"Todd Keisling runs at the front of the pack."

—John Langan, Bram Stoker Award-winning author of *The Fisherman*

About fifteen miles west of Stauford, Kentucky lies Devil's Creek. According to local legend, there used to be a church out there, home to the Lord's Church of Holy Voices—a death cult where Jacob Masters preached the gospel of a nameless god.
And like most legends, there's truth buried among the roots and bones.

In 1983, the church burned to the ground following a mass suicide. Among the survivors were Jacob's six children and their grandparents, who banded together to defy their former minister. Dubbed the "Stauford Six," these children grew up amid scrutiny and ridicule, but their infamy has faded over the last thirty years. Now their ordeal is all but forgotten, and Jacob Masters is nothing more than a scary story told around campfires.

For Jack Tremly, one of the Six, memories of that fateful night have fueled a successful art career—and a lifetime of nightmares. When his grandmother Imogene dies, Jack returns to Stauford to settle her estate. What he finds waiting for him are secrets Imogene kept in his youth, secrets about his father and the church. Secrets that can no longer stay buried.

The roots of Jacob's buried god run deep, and within the heart of Devil's Creek, something is beginning to stir...

Made in the USA
Middletown, DE
01 April 2022

63474817R00168